Claimstake

by

Prudence Macleod

Book four of the Nova Series
second edition

CLAIMSTAKE

First edition. December 10, 2023.

Copyright © 2023 Prudence MacLeod.

ISBN: 978-1927478394

Written by Prudence MacLeod.

Taken

The child was miserable as they bounced along. He was bound hand and foot, gagged, beaten, then thrown across a shoulder and carried off. Tears of fear and rage ran down his face as he moaned in pain for his mother. She would come for him; they all knew it.

"Faster, dammit," growled the man in the lead.

"I can't, Borry. Damn kid's too heavy," panted the second man. "You carry him for a while. Better yet, make him run on his own two feet."

"Don't be stupid, Dunc," growled the leader, as he stopped to catch him breath. Gratefully, the second man dropped his squirming cargo on the hard ground. "The brat killed two men and maimed a third. We can't let him loose and we have to get away from here."

"Where'll we go? They'll find the bodies and Jass will talk. You know the witch will make him talk. We'll never get off the damn planet. We're as good as dead right now; those freaks are probably already on our trail."

"Just shut up and let me think. We need a new plan."

"Well think fast, Borry; we're running out of time."

"All right, we'll do the last thing they'd think of."

"Oh yeah, what's that?"

"They'll be expecting us to try to get off planet. Instead, we'll head for the eastern continent. We'll go to my place and grab that old speeder I've been working on. Senni can come with us to look after the brat."

"Are you nuts? That continent is nothing but scrub forest, rodents, and bugs."

"There's lots of abandoned mines and town sites there as well. We'll find a hideout and then contact the slavers. They can send someone in to get us. We'll still get rich and we'll only have to split the money two ways."

"Who knew anyone would pay that much for a Spawn brat?"

That stung the child deeply. He knew that some people hated and feared the Guardians, but to be called Slime Spawn truly hurt. He was old enough to know that some people actually believed Lady Arlessa had made the Guardians out of slime worms. He squirmed and tried to kick at them, but the man danced away then delivered a kick to his belly, driving the air from his lungs and the hope from his heart.

The boy was hauled up and carried off. Later he was stuffed into the cargo space of a small speeder and whisked away.

———— ◉ ————

IT HAD BEEN NEARLY twenty years since the Battle of the Gap, as it was called. When the witches of Nova exploded a star to keep the empire at bay, they had inadvertently created a gap between Sector Nine and the rest of the galaxy. It was a wide stretch of space riddled with pockets of radiation and Erratics, as the wandering planetoids were called. Other unexplainable things happened in the Gap as well; things that could drive a person insane.

A few hardy souls had found their way through that maze and often made trade runs. Others just worked salvage on the ones that failed, while still others stooped to outright piracy. Collectively these people were known as Gap Runners. The majority of the trade was conducted by the Runners' Guild; a company of traders on this side of the gap and a network of smugglers on the other.

The Guild was owned and operated by a woman named Kella. When the Guild made a run it was usually escorted by a crew of super mercenaries from Nova Prime. No one ever attacked one of their convoys. At least, none lived to tell of it.

In the Borelian Free States, things had soured somewhat for the Novans. At first Micha and crew were hailed as heroes, but Micha's hard stance against slavery soon had the people divided. Nova, and the five nearest systems it claimed as protectorates, had become somewhat isolated.

Both Lady Marla and Chieftain Lortax had tried to stay out of it but failed. The new Chieftain of Sega Clan had pressured Lortax to command Lessa and Micha to reverse their stance. The next in line for High Priestess had backed them. They said it would keep peace in the sector; that the changes should come slowly over time, through diplomatic means.

Novans responded by removing their Nara tattoos and adding a Nova sunburst instead. Those people who chose not to remain were helped to relocate elsewhere.

Severing their ties with the Nara further isolated the Novans. After Lady Marla retired, the new High Priestess tried to enforce her will by calling on Nova Temple to comply. After a short but private conference with both Arlessa and Norlene, she rescinded that command.

Micha and the Guardians watched as politics and greed tore apart the sector while on Nova Prime things had begun to deteriorate as well.

It all began with the children. The offspring of the Guardians were far too strong physically to allow them to play with the normal children. That interaction only happened under strict supervision.

Worse yet, the Guardians taught their offspring to protect the other children and to both ignore and endure any and all taunts the others might throw at them. This only made things worse as the parents began to grumble. "Damn things think themselves so superior, even their kids won't tussle with ours," muttered one father. "They just ignore them and treat them like they're inferior."

Not everyone felt this way of course, some were just the opposite. "I like the Guardians," said one man. "Yesterday my son and I were struggling to put the bull in the pen, but we couldn't handle him. Rathbone was walking by. He grabbed the bull by the horns and dumped him on his back. That bull was a lot easier to handle when Rathbone let him up.

"He saved us a lot of trouble and possible injuries. They keep the slave raiders away, help with the work, and lots more. Sorry friends, but I just can't see the bad here."

"What if they turn on us?"

"Why would they? They protect us and we provide the food. Everybody works together and we all prosper. Where's the bad in that?"

The arguments went on. Over the years they became more intense, and the population of Nova slowly became divided. The crew and families tried to ignore it, but that only emboldened the troublemakers. They began to shout insults openly and the Guardians had to break up many fights between the dissenters and their supporters.

It eventually began to wear thin as the Guardian's younger children started to retaliate, at least verbally. It was in this environment that, with the promise of great riches ringing in their ears, five men kidnapped the youngest child of Micha and Edie.

Micha and Edie had taken the older children to a celebration gathering at a farm about an hour away. The farmer was a friend and strong supporter of the Guardians. He had invited them to see his daughter's new son and they all went, all except Kon. The boy hadn't felt well so Edie had asked a neighbor's daughter to stay with him.

They arrived home late to find the girl injured and unconscious on the floor. In Kon's sleeping room there were two dead bodies and a man trying to crawl out the window. He had failed. The man was too badly injured to escape but the boy was nowhere to be found. Micha shifted to warrior instantly.

"Someone took him. Edie, tend the girl. Michella, find the trail. Allore, fetch my comm then go help Edie."

Everyone sprang into action. Michella, the eldest daughter at twenty was much like her father, and she had a real flair for the things Miriam taught them about tracking and survival. Allore, the second child, was thirteen and determined to be the greatest healer in the Sector.

Micha's voice was steady, but barely controlled as he used the comm. "Micha to Ravage, come in Ravage."

"Ravage here, Sir." It was a child's voice.

"Ravage, order seven, inform your captain at once."

"What's up, Boss?" Jorge was instantly on the comms. He often took his youngest son with him for a night patrol and Micha usually enjoyed hearing the boy, but not this time.

"Kon's been taken. Nothing leaves or lands on the planet until further notice. Nothing."

"Understood." Jorge hit the ship-wide comm and informed the crew of the new orders. Gunners were at the controls in moments. Within an hour the Freedom should be home to help.

"Micha to Zartah, wake up Zartah." At Micha's second call he got a sleepy reply.

"Zartah here, Boss. You been partying?"

"Kon's been taken. Michella is finding the trail, but I want Miriam just in case."

"Understood. Coming."

"Please, I need a healer..." begged the injured man, but Micha ignored him. "Micha to Brenna."

"Micha, what happened?" Brenna knew he'd never disturb them late unless he had to.

"Kon's been taken. I may need a dispatcher."

"On my way."

"Please, a healer..."

"Shall I see to him, Micha?" Edie had just returned to the room.

"Not yet, my love. Report." His voice was gentle as he spoke, but his posture did not soften.

"Allore is taking Nella home. She'll be fine in a few days once the bump on her head goes down, but I'll ask Lady Arlessa to check on her anyway. I'll go help Michella now."

"Not yet." Edie stopped but said nothing. Micha's cold warrior stance was keeping her panic under control. As badly as she wanted to go find her son, she knew letting Micha take control was the fastest way to get him back. Reluctantly she held herself in check.

"Have you questioned him yet?" she asked.

"No."

"Are you going to?"

"Yes, as soon as Ena gets here."

"You called Ena?"

"I called Zartah."

"That'll do it."

Just then Brenna came through the door with Lessa. Zartah and Ena were close behind. "Miriam's on the trail, Boss. Murtah, Rathbone, and Keira are with her. Gorda took a fighter up to start searching the area."

"All right, you," said Micha, as he finally acknowledged the presence of the wounded man, "I want to know the full story here. Lie to me and this woman will know. This woman is a dispatcher. Tell the truth and she'll ease your passing. Lie and I'll make your passing more painful than you can imagine. Now start talking."

The man was already in great pain. Lessa touched him lightly and the pain subsided. "That will allow you some relief," she said gently.

Suddenly she shifted into that terrible voice from a darker realm. "*If you lie, Micha will let me play.*"

The man swallowed hard then started to talk. Suddenly he was babbling, and the full story came tumbling out of him. The old Empire was being rebuilt by Loran the Second. They called him the Iron Emperor. He'd sent agents to a slaver offering a princely sum for a live child of the Slime Spawn. Micha ground his teeth at that phrase, but he said nothing.

"There were five of us," the man said. "We were making plans when we heard you'd left the boy home. That was our chance."

"What happened?"

"We got in easy and found them in here. The damned girl screamed and attacked us. The boy tried to help her. He stuck Zale with that stone spear thing and brained Egger with that ball bat. Monk grabbed him, but the kid got loose, grabbed Zale's blaster and shot me. Thank the gods it was set on low stun."

"Low stun?"

"We thought it would knock out the kid, but it didn't even slow him down."

"Where are they taking him?"

"Zale's farm, the slavers will be waiting there to take him back through the Gap."

"Zale's farm," said Edie, as she nudged one of the bodies with her foot. It rolled onto its back, cold glassy eyes staring blindly at the ceiling. Kon's stone dagger was still embedded in its chest. Kon had been proud of that knife and had kept it beside his bed. "I've been to his farm several times to tend his sick children."

"Take us there," said Micha, as he turned toward the door.

"What about him?" asked Brenna.

"Dispatch him."

"No, please..."

"I can't Micha. He's not attacking me, and he hasn't asked for release."

"I can change his mind," said Lessa.

Micha whipped out his blaster and shot the man. The body jerked hard then went limp. "Quickly, Edie." She hurried outside and climbed into the fighter ship Micha always kept at the farm. The others were right on her heels. They had never seen Micha coldly kill a man like that and it frightened them.

Edie was at the controls as the ship leaped into the air. Micha grabbed the comms. "Michella, they're headed for Zale's farm."

"No they're not, unless they're going the long way around."

"Stay on the track."

"Understood."

MICHELLA, AFFECTIONATELY known to the other Guardians' children as Mamma Hen, leaped from the house at her father's command. A shrill whistle brought a huge dog bounding toward her. There had been such a dog at her side from the time of her birth. This was the third such beast. Eyes shining and tail wagging, he was ready for whatever adventure she had in mind.

"Find Kon, Jak," she urged, as she searched the ground for some sign of the intruders. The dog started for the house, but she called him back. "Find Kon, boy. Find Kon." Getting the idea, he began to snuffle the ground near where she was searching. A moment later he bayed once, then set out on the trail, Michella close behind.

The two moons of Nova gave enough pale light for her to keep from falling, but only just. Several times she called for the dog to wait. Finally he stopped for a moment to search an area, and then he was off again. The trail had followed a path leading southwards, but now the dog was travelling in a new direction over broken land. They soon came out at a rundown farm.

Jak snuffled his way up to the house, but did not attempt to go in. Instead, he made his way towards the barn which stood silently with open doors. The trail ended there. After a few minutes of trying to find the scent again, the big dog sat down and howled once. He gazed at Michella with sad eyes. He had failed her.

The girl hugged the dog and reassured him that it was fine, and his tail began to wag. She was reaching for her small comm unit when a fighter ship swept in and landed in the farmyard. Miriam, Zartah, Keira, and Rathbone spilled out of it. They were armed and ready for battle.

"Michella to Micha." Her voice was cold and tightly controlled; Edie didn't like the sound of it. The girl was a lot like her father when she was under pressure.

"Micha here. They were headed for Zale's farm and so are we."

"Negative. They came to a rundown farm to the east. They must have had a ship hidden in the barn. They're gone."

"Stay there. Learn what you can."

"Understood."

Michella's shoulders slumped as she turned to the new arrivals. "How did you guys find me? Wait, Jak's collar; you followed his signal."

"Very good, Little Micha," smiled Miriam. She reached for her own comm unit. "Miriam to Ravage; Jorge, are you still tracking that ship?"

"Ravage here. It's well out over the ocean now and still headed east."

"Stay with it," she replied as she passed the comm to Zartah.

"Zartah to Micha."

"Micha."

"We're with Michella. They had a ship of some kind. Jorge is tracking something that left this area headed east. It is well out over the water now."

"Understood." Zartah passed the comm unit back to Miriam as he followed Michella towards the dilapidated farmhouse. "Michella, what are you going to do?"

"I'm going to find my brother and kill the men who took him." She whirled around and faced them all. "Don't try to stop me or interfere."

"I will hunt with you." Miriam stepped up to the angry, frustrated girl. "Remember what you've learned; remember who you are."

Michella's shoulders relaxed a bit as some of the defiance left her face. "I will, Aunt Miriam."

"Count us in." Rathbone and Keira stepped forward, as did Zartah.

"This is Michella's hunt," said Miriam. "What do you want us to do?"

"Should we search the barn?"

"No, Uncle Zartah. If they were still there, Jak would have found them. No, they're gone, but someone might be inside who knows where they'd go. I intend to ask, and I don't plan to be gentle."

"Michella?"

"Just don't let anyone escape." She spun and leaped up the rickety steps to the door and kicked it in. A block of firewood struck her chest as she entered. In the dim moonlight she could see a girl of about her own age standing in front of two small boys. The girl held up another piece of wood threateningly.

"I won't let you hurt them."

For a moment the rage flared in Michella's heart, but she fought it down. She knew this girl, she'd had a crush on her for months, and could see she was only trying to protect her own brothers. "Deann, you know me, and you know what I can do. I don't want to hurt you and I won't, if you tell me where they took Kon."

The girl didn't move or respond; she was too frightened. Michella picked up the stick that had been thrown at her. She twisted it in her hands until it shattered into a thousand splinters.

"It's over, Deann; I'm not a Guardian anymore. I won't hold back, and I'll kill anyone in my way. I want my brother back; you'd do the same. Please don't make me hurt you."

The girl's shoulders slumped, and she dropped her stick of wood to the floor. "Please don't hurt them, Michella. They didn't know what was going on."

"Did you?"

"No, not until they dragged Kon in here tonight. I tried to call you, but Borry smashed my comm unit and said he'd kill me if I tried to contact anyone. He made my mother go with them to take care of the boy."

"Where did they go?"

"They said they were going to the eastern continent to hide out and send for the slaver to come for them. They think they're going to be rich, the fools. The slavers will take them too or kill them."

"You're a lot smarter than your father, Deann. That's exactly what will happen. Who was the other man involved?"

The girl hugged the two boys to her. "There were four more. They were always out in the barn, working on that old speeder of his. He's not our father, Michella; our father left us ten years ago or more."

"Two of those men are dead and Poppa has the third."

"Then Dunc is the only one with him. I heard his voice and he sounded scared."

"He should be." Michella turned to go, but the girl's voice called her back. There was a note of pleading there that touched her heart and cut through the rage.

She turned to see a teary-eyed Deann holding her brothers close. "Michella, Borry isn't our father. I don't care what you do to him.

Mamma had nothing to do with this; they made her go. Please don't hurt her."

Michella's cold rage melted in the warm glow of those tears. Dammit, this was no time for hormones or weakness. She turned away towards the door. "I make no promises, but I'll bring her back to you if I can." With that she was out the door.

Outside there were two more speeders on the ground and several of her friends waiting for her. All were the children of the Guardians. "Did you find him?" asked a tall muscular boy of about seventeen.

"No, Palentine, I didn't, but I will."

The boy flinched at the use of his full name. This was it; Michella was angry; the day had come. They all wanted it, but they had waited for Michella. He'd always known it would take a lot to shake her, but he knew it would happen. He was ready. "I'm with you, Chella, and so are the others."

"What's going on, son?" asked Rathbone, as he stepped up to the young giant.

"Chella will explain, Poppa, but not now. Now we have to find Kon."

"Agreed."

"They're headed for the eastern continent. They've taken Deann's mother with them to look after Kon. I wonder if we can track them."

"Jorge's tracking something headed out over the ocean now, Michella," rumbled Rathbone. "Probably them." Just then Micha's ship landed and Edie leaped out.

"Report," Micha barked as he reached the ground.

"They're headed for the eastern continent," said Michella. "They've taken a woman to care for him, so he is still alive. They plan to hide from us, and then call for the slavers to come pick them up. The Ravage is tracking them.

"Father, this foolishness has to stop now."

The entire area fell silent under the pale moonlight as father turned to face daughter. "Foolishness?"

Michella took a deep breath then squared her shoulders. "You've always taught us to defend the humans, to protect them. We've been forbidden to harm them in any way. We endure their blows and insults and still try to protect them. Because of this they don't respect us. Father, it has to stop." Palentine and the others had stepped in behind her to show their support.

Micha gazed at her for a long moment without speaking. Finally his shoulders sagged. "You have your mother's passion, Chella. I love that about you, but you must never let it take control. Sadly, I can see your point and must agree. I was wrong. However, we're also humans; we need to bear that in mind. You're right, this foolishness must stop. So, what do you suggest?"

"I suggest we be free to defend ourselves and our friends, but no others unless we choose to do so. I suggest you let me find my brother in my own way."

He didn't respond for a long moment and not a sound was heard. Slowly, Micha began to nod his head. "All right, Michella. You mission is to retrieve your brother; my crew and I have another errand. What do you need?"

"A ship and weapons."

"Take my ship," said Micha, as he unbuckled his weapon's belt and passed it to her, "and my healer. Kon will want her when you find him. Do you need more crew?"

"I have a crew," she replied, nodding to Palentine. Silently he climbed aboard the fighter ship as she slung her father's weapon's belt over her shoulder. At her hand signal Jak leaped aboard the ship as well, followed by two powerfully built young men. Grinning, Zartah tossed his weapons belt to his sons.

"You may need a witch on your crew, Chella," suggested Lady Arlessa.

"Thanks, Auntie, but I already have two." She nodded at the two excited girls who squealed and leaped aboard the ship. Michella followed as Micha kissed Edie's cheek and winked at her.

"Micha..."

"Kon will need you, my love. Chella is ready and we have another errand." Edie, looking worried, followed her daughter aboard the small fighter ship which was already running. As soon as she was aboard, it leapt into the sky and streaked eastward.

As the ship disappeared from sight Zartah was heard to whisper to Miriam. "I don't know, love, but something must be up for the boss to stay behind on this one."

"Think about it, Zartah," sighed Micha. "If you wanted to divert the attention of the Guardians, how would you do it?"

"So you think somebody wants all of our resources pointed somewhere else?"

"Yes, my old friend, that's what I think."

"If they come on the ground, Norlene can handle them," said Lessa. "We need to be in the air."

"Agreed." Micha reached for his comm unit. In less than an hour the two Arcalian fighter ships were in space. As soon as Michella had the coordinates of her quarry's landing site, the Ravage turned to join them.

Retrieved

Michella was nervous and it was showing. She was nibbling a strand of her hair as the ship sped over the water. Suddenly a small hand rested on her shoulder and a wave of healing energy flowed through her. "You can do this, Mother Hen," a voice whispered in her mind. "This is our chance to prove ourselves. We need you to lead us as you always do." She patted the hand on her shoulder and straightened her back.

Only a few people knew of this particular talent of Nellie's. Nellie was Brenna's daughter. Lessa and Brenna had each born a child of their united DNA. Nellie and Ellie were born two weeks apart of different mothers, but were as identical as any twins. They both had Brenna's small stature and Lessa's lighter coloring, as well as her gift for magic.

Lady Norlene spotted the talent early and became their tutor. Both girls were strong witches at the tender age of eighteen. Considering who their mothers were, it's no surprise they were strong willed and independent as well, but for some reason they always looked to Michella for leadership and approval.

"Relax and focus, Chella. You need to be focused to get this done." Edie was lightly gripping her daughter's hand. "I know having your mother along on your first mission is tough, but I'm not here to judge you or to take over. I know you're the right one to get this done; I just need to be there to help get my son back and to make certain he's unhurt." Michella gave a weak smile and nodded then returned her attention to the vista of endless waters churning beneath their ship.

Behind her the young witches mentally rehearsed spells they might need while trying to hide their excitement. They knew it was a grave situation, but it was exciting. The other two young men weren't helping. Tarah and Barah, Miriam and Zartah's sons weren't hiding their excitement very well. They kept punching each other on the arm and wrestling with Jak. It took Michella's disapproving glance to settle them down a bit.

"Land ahead," announced the young giant at the controls. Palentine of Nova was his was name, but everyone called him Pally. From the very first he had always been there to enforce Michella's will on the others. Together they'd kept all the enhanced children from hurting the normals, but as they grew older it became harder for them to justify that rule. "There's their speeder; looks deserted."

"Land beside it; Tarah, Barah, check it out, make sure it isn't booby trapped."

Edie had a ghost of a smile on her lips as Michella slipped into command mode just like her father. "Yes, Micha," she thought, "she has my passion, but she's your daughter."

The ship barely touched the ground before the two young men leaped out and cautiously approached the speeder. There were clear tracks in the sand leading up to the forest. A swift inspection proved the speeder to be empty and safe to approach. As Michella reached them she heard Tarah mutter. "This thing isn't going anywhere."

"It is a wonder it didn't explode before they reached land," agreed his brother. "Chella, all clear here."

"Take our ship up and keep an eye on us from above, Barah. Tarah, go with him and man the guns; I'm sure you know how."

"I do," he grinned.

"If they have another ship, force it down but don't blow it up."

"Aye, Boss." Both boys were grinning with delight as they boarded their own ship. It leaped into the air and hovered high above like a hunting hawk.

As they rose into the air Michella was already following the tracks at a run. "Find Kon, Jak; find Kon." The big dog was well ahead of her again, his nose close to the ground. He had caught the scent as soon as they landed and was itching to go. It didn't take long to find them.

They followed the track where the kidnappers had fought their way through the scrub forest towards the abandoned mining town that brooded silently ahead. The going was a lot easier for them than for their quarry.

Suddenly the dog gave a startled yelp and leaped aside. The strange lizard that had tried to ambush him missed and stood in the track hissing. "Careful, it's poison." Pally easily sidestepped the lizard's attempt to bite him.

A few quick moves near it and he had the creature's complete attention. A feint to the left, a lightning move to the right, and the lizard lay still on the ground, stunned. They continued on. There was blood on the ground now.

The trail ended at a weathered building with a freshly kicked in door. Michella called Jak back and held him. At her nod Pally slipped around to the side of the building, Ellie right behind him. Michella cupped her hands to her mouth and called out. "Hello, the house. I'm Michella and I've come for my brother. Send him out unhurt."

A blaster fired in response, but the front of the building absorbed much of the energy and Michella was unhurt. "Stay back or I'll kill the kid," shouted a voice.

"That would be stupid," replied Michella, as she moved easily to the side. "Then I'd have no reason to keep you alive."

"I'm not joking," shouted the man, as he staggered through the door holding Kon by the collar. The boy was a mess and both Edie and Michella gasped as they saw him. Before the man could say anything more, his blaster crumpled in his hand, and he dropped it.

Pally was on him, the man was down and disarmed, and Kon was carried gently to his mother.

Edie was crying as she cradled her son in her arms and untied his bonds. His ribs were broken, he had a fever, and had badly soiled his clothing. Someone had obviously tried to clean him up and bandage him, but hadn't untied him to do it.

Michella gestured for Pally and Ellie to check the building as she grabbed her comm unit. "Tarah, we've got Kon. Come down."

"Understood. Coming down." The ship dropped swiftly to the small clearing. Nellie sent Kon a wave of healing energy as Edie carried him to the ship. The boy sighed and slipped into a peaceful sleep.

"Barah, take Mamma home then come back for us. Nellie, go with them." Michella turned to see Pally dragging a reluctant woman out of the shack.

"The other one's gone, Chella. I found this one hiding inside." Pally dropped the woman at Michella's feet.

"You're Deann's mother."

"Yes. Please don't hurt me; I tried to help him. Borry made me... They wouldn't let me untie him to ..."

"Understood. I won't hurt you, but you have to tell me everything." Michella reached out and helped the woman to her feet. "How long have you known what they were planning?"

"I didn't. I thought they were just out there drinking and blustering. Every time I asked I was told to shut up. One time he hit me and told me to stay out of mens' business. Last night, they disappeared, and then he came in dragging the boy. I tried to help him, but Borry hit me again for trying to untie him. I couldn't..."

"Is that Borry?"

The woman sniffed and drew a deep breath. "No, that's Dunc. Something bit him and he started to get sick. Borry left him with me and went to find food."

"What was the plan? What were they going to do with Kon?"

"They were going to sell him for millions. Borry said the slaver told him the Imperials would pay fortunes for one of the special children."

"What's the slaver's name and where do I find him?"

"I don't know; I swear I don't know..."

"Accepted." Michella had already turned away and was studying the ground. The man on the ground moaned and asked for water. Michella rolled him over with her toe. "Tell me the name of the slaver and I'll give you water."

"Mortan, his name is Mortan..water..."

Michella nodded. Pally knelt and pressed a water bottle to his lips. He left the water in the man's hands as he stepped back from him.

"Where do I find this Mortan?"

"I don't know," wheezed the man. "Borry was his contact. He'll know. Please, you've got to get me to a healer."

He was already talking to Michella's back. She was searching the ground for Borry's tracks. "It's way too late for a healer," said Pally. "The poison works slow, but there's no way to stop it."

"I have the trail," called Michela. "Come on, and bring her with you."

"Let's go," said Tarah, as he took the woman's arm and propelled her after Michella. "Don't try anything stupid if you want to stay alive and get out of here."

"I won't." She whimpered as she cringed away from him.

"Go easy," said Ellie. "Tarah, we've been set free to defend ourselves, not to become the bullies." One look at the fierce little witch's eyes and he relented.

"Sorry, Ellie, Ma'am. I meant stay close so we don't lose you when we're ready to leave."

"Much better," said Ellie, as she punched his arm and winked at the frightened woman. "Stay close to me; I won't let him hurt you." The woman thanked her and moved closer. She didn't see the sly grin Tarah gave Ellie. He'd set it up perfectly. If the woman had any more information Ellie would get it out of her now.

Dunc tried to rise and follow, calling for them to wait, but he was too weak. They disappeared into the trees just as another large lizard entered the clearing from another direction.

Borry wasn't much of a woodsman and his trail was easy for Michella to follow. He'd fought his way through the trees to the edge of the abandoned city. Once there he started to rummage about looking for old packaged food. He'd found a few things, but by what was scattered about, it was clear he hadn't found anything useful.

Borry stepped out of a building, still cursing as he tried to pry open a rusty container. He froze in place as he saw Michella and her companions. With a sudden desperate move he threw the can at her head and fled. In less than a heartbeat she had him by the collar and rammed him into the side of a building. He groaned as the air left his lungs.

Michella thrust him against the wall again, then stepped back. "Where do I find Mortan?"

Borry just shook his head as he tried to get air back into his lungs so he could speak. He sank to the ground for a moment then struggled back to his feet. He leaned his hands on his knees, drawing in great gasps of breath. Suddenly he straightened up and hurled a fist full of sand into Michella's eyes then fled. He didn't get far.

Borry had managed only a few steps when his body froze in place. Horrified, he struggled in vain as he was lifted into the air about ten feet then suddenly dropped back to the ground. He landed with a thud. A shiny dagger was pressed to his throat, and he was hauled back to his feet.

Pally held him easily and spoke softly. "Answer her questions or I'll feed you to the lizards. Your only hope of survival is to cooperate. Try anything else stupid, I'll kill you. Lie and Ellie will know. She'll drop you from a hundred meters up next time."

"Count on it," said the fierce little witch, a fire dancing in her deep brown eyes.

"Let him go."

"Chella?"

"This is personal; he's mine. He hurt my brother and now he pays. Tell me what I want to know and I'll let you go. If you lie to me, I will get truly nasty." She was still trying to get the dirt out of her eyes and by her look he knew she was unhappy.

"Mortan's on a ship, dark side of Lude. That's the second moon."

"I know what and where Lude is," she snarled. "Give me his contact codes." Trembling, he carefully pulled an info stick from his pocket.

"The code is there; I just have to send it then send the coordinates. They'll come for us in the ship."

"Send it."

"What???"

"Send it. If he gets past the Ravage he's mine. Send it." With trembling hands he obeyed. "Now run. If I ever see your face again I'll kill you with my bare hands."

Michella grabbed his collar and propelled him to the trees then turned away. There was a sudden flash of something passing her head then a crunch behind her. She turned to see Borry on the ground with Pally's dagger in his skull. Borry had a knife in his hand.

"Never turn your back on an enemy, Chella," the young giant rumbled softly as he retrieved his knife and wiped it on the dead man's shirt. "What's our next move?"

Michella swallowed hard as she gazed at the dead man on the ground. Finally she roused herself and turned away, fighting to keep her stomach contents down. "Now I contact Father to report, then we wait."

Her hand trembled slightly as she reached for her comm unit. "Michella to Micha."

"Report, Chella." He sounded distracted and busy.

"Kon's safe, the kidnappers are dead, and the slaver has been contacted. He's on a ship behind Lude. His name is Mortan. Orders?"

"If he gets through, he's yours. Chella, information is more useful than dead bodies."

"Understood. Chella out."

They made a fire and waited for their ship to return. "Well, how did we do, Mamma Hen?" Pally settled to the ground beside Michella as he spoke. They'd all been silent for some time, each lost in their own thoughts.

Michella sighed and poked at the fire before tossing on another stick. "You did great, Pally; all of you. So, are you guys feeling as weird about this as I am? I mean, we've spent our whole lives learning to protect them and now we've just killed two."

"Only one, Chella; the other would have died of the poison in a few hours anyway. We couldn't help him if we'd wanted to."

"I didn't want to, Pally. Did you see poor little Kon? What they did to him? They wouldn't even let her clean him up properly. I wanted to hurt them; I'm just feeling strange about it."

"We all are, Chella. This is new for all of us, but somehow I know it's right. I'll keep an eye out for lizards." Palentine rose easily and began to patrol the area, throwing heavy stones at a lizard that had come to investigate. "They're getting curious; we should head back to the beach where we can stay out in the open."

They all agreed. Tarah kicked dirt over the fire until he was certain it was out then they headed for the beach where they'd first landed. "You know, Mamma Hen, we're still the Guardians; it's just that now we're guarding our own people. Humans don't have to be afraid of us as long as they don't attack us."

"Tarah's right, Chella," agreed Ellie, as she tucked her arm through his. "We knew we'd have to toughen up."

"This didn't affect you, Ellie?"

"Yeah, it did, but look at the lives our parents had. If we're going to be worthy of them, we'd better grow up, and fast."

"You're right, Ellie. Okay people, there's the beach."

"Find a defensible spot," shouted Palentine, as he dropped back. "We've got company. These damned things are most active at this time of day. Whatever you do, don't get bitten; it's fatal. The sound of his blaster hissing testified to the danger.

Just then Michella's comms came to life. "Nellie to Mamma Hen; where are you?"

"We're at the beach landing. Make a strafing run to keep our friends at bay then pick us up."

Barah's wild yell of glee could be heard over the comms as the fighter swept in and raked the beach with bullets. Several lizards were killed or wounded, and the rest fell on them to make an easy meal. A few moments later the young crew was back in the air and headed for home.

"What are you going to do with me?" The woman sat quietly at the back, her head down. She was terrified and her voice betrayed that.

"I'm taking you home," sighed Michella, as she turned in her seat to face the woman. "I promised Deann I would. After that I'm going back to wait for that damned slaver."

Diversion

Once Michella was on her way, Micha had boarded Zartah's speeder. The others followed; they headed straight for the Ravage. As soon as they were on board, they set about readying all the fighters for battle. Once prepared, they settled in to wait.

Everything seemed quiet for a long time. Zartah began to pace about the bridge, but Micha relaxed in the captain's chair. "Give it time, Zartah; it'll get interesting soon enough."

"Are you sure about this, Boss?"

"I'm sure. Chella and her crew of savages will catch up and retrieve Kon. I just hope they stay cool long enough to spring the trap."

"Trap?"

"When the kidnappers call for help, whoever is hiding out there will attack, thinking we're all occupied with something else."

Just then the comms came to life as Michella reported in that she had succeeded. Everyone raced back to the fighter ships. They were barely aboard when Jorge's voice came over the comms. "Fifteen ships incoming, unknown design."

"Understood. Launching."

"Freedom is inbound, but she ran into trouble and just shook it. She's an hour away at best speed."

"Understood. Looks like we're on our own folks."

The two aging Arcalian fighters pulled out in front of the Ravage, facing the approaching ships. As they neared, Micha went on the comms. "Approaching ships, you're in Novan space. Nova is temporarily out of bounds. Hold your position and state your business."

"Always the perfect diplomat," giggled Brenna. Micha shot her a look, but she ignored it.

"Is this the witch's hound?"

"Stall for time, Micha," hissed Lessa as she squirmed in the gunner's seat, trying to get comfortable. "Keep him talking until the Freedom gets here."

"I'm Micha of Nova, is your business with me?"

"Oh yes it is, slave. I've waited for over twenty years for this day. You should be on the ground, looking for something you've lost. Why are you out here in that old ship?"

"State your name and business," Micha replied through clenched teeth. Something about that voice seemed vaguely familiar.

"As you wish, slave. I'm Mortan. You and that thrice damned witch ruined me years ago and I have gone through hell and back again to get to this point. I have your only son, slave. You will surrender to me now or my men will cut his throat."

"Ah yes, now I remember you. You're the man who killed his own brother and abandoned a group of children on a doomed ship. You're also the man who was slave raiding on Kora Six. We stopped you there and gave you a taste of your own medicine. Did you enjoy your time as a farm slave?"

"I spent that time planning your death, yours and the witch's. Surrender and your son lives. Do it now."

"Actually, my mate has my son safely at home. My daughter and companions found your men, forced them to contact you, and then eliminated them. You've failed again. I give you one chance and one chance only. Leave here now and I'll give you a one day head start before I hunt you down."

A long stretch of silence followed that statement. "Stay sharp," cautioned Micha. "He'll try to contact them and when he can't, he'll attack."

Behind him Micha heard the sounds of Lessa and Rathbone settling into the gunners chairs while Miriam kept a sharp eye on the scanners. "There are no more ships showing up, Micha. I only see these, fifteen in all."

"Thanks, Miriam; take the tail guns now. This will break open soon." She nodded and slipped back to the tail gunner's seat.

Micha was studying the scanner panel, trying to make sense of the enemy formation. "Lessa, are you thinking what I'm thinking?"

"He'll be in that bigger ship that's holding back behind the others."

"That was my first thought. Can you reach him from here?"

"I'd like to be a lot closer."

"I'll see what I can do. Rath, is she up for it?"

The big cyborg just chuckled. "Aye, Boss, I just tuned her up yesterday. One hard burst, then full jets should put us in the middle of things."

"All right folks, brace yourselves. He'll make his move any second now.

Micha's assessment was bang on. His years of experience gave him a huge advantage, their superior physical bodies greatly increased that advantage but even then, five to one odds weren't good. They needed something more; the element of surprise. Before Mortan could give the order to attack, Micha's ship was in motion.

As the Arcalian fighter leaped at them, Mortan bellowed for the attack. The waiting was over and the battle was on. In the breath or two it took for the slavers to react, Micha's ship was among them, his guns blazing. The Ravage and the second fighter ship were only a heartbeat behind. To Mortan's horror, Micha's ship wove through the mass directly at him.

Witchfire lanced out from the fighter, but another ship wandered into the line of fire and Mortan was saved for the moment. The other ship wasn't so lucky, it was sliced to ribbons. Mortan opened fire, targeting Micha's small ship and trying to keep another between them as a shield.

The element of surprise helped, but it wasn't enough. The Guardians were too greatly outnumbered, and they faced new modern ships. Before long, Micha's ship was crippled and she was scooped up by the Ravage. The crew boarded one of the old Imperial fighters in the fighter bay and launched out again.

They managed to get the enemy down to five ships, but Zartah was out of the battle and Micha was trying to keep the others off him long enough for the Ravage to haul him in. It was looking bad when a new ship appeared on sensors. It was the Freedom, coming in at full burn, but she was being chased by another half dozen ships.

Without hesitation the Freedom hurled herself into the fray. So did her pursuers; six shiny new fighter ships of Arcalian design. The battle was soon over with the remaining three Slaver ships surrendering. Dozens of escape pods were floating freely in space and the Ravage began to gather them up.

"Looks like we're done here," said Micha, as he landed his small fighter in the cargo bay of the Ravage. He led the way back to the bridge and settled into the captain's chair. He grinned as Jorge's young son vacated the chair to make a place for him. "Comms, shipwide, Ensign."

"Aye, Boss," replied the boy, as he raced to the comms position. "Shipwide, Sir."

"Report. How are we doing people?"

"Our fighters are out of commission for a while," came Rathbone's voice, "But the Ravage seems to be intact."

"Lessa, you in the infirmary?"

"Here, Micha."

"Casualties? Injuries?"

"We took no casualties; just a few minor injuries. A few of the prisoners are in bad shape."

"Understood. Is Keira there with you?"

"Yes, she and Brenna are on guard."

"Very good. Ship-to-ship, Ensign."

"Aye, Sir, ship-to-ship." The boy's grin grew even wider as he spoke.

"Freedom, Micha here. Report."

"Dav here, Micha. We met with a bit of resistance, but His Majesty happened to be going our way and set things right. Sorry we're late to the party."

"No problem, Dav. Casualties?"

"None, but we've taken a bit of damage. Those are fancy fighters for slavers."

"Indeed they are, and with very determined pilots. I really would like to know what's going on here."

"I think I can shed some light on that for you Micha," came another voice.

"King Borad? Is that you?"

"Guilty as charged, Micha. I was on my way to Nova to present you with six of the High Guard's newest fighters when we happened upon the Freedom. She was battling the slaver's back up."

"Six new ships? A gift?"

"A down payment, Micha. I have news and a proposal, but I should like to save that conversation until my poor battered yacht catches up. She took a bit of damage in the original skirmish."

"Agreed. Please proceed to Nova under Freedom's escort. We'll finish up here and join you as quickly as possible. Micha out."

"Now what in the nine hells is he up to?" Micha was on his feet and pacing as he muttered to himself. Finally he stopped and raised his eyes from the deck. He could feel the others watching him. "What?"

"Are you all right, Micha?" Brenna asked softly.

Micha sighed and sank back into the captain's chair. "What's on your mind, Brenna?"

Lessa stepped forward and laid a gentle hand on Micha's shoulder as Brenna responded. "You ordered me to dispatch that man at your farm. Micha, you knew I couldn't do that."

"I knew. You're also concerned about how I shot him. Brenna, I'm all too familiar with the dark side of slavery. Those men attacked my home and stole my son to be slaved out or worse. I wanted him to know he was going to die, but I didn't expect you to do it. The problem is how badly I wanted to do it. Right now I'm wrestling with the mad desire to run down to the brig and see if Mortan is there so I can kill him in person.

"That's the big problem here; this is getting personal, and I can't function like that. I have to keep a clear head."

"Is that why you sent Michella after Kon?"

"Yes, that's why. Michella has her mother's passion, but she can still function when the emotion grips her. I envy her that."

"So, what else is going on in that head of yours," asked Lessa, as she squeezed his shoulder affectionately.

"You're not going to like it."

"I already knew that."

"I'll tell you later, but you'll have to protect me from Norlene."

"Norlene?"

Further discussion was cut short as Zartah came over the comms. "Mess is all clear, Boss. We've got Mortan in the brig. Shall I shoot him, or do you want to?"

"I want to," replied Micha, already on the move towards the door. "I'll be right there." Lessa was close on his heels.

A grizzled and sour looking old man sat glowering at Zartah as Lessa and Micha swept into the room. Lessa thrust out her hand and the man was hurled back against the wall. She paced slowly towards him, her hair blowing back in a breeze only she could feel.

He struggled against the force that held him, but he was helpless. Zartah flipped a switch so all would be recorded.

"Be still." Mortan stopped struggling and wet himself. That voice could not have come from a human woman's throat. She reached up and blew a greenish powder in his face. He choked, but couldn't avoid breathing in some of the powder. His eyes went blank and she dropped him to the floor. "You will answer all questions truthfully."

"Yes," he responded in a flat emotionless voice.

"He's all yours, Micha."

Micha nodded then sat on the floor facing the man who had attack him and his people more than once over the years. "You organized the capture of my son."

"Yes."

"Why?"

"More money than you can imagine, and for revenge on you and the witch."

"Who would pay you this money?"

"The Imperials. Emperor Loran the Second wants a Spawn brat to study."

"Where did you get those fighter ships?"

"From the Imperials; they're a new design."

"How did they get them through the Gap without Kella knowing?"

"Thornk brought them through. He lost three in the Gap, but he got the rest through. Kella trusts Thornk. She believes what he tells her."

"Do you have allies on this side of the Gap?"

"Yes."

"Name them."

"Kemge, of Sega Clan and Lady Elaia set up a base for me on Praxi Three. My people are there."

"Who is your contact with the Imperials?"

"Harborne of Elliston."

"Is he on Praxi Three?"

"Yes."

Micha rose to his feet and turned to Zartah. "Send a copy of that interview to Lortax. I'm sure he'll be interested. Lessa, are you all right?"

"Micha, he just said the high Priestess herself was involved. Mortan, have you spoken personally with Lady Elaia?"

"Yes. She was with Kemge when I met with them."

"Exactly what did she say?"

"If you get the chance, Slaver, kill Arlessa for me."

"You get that last bit Zartah?" asked Micha.

"Got it Boss. Sending now."

The man on the floor groaned and began to stir. "It's wearing off," sighed Lessa. "Shall I put him out again or let him wake up?'

"We're done here," said Micha. "Let him wake up."

"What did you people do to me?" groaned Mortan as he struggled to his feet.

"We drugged you," replied Micha. "You sang like a lark. Now I'm going to do something I've never done before. I'm going to sell a slave. I'm taking you to Dornal; they're always looking for training slaves."

Pale and trembling, the aging slaver made a desperate lunge for Micha. Zartah's blaster sizzled and the man was hurled against the wall, dead. "Boss, what's a training slave?"

"The old and useless, Zartah. They use them for young guards to practice their whipping techniques on. A training slave usually only lasts a day or so, but it is a hard way to die. They cut out their tongues first so they don't have to listen to them begging for mercy."

"Micha, how do you know this?"

"My Grandsire was sent there because he broke his leg and it didn't heal right. Our owner took great pleasure in explaining all about it. He felt we needed to know what he did with lazy or useless slaves."

"You never told me..."

"There's a lot about slavery I haven't talked about, Lessa, but now you know one of the reasons I want to make it stop whenever I can." She didn't speak; she just nodded, hugged him gently for a moment, and then released him. Micha gave her a weak smile then left for the bridge.

Micha strode onto the bridge and sank into the captain's chair. "Report."

"Mess is cleaned up and bundled, Boss. You can see it on screen." Jorge flipped a switch as he spoke and the screen came to life. All the debris from the battle was bunched up and free floating in space. Micha's favorite Arcalian fighter was in the rubble.

"I'm going to miss that ship," he sighed. "Did we salvage anything useful?"

"Rath has three of those new Imperial fighters in the bay. He says we can use them."

"All right, Jorge, blast that lot then head for home. The King doesn't like to be kept waiting."

"Aye, Boss, blasting." An energy beam lanced out from the Ravage and the rubble began to melt down in space. The metals twisted and buckled then began to collapse in on itself, creating one solid mass. The beam stopped and a torpedo streaked towards the mass, detonating right at its edge. The mass began to move very slowly.

"That should do it, Boss. It'll reach the star in a couple of days. Heading home."

———◦———

THE SHIP TOUCHED DOWN in the farmyard. Michella leaped down and raced through the door of the house. Kon was in his accustomed chair sipping his favorite soup, Nella, head bandaged, was beside him. Edie fussed about, tidying a house that was already tidy. The neighbours had dragged the dead bodies out and cleaned up the mess before they'd returned with the boy.

Michella let her shoulders sag as she finally relaxed. She got herself a bowl and indicated that her friends who had followed her in should do the same. They were all gathered at the table when Micha returned with his crew.

Micha stepped through the door and Edie threw herself into his arms. He held her tightly as he gazed at his son for a moment then watched as his crew served themselves and sat to the huge table. "Report, Edie. How's our boy?"

"He's a little beat up, but he'll be fine in a day or two. Micha, what happened up there? Did you get the slaver? What's going on?"

"Okay, okay, I'll talk." He grinned as he slowly released her from his arms. "For a bowl of that soup."

"Sit," she laughed, as she slapped his arm then turned to the large pot at the stove. She served him then sat beside him. "All right, Mister, start talking."

"Yes, Ma'am," he grinned as he told her the story of what had happened. He had barely finished when his comm unit squawked.

"Micha here."

"It's Norlene, Micha. Gorda and the king are in the guest quarters getting drunk as lords. I'll stay here to protect the young priestesses. It'll take them a day to sober up and another to recover from the hangovers. You have a bit of time; get some rest people."

"Yes, Ma'am," grinned Micha. "We hear and obey."

———◦———

THE TALL MAN STOOD gazing out the window of his office high above the surface of the planet. There was nothing but city as far as the eye could see. With his hands clasped behind his back, he sighed and spoke without turning around. "What is it?"

The woman knelt and lowered her eyes. "I have the report from Sector Nine, Sire."

"Failure as usual?" he asked.

"As you predicted, Sire. The Hound regained his child and destroyed those who attacked him."

"In that case, there was no failure," smiled Emperor Loran, as he turned to face her. "Rise. Tell me all."

"There is little more to tell, Sire," she replied, as she rose easily to her feet. "The attempt failed as you knew it would."

"Yes, but it's the results of the attack that interest me most. The Hound knows he's vulnerable now. We've stirred up enough resentment against him that he knows his own people will betray him. He will leave Nova. The big question is, where will he go? Exile? Perhaps, but I doubt it. Life is never that easy.

"No, my old enemy, you will flee, but where will you go?" He began to muse to himself and she slipped quietly out of the office. "I've had a better body built, Hound, one without the weaknesses of the earlier version. I won't be so easily defeated at our next meeting. Next time you will be the one to die, and there will be no resurrection for you.

"I know, I know, the witch has the remote that shuts me off, but that damned fail-safe wasn't the only trick the mad doctor built into me. No, he also put in a thin membrane that isolated the brain and kept it alive for weeks in stasis. I call myself Loran the Second because this is my second body, but it's still me. It's still me, Hound..."

Endings and Beginnings

Michella slept the clock around and awoke hungry. As she entered the warm kitchen, she found her father and his crew gathered at the table. The others were talking softly, but Micha was listening quietly, his mind working at light speed as usual. She gathered some meat and cheese, and then abandoned the kitchens for the orchard. She picked an apple then settled down under a tree to enjoy her meal.

Before she could take a single bite Jak began barking furiously at a nearby tree. A woman's scream was easily heard above the dog's noise. Michella leaped to her feet and raced to his side. One look into the tree and she lost all focus entirely. She was staring open mouthed at a pair of long slim legs dangling from a branch just up out of the dog's reach. It was Deann.

Michella was lost in the delicious spectacle before her, hormones racing through her body and clouding her mind. The girl's feet were encased in soft leather boots, but her legs were bare, and her skirt had caught on a branch as she lost her footing. Deann was bare to the waist and hanging just above eye level.

"Michella, stop drooling, call off that damned dog, and get me down out of here. It hurts and it's embarrassing."

"Oh yes, it is," grinned Michella, as she motioned for the dog to back away, "and may I say you have a fine ass to embare?"

"Shut up and get me down," laughed Deann.

"All right, if I have to." Michella climbed easily into the tree, checking her footing before setting her shoulders under Deann's feet. "Okay, let go and slide down onto my shoulders.

Deann slowly, fearfully, released her hold on the branch, fighting to release her long skirt as she did. Her squirming caused her to turn just as she began to slide down to Michella's shoulders.

Michella lost all sense of reality as a silken thigh slid along her cheek until her nose was buried in the girl's pubic hair. She gasped then drew a long deep breath, savoring the sweet scent of woman and allowing her mind to go several naughty places at once. The skirt fluttered down over her head leaving her in darkness and awash in that glorious aroma.

For a moment those warm thighs gently squeezed her head, then Deann's admonishing voice broke the spell. "Stop that, you pervert. Get me down before we both get killed."

"I can't, see, Sweetheart," giggled Michella. "You'll have to lift your skirt so I can see." Slowly, almost painfully slowly, the skirt slid up and revealed the world to Michella once again. She nuzzled Deann's belly once, then turned her so she could slide down and ride piggyback. With the girl clinging to her back, she climbed back to solid ground.

Once on the ground, Deann slid slowly off Michella's back until her feet touched solid earth. She was a bit slow to release the tight grip she'd had around her rescuer's neck. Jak came over and tentatively sniffed at her legs as the skirt slid back into place. "Sorry big guy, I didn't mean to scare you like that," she said, as she scratched the dog behind the ear and made friends.

"So, what happened there anyway?"

"What happened, Chella? Your dog chased me up a tree, where I got trapped with my skirt around my ears. You came along and took advantage of me before you helped me down. Stop laughing at me."

"I'm sorry, Sweetheart." Michella was giggling and there was no hint of contrition in her voice. "You were far too delicious to resist."

"Oh sure, I'm so irresistible. Sweetheart?"

"Well, considering how intimate we've become lately, I thought it appropriate."

"Stop laughing at me, Chella. Intimate? I threw a block of wood at you after you kicked in my door and now you take advantage of me when I can't escape. That's intimate?"

"Well, the last part was," giggled Michella.

"You're awful, you know that?"

"I know; I'm bad. If I share my lunch with you will you forgive me?"

"Okay, but only if it's good," grinned Deann.

Michella was gazing into those large brown eyes and getting lost. Deann's scent was still in her nostrils and her desire was plain on her face. Reluctantly she shook off the spell and led Deann back to her abandoned lunch. They sat beneath the apple tree and shared the food, gazing into each others eyes, but not speaking.

Finally, Michella broke the spell. "Deann, what happened back there? I've never known Jak to do anything like that before." The dog was now lying between them, his huge head resting in Deann's lap.

"That was my fault, Chella. I was coming over to thank you for bringing Momma home safe and sound. As usual I had my eyes on my vid game and not on where I was going. The big guy was asleep and didn't hear me coming, I guess. Anyway, I must have stepped on his tail. "He jumped up and barked which scared the bejebbers out of me. The next thing I knew I was climbing the tree and my foot slipped. The rest you know."

"So, you came to see me and didn't wear underwear?"

"Stop it, Chella."

"Come on, Sweetheart, confess."

Suddenly, Deann leaped to her feet and fled. "Stop calling me that," she sobbed as she ran from Michella. She hadn't gone far when she realized that Michella and Jak were keeping pace with her easily.

She stopped running and turned away. "I guess I can't get away from you, can I?" she sniffed.

"Why can't I call you Sweetheart?" asked Michella, as she took Deann's arm gently to turn her. Deann hissed in pain and shrank away. "Deann, I'm so sorry. I didn't mean to hurt you. I would never hurt you..."

"No, Chella, you didn't. I scraped my arm and side on the tree, and it stings. You didn't hurt me."

"I didn't?" Michella gently took Deann into her arms and hugged her. "If I didn't hurt you, why did you run away from me? Why don't you want me to call you Sweetheart?"

"Because you don't really mean it." Deann burst into tears again and sobbed into Michella's shoulder.

"Are you so sure I don't mean it, Deann?"

"You can't really mean it, Chella. I'm not one of you..." Michella stopped her with a kiss. She hadn't meant to kiss the girl, but holding that firm female body in her arms and the scent of the girl's hair made her lose all control. Deann whimpered and melted into Michella's arms.

Michella forced herself to hold the girl gently, even though her knees were trembling under the fire of that kiss. "You can hold me tighter, Chella. I won't break, I promise."

"Deann, I..."

"Oh Chella, I've been trying to get you to notice me for so long..."

"Notice you? Silly woman, I haven't been able to take my eyes off you for months. It broke my heart when we tracked Kon's kidnappers to your farm."

"Chella, I didn't know... I tried to warn you, but he hit me and smashed my comm unit. I..."

"I know, Sweetheart, I know. Yes, I said Sweetheart, but you kissed me, now I have the right."

"I kissed you?" Deann leaned back to make eye contact, trying to keep her face stern and failing. "You kissed me first."

"I did?" Michella was trying to look innocent and failing. "Oh dear, what are you going to do about that?"

"I'm going to get even with you, lady." Deann kissed Michella and Chella crushed the girl to her. Deann moaned with pleasure and tightened her grip on Michella. "Please don't ever let me go, Chella," she whispered as their lips slowly parted and she buried her face in Michella's neck.

"I won't, Sweetheart; I won't. You're far too delicious to let go."

"Promise? Promise me, Chella. I know you'll keep that promise."

"I promise I'll keep you as long as I can or as long as you want me to, Sweetheart. I will never force you to stay if you don't want to, but I can't imagine ever being willing to let you go. Come on, let's go back and finish our lunch."

"Okay. Chella, will you hold my hand?"

"What's going on in that head of yours?" asked Michella, as she took the girl's hand and laced their fingers together.

"Well, I'm not one of you and I'm a girl, so…"

"Okay, Sweetheart, here's the rules. My friends and family will accept you. It may be a bit tough at times, but we'll face all that together. I will not cave to pressure, but I honestly don't think there'll be any. I just can't see it being a problem."

"Well, I guess we'll soon find out, here comes your father."

Micha slowly approached the two girls, but his attention seemed to be far away. "Hi Poppa," smiled Michella. "This is my sweetheart, Deann. We're all brand new."

"That's probably not a good idea, Chella," he replied, as he turned away and swept his gaze over the fields of the farm and sighed deeply.

"Just what is that supposed to mean, Father? Do you disapprove of my choice? Would you care to explain why?"

The cold tone of her voice cut through his mood, and he turned back to her. He shook off the mood and focused. The fire in his daughter's eyes told him he was on shaky ground. He turned his attention to the girl cowering behind Michella. "Forgive me, Deann. My comment has nothing at all to do with you personally or with your gender. It has to do with the timing of events well beyond our control."

"Poppa, what's going on?"

"I'd rather not say just yet, Chella."

"Deann can keep a secret and so can I, Poppa."

"All right, Chella, Deann, but you can't say anything to anybody just yet." Both girls nodded so he continued. "The King of Arcalia came all the way to Nova to bring me six new ships. I can only assume that I'll soon be in need of them.

"Ladies, I don't like the way events are moving, but I have to face reality. We called ourselves the Guardians, but we've become outcasts. Instead of working with us and enjoying a peaceful life, most people have turned against us. I have this feeling that soon we'll have to abandon our beloved Nova.

"You two are new. Edie and I had only a moment before we were separated. You two may have only days or it may never happen. Just in case, enjoy each moment you have together as though it may be your last." He took a long sad look into the fields. "I will miss this farm." With that, Micha wandered off towards the barns.

"Michella, is he serious?"

"You saw his face, Deann. That's as close to crying as I have ever seen my father, and it scares me. It means he's already made the decision and accepted the consequences. He's already in mourning."

Deann clutched Michella's arm tightly. "I don't want you to leave, not now."

"I know, Sweetheart; me either, but he's made up his mind. I know my father. After what happened with Kon he'll go into defensive mode. He'll find some way to hide and protect all his people or he'll die trying.

"Poppa always says to hope for the best, but to prepare for the worst."

"Take me with you, Chella." She was clinging to Michella's arm and all her emotions were easily read in her eyes. Fear, loss, love, devotion, determination, all those and more raced through her then she settled into determination.

"I don't know if I'll be able to." Michella's voice choked, and she was hugging Deann tightly, her face buried in the girl's hair.

"All the others call you Mother Hen because you always find a way to keep them safe, protect them, and still get things done. You can find a way, and if you can't, I will."

"We'll find a way, Sweetheart; we will. Right now, I have to get you patched up." Deann had whimpered as Michella's arm tightened on her side. Michella took her comm unit from the pocket of her tunic. "Michella to Allore."

"I'm a bit busy now, Chella." Michella sighed. Allore was upset about something, and she'd have to fix it before anything else could be accomplished.

"Allore, I need a healer, now."

"You didn't need me before..." So that was it.

"Poppa sent Momma with me, Lore, you know that."

"Fine, but no more guessing games; am I, or am I not the medic on your crew?"

"Allore, you're a bit young..."

"Answer the question, Chella."

Michella sighed. It wasn't going to be easy to get this one past her father, but she had no choice. Allore could stay angry for months if she wanted to. The thing was, Allore was already a better medic than her mother. Why did everything have to be so damn complex all the time? "Allore, you're the official medic on my crew, you know that. Come to me now, I need you. I'll send Jak."

"She's a determined one, isn't she?" grinned Deann.

"You have no idea," sighed Michella, as she gently pulled Deann back into a hug. "Jak, go fetch Allore. Go fetch Allore." The big dog happily bounded away towards the house.

"I'm every bit as determined as she is, Chella. I'm going with you."

"What about your mother, your brothers?"

"She's already sold the farm, Chella." Deann sank to the ground and Michella sat beside her, taking her hand. "She's taking all of us to her brother's house on Borealis Two. They'll be fine there; they'll be safe."

Jak came bounding joyfully across the field, followed by a laughing Allore, her medic's kit bouncing at her hip. Edie had made it for her and put the Nova Crew sunburst logo on it. "Deann, why are you here? Are you hurt?"

"She's here because she's my sweetheart and we want to spend time together. Yes, she's hurt. Stop being so nosey and help her."

"Yes, Boss," giggled Allore, as she knelt beside Deann and opened her kit. "Sweethearts, huh? When did this happen?'

"A few minutes ago," grinned Michella.

"Did you have to beat her up to get her to agree?"

"Just shut up and help her, Allore."

"Yes, Boss. Deann, show me the injury."

Blushing furiously, Deann raised her tunic and lowered her skirt to show Allore the angry red scrape down her side.

"Oh, that looks nasty; I'll put some of this Magic Skin sealant on it." Allore popped the lid off a container and lightly sprayed a filmy substance over the scrape. Deann sighed with relief as the filmy substance congealed into something like skin. "Over the next few days your natural skin will reform and absorb that. In the meantime, be gentle with it. So, why aren't you wearing any underwear?"

"Allore!" exclaimed Michella, then she giggled and turned to Deann. "Yes, Deann, why are you not wearing any underwear?"

"Stop it, both of you. It is all in the laundry, okay?'

"Oh, yes, of course," giggled Allore.

"There, Allore, you see, she had a perfectly good reason."

"Stop it, both of you," blushed Deann, as they both giggled helplessly. "Okay, fine. Look in that tree where the dog chased me; they're hooked on a branch there. They tore off when I slipped." She was laughing with them now.

"Well, I expect you two want to be alone now," said Allore, as she arose and began repacking her kit. "I'm going back to the house to see if I can figure out what's going on with Poppa. He's off his game, if you know what I mean, and I have a kitten with a broken leg..." her voice trailed off as she trotted away, Jak loping happily at her side.

"Come with me, Deann," said Michella, as she rose and gently pulled the girl to her feet. "I want to show you the rest of the farm."

"The rest of the farm?"

"Yes, the hay loft in the barn is particularly interesting."

"Oh, well then, I can't wait to see it," laughed Deann, as she laced her fingers through Michella's.

Decisions

Two days later the call came in. They were required on Borealis Prime in five days. Micha and crew refused to go, citing the attack on them and Nova as reason. To Micha's surprise, the conference was relocated to Nova one week later. Something big was up.

Three days before the conference was to convene, Lessa sent for Micha. The King of Arcalia was ready to talk. "It's about time," muttered Micha, as he contacted his crew. No one was truly surprised to see Michella arrive with them. She had led a crew on a successful mission; she was now a crew boss of Nova.

They filed into the audience chamber of the temple where Norlene sat as High Priestess. Lessa had elected to sit as part of the Crew. The members of Michella's crew slipped into the room and quietly sat in the row behind her. Micha glanced at them then gave Allore a hard look. She held up her medic kit with a look of defiance. He looked to Michella who nodded. He turned back as Norlene cleared her throat.

Resplendent in flowing scarlet robes, Norlene rose and held up her arms. The room fell silent. She lowered her arms and spoke in a clear steady voice that easily reached every nook and cranny of the room. "Guardians of Nova, we are gathered in the hall of audience this day to hear the words of our honored guest, His Majesty, King Borad of the Arcalian Alliance. We will now hear his words." She sat back down and nodded to the King who was sitting in the seat of honor to her left.

"Greetings, people of Nova. May I begin by saying I'm quite surprised at the formality of the meeting. I had hoped for something a bit more intimate."

"I warned you," grunted Gorda. Micha shushed him.

Norlene turned to Micha. "Would you care to address this, Micha?"

Micha rose to his feet and grinned. "I thought to save a bit of time, Sire. If the whole crew is here then I don't have to repeat everything to them afterwards." There was a round of chuckles at that.

"And the children?" asked the king.

"The young people behind me are Nova Crew Three. They've proven themselves in the field and their concerns will be heard before I make any decisions. Forgive me, Sire, but I have a damn good idea why you're here in person instead of sending for me as usual. What you have to say concerns all of us."

The king nodded his head and let his shoulders sag a bit. "Understood and accepted, Micha. Alright people, here's the situation. You led us to victory at the battle of the Gap. However, the Gap was created at that battle, and it is expanding, albeit slowly.

"Most of you have been through that Gap and know full well the dangers. However, in recent months, things have gotten a lot worse. Stranger and stranger things are happening there. More and more pirates are getting through and so are Imperial spies.

"As you all know, the Gap is primarily along my outer borders. On my other borders, the forces of Sega Clan are pressing me. Oh they haven't actually started anything that would warrant calling in the Viceroy, but they're building up a presence. Every small planet along our borders with them now has a large contingent of Sega military personnel visiting on a regular basis.

"I can't properly defend my borders from Sega Clan and all of Sector Nine from the Gap at the same time. I need help; I need an ally. That's why I've come to you. I tried to get here in time to head off the attack on Nova, but I was too slow."

"You knew about this and didn't warn us?" Micha had leaped to his feet, but Lessa put a restraining hand on his arm.

"Micha, I swear I didn't learn of it in time. I was almost to Nova when I got the word."

"Accepted. So, why were you coming to us?"

"I brought you six new warships as a gift. You'll need them regardless of what you decide to do. I have more, though. Micha, I need you to move your crew to the Gap permanently. I know what you ask for fees, and I'll bankrupt my kingdom to pay it if I have to. I'll provide you with a planet of your own, supply bases along the Gap, and anything else you may need."

"You want us to uproot our families, abandon our farms and homes?"

"Yes. Micha, I've got spies everywhere as you know. I've watch for years as things on Nova deteriorated.

"Listen to me, now. You and Lady Arlessa had a vision of restoring Nova Prime and bringing her people home. You accomplished that, but you were changed in the process and the Nova of reality isn't the Nova either of you envisioned.

"I suggest to you that your Nova is not this planet; it's your people. You wear the sunburst tattoo now, and it's well known you've withdrawn from Nara Clan. I suggest to you that your Nova is Nova Clan; you and your people. That Nova will be wherever your people are.

"Please think this over. If I fall then Sega will be spread too thin to control the Gap. Sector Nine will be wide open to the Imperials and anything else that finds its way out of that rift in time and space."

Micha didn't respond for a long moment and the king began to sweat. He desperately needed these folk. Micha and crew were only a handful of people, but they had proven themselves to be a force of nature. With them guarding his back and plugging up the Gap, Arcalia would be too strong for Sega Clan to attack. He could concentrate all his forces to that border and defend it easily.

Finally, Micha rose to his feet again. "All right, folks, you've heard it. Opinions, options?"

"Nova Clan, now I do like the sound of that," grinned Zartah. "This could be exciting." Micha grinned and shook his head. Leave it to Zartah to put a happy face of it.

"Gorda?"

"King Borad's right, Boss. Right now we're out in the open and easy targets. Personally, I wouldn't mind having a friend watching our backs."

"Rathbone?"

"Gorda's right, we're in a vulnerable position here. However, this is your home, more, this is Lady Arlessa's home and dream. Whatever you decide, I'm there." Keira pumped her fist at that and grinned her agreement. There was a round of ayes at that.

"Dav?"

"Sorry, Micha," grinned Dav. "You want the bad news now or later?"

"Now Dav."

"I'm here to represent the cyborgs by mutual agreement. We're retiring. Our cybernetic enhancements are starting to work our human parts too hard. We're all long past military retirement age. Now we just want to find a place to soak up and enjoy our declining years."

Micha nodded his head thoughtfully. "King Borad, have you got someplace for these men and their families to live in safety?"

"Consider it done," replied the King.

"Michella, your thoughts?"

Startled, Michella stood up slowly, glancing at her friends for support. They all nodded. Whatever Momma Hen decided was good with them. "If we're Nova Clan," she replied slowly, "then you're clan chieftain. I and my crew will follow your decision. We don't want to leave our homes and friends, but things are such that we'll understand if you decide to go."

Again Micha nodded thoughtfully. "Michella, Dav and his men are retiring. The Freedom is yours." Michella gasped and didn't respond. "Take your crew and inspect your ship. Dav, show her around please."

"On it, Boss." He grinned and stepped to Michella, offering his arm. "My lady." Blushing, she took the arm and filed out, her crew close behind her. Micha turned to Lessa.

"Lady Arlessa, your thoughts?" he asked gently.

"Sadly, His Majesty is all too correct in his assessment of our situation. He needs us, but we need him as badly. I've seen this coming for some time, Micha. As Michella said, we're Nova Clan, and you are chieftain. I'll abide by your decision, but I do recommend we accept the King's offer."

Micha nodded and slowly turned back to face the king. "It seems as though Nova Clan is ready to go, but I'm not so ready. I was born and raised a farm slave. I hate slavery, but I love farm life. For me, the joys of my life are tied to that farm you ask me to abandon. It's my one place of peace.

"Personally, I'd prefer to load up my crew and head straight for Exile. We'd be safe there; we'd be welcomed. You're asking me to commit my people to untold generations of danger and combat, if we manage to survive.

"I need time to think. Lady Norlene, will you grant me two days to make a decision."

"Granted, Micha. Is there anything further? No? Then I wish you all god speed and success." With that she rose and left the dais followed by two young priestesses in training.

AS ALWAYS WHEN SOMETHING big was in the wind, the crew gathered at Micha's farm. They talked softly among themselves, but he hadn't spoken or even averted his eyes from the window for over an hour. Edie stepped up to him and put her arms around him from behind, resting her cheek on his shoulder. "What is it, my love?"

"Mmmm?"

"You already had your mind made up, what prompted you to ask for two days to think it over?"

"What? Oh, sorry Edie. It's a bargaining ploy. The king will be easier to deal with if we don't appear too eager, and the kids need time to get the hang of their ship." There were chuckles from the table at that.

"Why did you give them a ship, Micha?" asked Ena. "Do you think they're ready?"

"No, they're not ready, but they will be all too soon. We've protected them and sheltered them for too long and I'm not so sure we did them any favor."

"What else is troubling you, old friend?" asked Lessa.

"Lessa, you've always been way too good at that," he chuckled.

"I'm a witch; I know things. So talk to us. Show us what's missing here."

Micha turned from the window and with his arm around Edie's waist, returned to the long table and sat with his friends. Edie sat close by his side, holding his hand tightly. "Nova Clan is in for a long hard haul," he began.

"I'll petition the rest of the clans for recognition, but I doubt it'll happen. We're forced to leave our own home world, or to subdue it and rule it by force. I won't do that; it's not our way. King Borad has offered us a planet to make a home, but it'll be no different there. We'll still be the target of the fearful and troublemakers. Being that close to the Gap will just make it easier for us to be attacked."

"What are you saying, Boss?" Murtah's voice betrayed his fears.

"You know as well as I do what has to happen, Murtah. We have to become nomads; the ships will be our homes. We'll roam the Gap for generations until our numbers increase to where the clan can occupy and hold a planet of its own. Only those of our greater physical attributes can hope to survive this.

"Borad knows this, of course. That's why he came in person. The King's a friend; one of the few we seem to have left."

"Nomads, they're hard to attack because they're hard to find and you never know where they'll show up." grinned Zartah. "Sounds exciting."

"Much like I was on Exile," agreed Miriam. "My darling Zartah will never be bored again."

Micha chuckled at that. "Opinions, options?"

"We don't like it any more than you do, Micha, but there are no options. Even if we retreat to Exile they will eventually come for us." Lessa had tears in her eyes as she spoke. Brenna squeezed her hand reassuringly. "I tried to create something beautiful. I enhanced you all because you're beautiful people. I saw you as the beginnings of a new way of being for everyone. How did it all go so wrong?"

"Human nature," rumbled Rathbone. "I agree there are no other options. Now the question is how do we make the best of this?"

"We'll need ships and weapons," signed Keira.

"Yes, and allies," agreed Brenna.

"No, no allies," said Micha, his face hardening into the look of the warrior. "An ally can call you into a war you don't want to fight. No, Nova Clan will be completely independent."

Lessa reached out and gently gripped his shoulder. "Don't write off the clans yet, Micha. We'll also need King Borad to watch our backs, and we'll need Kella and the Guild."

"You've got Kella and the Guild," said Kella as she stepped through the door. She looked tired and beaten, yet defiant. "The guild's a bit smaller these days, but we'll work with Nova Clan or I'll personally gut the lot of them."

"I see you got our message," Lessa said as she rose and took the tired woman in her arms. Kella sighed as Lessa sent a wave of healing energy through her. She gave Lessa a gentle hug and breathed a soft, "Thank you."

"Yes, I got your message. I trusted that man with far more than I should. I've cleaned house as best I can, Micha, but the Guild is somewhat smaller, and I have no idea what the situation on the other side of the Gap is like."

"Thronk seemed like a good man, Kella. Did he say why he did it?"

"No, but his friends did once Thronk's speeder malfunctioned and exploded," replied Kella, resting her chin on her fist. "It seems the New Emperor, Loran the Second, is a very generous man."

"You've cleaned house?" rumbled Rathbone.

"I have. Did I hear that right, Micha? Are you taking control of the Gap?"

"Yes, Kella, it seems we have no other viable option. Have you got any work for us?"

"You get my convoys through three times a year and I'll supply whatever you need anytime you want it."

"Deal," grinned Micha, as he offered his hand. They shook hands and he reached for his comm unit.

"Micha to King Borad."

"Here, Micha. Have you decided?"

"It'll cost you."

"Name your terms, Micha. I'm sitting down."

"One, we control the Gap completely."

"Agreed."

"Two, you keep us supplied as needed."

"Agreed."

"Third, we'll need our ships upgraded plus three more battle ships capable of carrying fifty plus. Each fully armed and carrying six fighter ships like you brought with you."

"Three more ships like the Ravage? Why so many ships?"

"Just in case the Gap swallows one or two. I want back-ups."

"All right, Micha, agreed. I'll send messages right now. Oh, since we're now official allies, my spy network is also at your disposal. The conference to be held here on Nova in two days' time will have a surprise for you. The Council of Clan Chieftains will meet here as well at the request of the Viceroy."

"Blast it. Thanks for the warning. How soon can I have those ships?"

"They'll be waiting for you when you reach Arcalia Prime, and so will I. I'll leave for home later today to make arrangements. When can I expect you?"

"When I get there," sighed Micha, "probably in a couple of weeks."

"I'll have everything ready and waiting. Borad out."

"All right family, we're committed, "sighed Micha. "This is the last time I make a decision like this without consulting the kids. They've formed their own crew; they deserve to be included." Micha picked up his comm again.

"Micha to Chella."

"Here, Poppa."

"Come home, bring your crew."

"Understood. On our way."

⸻ ● ⸻

MICHELLA AND HER FRIENDS arrived to find Micha and his crew waiting for them. Micha was pacing and waved his hand at the table where the others were gathered. There was a scraping and shuffling of chairs as the younger folks found seats. When all were ready, Micha spoke.

"You kids wanted, demanded changes. You've got them, sadly. When I was your age my life was suddenly ripped apart and I had to find ways to survive, we all did. Now that fate has come for you.

"We're leaving Nova forever. From now on, we're Nova Clan. I'll apply to the council of chieftains for admittance to the council, but I doubt they'll let us in. Most of the Clans number in the billions of people. We number thirty-three souls in total. I expect to get laughed out of the room on that one.

"So, we'll be the outcast clan, we few. We'll claim territory nobody else could handle. We'll live a life no one else would want. We'll become the Nomads of the Gap. Michella, I made this decision without your input; I won't hold you to it. If you'd rather take your crew and head for Exile and safety, you may go with my blessing."

Michella didn't speak; she just looked from face to face of her own crew. Each shook their head in turn. At last, she turned to Micha.

"We were all born with the Nova Sunburst mark. We're Nova Clan born. Wherever the clan chieftain leads we follow. Look at who our parents are. How could we run and hide? You all fought so hard to give us a good and safe life. Now it's time for us to carry our share of the load. What's the plan?"

"First, I want you kids to know I'm proud of the way you handled Kon's retrieval. That was well done. That earned you crew status." Micha was grinning now. "The plan is this. We'll leave as soon as the conference is over. You'll be carrying mostly supplies in the Freedom. The Ravage will fly point guard.

"Our first major stop will be Arcalia Prime where there'll be more ships waiting for us. Kella, can you have pilots you trust help us with the extra ships until I'm ready?"

"I can, Micha. Consider it done."

"Good. Once we pick up our extra ships we'll move on to the Gap. For the next three days all of you will have to learn everything you can about the running of a ship. That includes routine maintenance and repairs.

"I expect there'll be a few foolhardy folk who'll want to come with us. They'll fly on the Freedom. The Ravage will be the battleship."

Michella stood up, looking as though she might protest, but Micha held up his hand. "Chella, your crew will be carrying what's left of our lives with you. All our few special treasures, mementos, and such will be on your ship. You will also have to keep a few civilians safe until we arrive at the Gap, then we'll gather and make a new plan."

She sank back into her chair, placated. "What's our fall back plan?" she asked.

"If it all goes to the nine hells sideways, cut and run for Exile. You'll be safe there for a few generations."

"Why not go there now, Poppa? Why should we protect them from the Gap?"

"We made the Gap, honey," sighed Micha, as he laid his hand on his daughter's shoulder. "I gave the command that made the Gap. I committed the act that made that order necessary. It's my creation; I'm responsible for it."

"As are we all," said Lessa, as she rose and stood facing Micha. "My dear friend, we all have had a hand in its creation, especially me. No, people, the Gap is ours; it's time we went to claim that which we've created."

———— ◉ ————

MICHA STOOD CALMLY before the Council of Clan Chieftains. He'd made his plea for membership in the clans and now it was time for the vote. Lortax had seconded his application and that would carry weight, but as chair of the meeting, he could only vote to break a tie. Micha had no illusions. Still, he had a small back up plan just in case he got lucky.

When the vote was called, Kemge of Sega Clan leaped to his feet. "No bloody way," he roared. "Good gods, there's barely a handful of them and he wants equality with the rest of us? No, I say." The two men beside him agreed.

The room fell silent when Haral, of Gemsa Clan, rose to speak. A tall woman with a long mane of iron grey hair and wearing full Clan regalia, she cut an impressive figure. As Chieftain of the largest and most powerful clan, her word would carry a lot of weight.

"Why not, Kemge?" she said. "In the beginning, all the clans were small. You, me, and everybody else in this room owes this man a debt of gratitude. Without him we'd all be in slave collars right now. Micha deserves a place at the table.

"There were always thirteen clans until a few hundred years ago when Sega absorbed Morna Clan. I say yes! Let's welcome Nova Clan to the fold and restore the tradition." She turned and winked at Micha as she resumed her seat.

The room was quiet for a moment, then a big burly fellow rose. "Micha cut down the Imperial ship that was about to roast me. I'd rather have him with me than against me. I vote yes." Slowly but surely, the momentum grew until there were seven yes votes, three against, and one abstained; Nova Clan was official.

"The yes vote carries," declared Lortax, grinning. "Chieftain of Nova Clan, define your territorial boundaries. The Council will then hear objections and make adjustments."

"We claim the Gap, nothing more," said Micha, as he rose to his feet.

"Objections?" asked Lortax. There were none. "So be it, the Gap is Nova territory. Is there any further business for the Council to consider?"

"I have a grievance," said Micha. All eyes suddenly turned to him again.

"State your case."

"My family was attacked, and my son taken. The attack was engineered by the Chieftain of Sega and I can supply proof. However, I'm content to speak to him directly with this company as witness."

Kemge jumped up and began to protest, but Lortax silenced him. "Speak, Micha."

Micha turned to face Kemge. "You have two options here. Option one, stay away from me and mine from now on and no more will be said about it."

"What's the second option?" sneered Kemge.

"Come at me again," Micha replied coldly, "and I'll hunt you to the death. There's no magic, no military force strong enough to keep me from killing you with my bare hands. The former Viceroy couldn't stop me, the Emperor himself fell to my hand, and so did his empire. Consider your options carefully."

"Ha," laughed Haral. "It's sad to be you today, Kemge. I sure wouldn't want the Hound of Nova on my trail. I'd take that warning to heart if I were you."

Kemge had sunk back into his chair, defeated. It was well known that Micha didn't bluff. Now that the conspiracy was out in the open he knew he was lucky to get away with a warning. His cousin hadn't been so lucky. She'd been stripped of her title as High Priestess and an inhibitor placed on her head. She'd spend the rest of her life in prison weaving baskets. Worse yet, with Gemsa and Nara clans throwing their weight behind Nova, he dare not openly attack them. Ah well, the Gap would be the end of them anyway.

EMPEROR LORAN SAT LISTENING to the general drone on. "We have all but sector three fully under control, Sire. There are still a few systems in Sector five that are resisting, but they will fall within the month. We..." the general got no further as Loran held up his hand to interrupt.

"Forgive me, gentlemen, but we must adjourn the meeting for an hour. Something has just come up." He rose from his chair and nodded slightly at the woman who had silently entered the room. One of the generals spotted her and shivered. None of them wanted to attract the attention of the Emperor's chief spy. The woman's enemies had a way of disappearing.

Loran waited until the room cleared, then he turned and led the way to his inner office. The woman followed closely. "What news, Lizera?" he asked, as she closed the door behind her. He waved his hand to indicate she should sit.

"There are a couple of interesting developments, Sire." She smiled as she sank into a chair facing him. "First, the Hound has left Nova as you predicted. The interesting thing is where he's gone."

"Oh? Do tell."

"The Hound and his few mutants have been declared and accepted as Nova Clan."

"Accepted? Into the council?"

"Yes, indeed."

"Hmm. That was unexpected. You say he's left Nova, where has he gone?"

"The Gap, Sire. Nova Clan has claimed the Gap as their territory. We seem to have new neighbours, figuratively speaking."

"The Gap? Well, well, that is a piece of good news. Did he take any normal humans with him?"

"He did. Unfortunately, he discovered our connection to Sega Clan and that door has been closed to us for now."

"That's irrelevant at this point, Lizera. Do you have anyone in their camp?"

"I do. We have one operative on his ship, but failed to plant one on his daughter's."

"His daughter's? She has her own ship? At her age?"

"Oh yes, and reports are she is even more deadly than the Hound. We must not underestimate that one, Sire."

"Do we still have connections inside the Guild?"

"Only one, Sire, the rest were purged when the kidnapping failed but there is a separatist faction within the Guild. We are now attempting to penetrate that faction."

"One should be all we need at this juncture, but see if you can plant a few more. Also, encourage that breakaway faction of the Guild."

"Already in progress, Sire," she smiled.

"Excellent. The Gap, hmmm? Perhaps we should see what we can do to welcome the new neighbours. I'll have one of the admirals send in a few ships to say hello. The results should be interesting."

On the Move

M icha walked out of the meeting after speaking privately with the Viceroy for a moment. As he emerged into the fading daylight he reached for his comm unit. "Micha to Chella."

"Chella here."

"We're in. Get your ship in the air. The Viceroy's flagship is in orbit right over the temple. Get in close to him and wait for me."

"I can't find Deann. As soon as I find her I'll fly."

"Get your ship in the air, Chella."

"Not without Deann, I have to find her."

"Michella. You wanted to be crew boss, well, this is what it's like most of the time. What you want is always secondary to the mission. Now use your head and deal with this, but get that ship in the air. I don't want to be caught on the ground."

Her response was curt, but he could hear the anger in her voice. "Understood, Boss." He grinned and winked at Edie.

MICHELLA'S CREW WAS all on the bridge of the Freedom; everybody heard the whole exchange. She turned with fire dancing in her eyes. "Pally, seal her up and lift off."

"Chella?"

"Do it. Nellie, Barah, get down to the fighter bay and prep a ship, I'll be along as soon as we break atmo." They left the bridge without a word.

"Allore, I want you in the infirmary. I'm going after Deann and she might be hurt."

"In that case, I should go with you."

Michella faced her younger sister for a moment then nodded. "Agreed. Go."

"Bird rising." Palentine's voice sounded like the bored voices heard on every military and civilian ship all over the galaxy. In spite of herself, Michella had to grin. He winked at her as he eased the controls and the ship rose gracefully into the air.

"Easy now, Pally, we've got a ship full of passengers."

"Aye, Boss." The lift off was smooth and the ship rose through the atmosphere without a hitch. "Clearing atmo now, Boss."

"The ship is yours, First Man." She grinned as she turned and ran from the bridge.

"First Man, looks like you just got promoted, Pally," giggled Ellie.

"Looks like. I think we'll have to sort out the job descriptions once we get on the way to the Gap. I was hoping for engineer."

"In the meantime, there's the Viceroy's ship," said Tarah. "Tuck us in beside her then I'll take over as pilot. You get the captain's chair until Chella gets back."

Pally nodded as he brought the ship in close beside the massive battle cruiser. As he did, the fighter bay hatch opened and a ship dropped out, hurtling toward the planet below. "Ellie, can you hone those sensors in on Deann's farm?"

"Should be able to, Pally. Just give me a minute or two. I won't be able to isolate Deann from anyone else, though."

"I know. This is just in case."

———— ◉ ————

BARAH WAS A BIT RECKLESS at the controls, but the mad speed that he loved was what Michella needed. Allore and Nellie were strapped in, but Michella was just hanging on tight. She was braced near the hatch. The ship dropped like a missile towards the farmyard, only slowing at the last second. The hatch was already opening as it touched the ground.

"Allore, Nellie with me. Barah in the air, locked and loaded." The ship touched down and the three girls were barely out when it rose into the air again, turned and the gun ports opened, aimed at the farmhouse.

Michella hit the ground running. She leaped up the steps, kicked open the door then charged inside. The woman screamed and flattened herself against the wall. "Where's Deann?"

"I don't know, she ran away." The woman was terrified and trembling.

"That's a lie," said Nellie, a wicked little grin on her face. She snapped her fingers and the hem of the woman's sleeve burst into flame. She screamed and beat out the flames then stared at Nellie with terrified eyes. "Lie to us again and I'll set your hair on fire."

"You already know what I'm capable of," said Michella, as she advanced on the terrified woman. "Now tell me where Deann is. I won't ask again."

Before the woman could speak, Michella's comm unit squawked. "Freedom to Chella."

"Here."

"There are four humans in the house and four more in the barn."

"Understood." Michella turned to the terrified woman. "Who is in the barn?"

"Please, just go away..."

"No. Who is in the barn? Last chance."

The woman burst into tears. "My brother and the boys," she sobbed. "Please don't kill my sons." Michella just grabbed her by the arm and dragged her outside.

"Chella to Barah," she said, grabbing her comm unit as they emerged from the house.

"Here, Boss."

"Blow that house halfway to Exile."

"Understood." The boy had trouble keeping the excitement out of his voice. There was an audible metallic click from the hovering fighter ship then a shell slammed into the house blowing it to smithereens. Michella marched her captive towards the barn. They were several paces from the huge doors when a shot rang out and a projectile kicked up the dirt at Michella's feet.

"That's far enough, Spawn. Don't take another step closer." The man's voice was nervous.

"Send out Deann and you won't be harmed," said Michella as she released her grip on the woman.

"The hell I will, no damned Spawn is getting their hands on..." he didn't get a chance to finish, they moved too swiftly. Allore darted around the side of the barn while Michella and Nellie charged right at it, dodging and weaving as they ran. He was shocked at their speed and nervously got off a single shot.

Michella hit him hard and ripped the weapon from his hands. He went flying and landed hard, groaning in pain. She heard a muffled scream of rage from the hay loft and swarmed up the ladder like a squirrel. A pitchfork was thrust at her face, but she battered it aside and tossed the boy well back into the huge loft of hay. The second boy dropped his pitchfork and backed away, terrified.

Deann lay bound, gagged, and half buried in the hay. She was struggling wildly, and it took a moment for Michella to get through to her. As she stopped struggling, Michella removed the gag and began untying her hands. Tears ran freely down the girl's face as she threw her arms around Michella's neck. "You came for me, Chella. Oh gods, you came for me. I was so afraid you'd leave without me."

"Leave without you?" grinned Michella, as she gently untangled herself from Deann's grasp and began untying her legs. "After tasting those lips? Perish the thought, woman. You're mine and I'm keeping you."

"Good," sniffed Deann, "because I do want to be kept." Michella helped Deann to her feet then Deann turned towards the back of the loft where her brothers had taken refuge. "All right, you two, come on out of there."

"No."

"Do you want Chella to come in and get you?"

"No." There was rustling of hay then the two boys struggled out to where they were. Deann just pointed at the barn floor and they obediently headed down the ladder. The girls followed.

They found the others outside, Nellie acting as the nurse as Allore tended to Deann's mother. "Keep the pressure here," instructed Allore, "until I get this sewn up. Chella, I want to take her to the ship's infirmary. This is the best I can do here."

"What happened?"

"Skeet for brains over there, shot her," snarled Nellie as she pointed to the large man who was standing by helplessly.

"I didn't mean to, I was just..."

"Trying to kill me," snarled Michella.

"You're destroying my family," he replied sulkily.

"You can't have Deann," one of the boys suddenly shouted. "She's our sister."

"Fine, then you can keep her," said Michella as she winked at Deann. She reached to her shoulder for her comm. "Barah, set her down, we have passengers."

"Coming down." The fighter ship sank to the ground beside them.

"Deann, get your brothers strapped in. Allore, what do you need?"

"Lift her gently into the ship and tell Barah to go easy on the way back."

"You've got it. Nellie, do your stuff." The small witch grinned as she focused on the injured woman. Slowly the woman rose into the air then floated into the ship. Allore followed her in and then Nellie followed Allore.

"I should kill you," snarled Michella, as she turned to the man, "but I won't. You can spend the rest of your life knowing I have your sister's children. If she survives she may contact you one day, but you can spend a few years knowing you shot your own sister, maybe killed her, and her children will be absorbed into the Spawn." With that she leaped aboard the ship and closed the hatch. "To the Freedom, Barah, gently now, we have wounded."

"Understood. On our way home." He grinned as he reached for the comm. "Barah to the Freedom."

"Freedom here."

"Coming home with wounded. Clear a path to the infirmary."

"Wounded?"

"Deann's momma took a bullet. Allore's tending her, but..."

"Understood. Path will be clear."

———◉———

THE TWO SHIPS LEFT Nova space together unobserved. The viceroy's ship had accompanied them while his fleet had prevented anyone from following. They'd set both ships down on PX19 to redistribute some of the passenger load and to take on supplies. A supply ship had been waiting, Kella was with it.

While the work was being done, Micha took his daughter aside. She knew he had something important on his mind; she waited patiently for him to work up to the conversation both would rather avoid. Finally he met her eyes and she read the concern there.

"Chella, I was younger than you when I became Crew Boss, but I had one advantage."

"Which was?"

"Every member of my crew was experienced and the best they could be at their jobs. You have a gifted crew, but they're inexperienced. This is no holiday, Chella. Your crew will gain experience faster than any of you would like, but right now you're vulnerable on this point. I'm sending over two people I want you to consider for your crew."

"Why? To babysit us?" she bristled.

"These people have skills you can use. Just consider them, 'Chella."

She let her shoulders sag. "Understood and accepted. Thanks Poppa."

"They'll meet us in about two days. Chella, believe me when I say I want you to succeed here. I believe you can, but I'm still allowed to worry about my kids."

"Momma made you do this, right?"

"She wanted to come and bring Brenna."

"Oh no, there is no way I'm having my mother and my school teacher looking over my shoulder every time I make a move."

"I figured as much," he grinned.

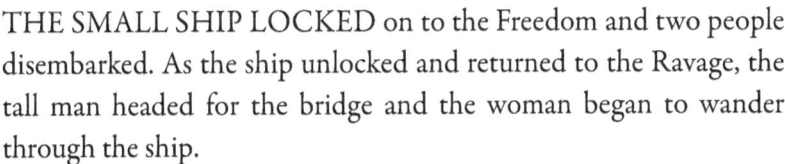

THE SMALL SHIP LOCKED on to the Freedom and two people disembarked. As the ship unlocked and returned to the Ravage, the tall man headed for the bridge and the woman began to wander through the ship.

Michella turned as he entered the bridge; he didn't make a good first impression. The man was tall with scraggly, limp hair and a tired slouch to his body. His movements were so loose it looked as though he might collapse in a heap at any given moment. That was the face of a man who had seen a lot of abuse in his life, most of it self-inflicted. Yep, this guy was definitely hung over.

"Sit down before you fall down," grinned Michella. "Nellie, Poppa just sent us two extra passengers. Would you see if you can find the other one please?"

"On it, Boss," laughed the tiny girl, as she offered the gangly giant her seat at the comm station. He ignored her saucy grin and gratefully sank into the chair.

Michella was getting irritated, but Nellie's soft whisper sounded in her mind. "Look at him closely, Chella."

Her eyes snapped back to the man for a second appraisal. The man was whipcord thin, but there was hard muscle under that combat uniform. He was hung over, but his eyes were still taking in everything and everyone on the bridge, soaking up every detail.

Michella relaxed and let her intuition reach towards the man, but she couldn't read him. This much she could sense: he was a dangerous man. Either she'd have to accept him or kill him. She didn't like either option.

"You got a name?" she asked.

"Dozens," he sighed. "Do you have to shout?"

"Name. Pick your favorite," she grinned, speaking softly.

"Thank you, Captain, you're a considerate woman," he said, his eyes still assessing the ship and crew.

"Name?"

"I've always liked Hawk. It's not one of my names, of course, but I like it."

"Hawk it is. All right, Hawk, my father sent you to me. I'm wondering why. First, let's get really clear on a few things. I want no one on my crew who isn't happy about being here. Two, never lie to me. Lie to me and Ellie will turn you into a kick ball and I'll boot you out the air lock. Three, this is my crew: I ask, you do first then argue later. Four, I need to know what you can do and what you won't do."

He let those pale eyes meet hers and he grinned. "So you are Micha's daughter after all. All right, in order, I volunteered for this post so I'm here because I'm willing to be. Two, lying is an art I've perfected, but I'll never lie to you, ever for any reason. Three, understood and accepted.

"Four, my particular skills. I began my career as a tactician in the royal fleet. I was also fleet hand to hand combat champion. After a few years, I moved into espionage. I've spent years as a spy and assassin. At this point I can honestly say I'm the best operative King Borad has at his disposal."

"So you're a spy."

"Yes."

"And you'll report everything I do, we do, back to the king."

"Yes, well, just the useful and important stuff. The king's a busy man. He likes the reports to be concise."

"Skeeter, blow him out the air lock, Chella," said Tarah.

"Easy, Tarah. I'm actually starting to like this guy," grinned Michella.

"All right, Hawk, we'll give this a try, see if we can work together. Go get some rest and clean yourself up. Come back when you're awake and functional."

The tall man chuckled and shook his head. "Boss," he said, "a spy who can't function with a hangover isn't very good at his job. I'm ready."

"All right, you're sitting at comms, may as well start there. It'll be easier to report to the king."

The big man met her eyes for a long moment then a small grin touched his lips. "Aye, Boss."

"Ship-wide."

"Ship-wide, aye." Hawk idly flicked a switch and nodded to Michella.

"Attention all passenger and crew, this is Michella. There is a new member of the crew. His name is Hawk and he looks the part. Treat him accordingly." She motioned with her hand and he flipped the switch back. A moment later Allore burst onto the bridge.

"Chella, what's going on here? New man on the crew? We're the crew. We're family, we've always been together. Who is this guy? Where did he come from?"

"I'm Hawk, Allore," the big man said softly. "All your questions are valid. I come from Arcalia Prime, I was sent here by the king and your father to help this crew as much as I can."

"How do you know who I am?" she demanded as she rounded on him, fire in her eyes.

"I've studied all I can about this crew," he replied easily. "You're Allore, daughter of Edie and Micha, sister of Michella, you're thirteen years old and you are already the best non-witch healer in three sectors. I tend to get beat up a lot; we'll have lots of time to get acquainted while you're patching me up."

"Four sectors, and you need a bath," she snarled, as she spun on her heel and left the bridge.

"You've really got to work on those first impressions, Hawk," chuckled Tarah.

"Momma used to tell me that," grinned Hawk, as he turned back to the comms.

A few moments later Nellie returned with a big woman in her forties. To say the woman looked dangerous would be an understatement. Her long hair was pulled back in a ponytail revealing the scars on her neck as well as the secret tattoos of the Guild. Her clothing was loose fitting and functional, her movements spoke of long years of combat training, and she was armed to the teeth. "This ship is a mess," she stated flatly.

"You can leave any time you like," Michella responded coldly. "Now would be good."

"Can't."

"Why not?"

"Kella gave me strict orders to get you shipshape and keep you alive."

"Did she? Well that tells me everything I wanted to know about you. Get off my ship or I'll blow you out the airlock."

"Why?"

"You just told me whose orders you follow, and you stated clearly that you intend to take over my ship. Give me a reason to keep you alive and I'll consider it for ten seconds."

The woman's face split into a wide grin. "You're Micha's cub alright, girl. Okay, here's why you want to keep me alive. I've spent the past eight years running the Gap. I've got more experience in there than anyone else alive."

"Try harder." The woman's grin faded as she looked into the hard eyes of the young captain.

"I have useful skills and experience," she replied, dropping the bravado.

"Name them."

"As I said, I have extensive experience in the Gap. I'm also the best scrounge in the business; Kella will attest to that. I have plenty of actual combat experience as well."

"I really don't give a fresh pile of skeet about your experience or skills," Michella said coldly. "I know everyone on my crew inside and out; I have known them and trusted them all their lives. Today I accepted one unknown onto my crew because he told me flat out where his loyalties lay. So did you; get off my ship."

"Wait, I'm sorry here, just give me a chance. Your father already..."

"I don't know what kind of a game you ran on Poppa, but I want you off my ship. Tarah, put her on a fighter and take her back to the Ravage. Barah, keep a gun on her and shoot her if she breathes wrong. Pally, get her weapons and put her in restraints."

"Now just a minute..." she got no further as Pally closed in. The woman suddenly leaped at Pally, drawing a dagger, but he swiftly overcame her and put her in restraints. She was actually laughing as he tied her up. She was a bit startled when he suddenly gagged her and started taking all her hidden weapons.

"Comms," barked Michella.

"Comms, aye," replied Hawk, putting his blaster back in its holster.

"Contact the Ravage."

"Aye, Boss. Freedom to Ravage, come in Ravage."

"Ravage here."

"Uncle Jorge, this is Chella. I'm sending you a passenger. Tell father he can take her back or I'll blow her out the air lock. Freedom out." She made a gesture and Hawk flipped the switch.

The comm came to life again instantly. "Ravage to Freedom." It was Micha's voice.

Michella nodded and Hawk flipped the switch. "Chella here."

"Chella, come over with your passenger; I want to confer face to face."

"On my way." She jerked her hand and Hawk broke the connection. "Pally, the ship is yours; I'll take her back myself. Ellie, keep an eye on Hawk; fry him if you have to."

The brothers seized the woman and hauled her to her feet then propelled her after Michella's retreating back.

"Fry him if you have to?" said Hawk. "Guess I have to earn my stripes on this crew."

"Yep," grinned Palentine, as he moved to the captain's chair, "and it won't be easy. Move to pilot. Ellie, you're on comms." Hawk grinned as he moved his loose frame to the pilot's seat. He'd have his back to both Palentine and the girl at that station. He was liking these kids more and more all the time.

THE WOMAN WAS STILL bound and gagged as Michella led her little band into the mess hall, her father's favorite meeting place. "My gods, Ayra, what the hells happened?" exclaimed Kella as she leaped to the woman's side and removed the gag. A swift pass of a knife and the woman's arms were free as well.

Micha saw the look on his daughter's face; this wasn't going to be fun. He kicked a chair over for Michella and she pushed it back, remaining on her feet. Micha sighed and Edie grinned. She'd warned him not to do this. "All right, Chella, what happened?"

"You sent two people over to my ship as potential members of my crew. I interviewed them, one I accepted, and one I didn't."

"Why? What happened?"

"Are you planning to take the ship away from me?"

"What? No. That's your ship and your crew. I just want you all to be safe."

"Thank you, Father, both for the vote of confidence and your concern. In future I'll choose my own crew, thank you. Now, is there anything further?"

Her jaw was set and he could see the anger in her eyes, but she was staying calm and Micha liked that. Perhaps his daughter was more mature than he realized. "Chella, what happened?"

"Two people entered my ship. One, hung over as he was, still managed to find his way to the bridge. We talked, he agreed to the terms of service on my crew, confessed that he is a spy for King Borad, gave me a short list of his skills and experience then said he was ready to go to work.

"I had to send someone to find that one. She came on the bridge and announced the ship was a mess and she was there to take over and straighten us all up."

There was a small grin playing at the corners of his mouth. "Then what happened?"

"I didn't like her attitude so I ordered her off my ship, she refused to go. She pulled a knife on Pally when I said to escort her off the ship. The woman is rude, ignorant, and she made it clear I could never trust her, nor would she follow my directions."

"You're leaving out some of the best parts, girl," laughed the woman.

Even with all her combat experience she was unable to react fast enough. Michella moved with the speed of a striking cobra. The woman was hurled against the bulkhead with enough force to knock the air from her lungs. She surged to her feet, grabbing a knife from the table, but one look at Michella stopped her cold.

Michella's posture said she was well trained, and her voice was cold and deadly. "Give me a reason. Please."

"That's enough." Micha almost magically appeared between them. "Kella, take Ayra down to the infirmary to get checked out. Chella, relax, Ayra was just doing what she was told to do." Edie winced as her daughter's eyes hardened even further.

"That was a test?"

"You have your mother's passion, Chella, and her temper. I need to know if you could stay cool when..."

"Are you satisfied?"

"Chella..."

"The spy already reported to you, didn't he?" With a snarl on her perfect lips Michella grabbed the comm unit at her shoulder. "Michella to Freedom."

"Freedom here."

"Put Hawk on, now."

"Here, Boss."

"You made your report to my father and maybe even the king. I don't know how and I don't care. You can report whatever you like to the king. Report to my father behind my back again and I'll personally throw you out the air lock."

There was only a slight pause before he answered. "You're sharper than I thought, Boss. Understood and accepted. It won't happen again."

She let her arm fall away from her shoulder. "Are we done here, Father?"

"Chella, you do need some experienced people..."

"Then give me two from your crew, people I know I can trust."

"Are you serious? If you are then pick them."

"Aunt Keira and Uncle Rathbone."

"Done. What else do you need?"

"Your faith in me."

"Chella..."

"Either you trust me to do this, or you don't, but make a decision now and stick with it."

For the first time anyone could remember they saw Micha back down and relent. The fight visibly went out of him. He reached out and put his hands on her shoulders. "I trust you to do this, Chella. I made a mistake here; it won't happen again. Go back to your ship, sort out your crew, then relax. We'll have little or nothing to do for a week or more, then we need to confer."

"Understood, Poppa," she replied, as she hugged him tightly. "I should beat you up, but I never could stay mad at you. Oh, don't think I don't know you did all this to get some of your crew onto my ship."

Micha chuckled at that. "So tell me why you chose those two."

"I need Uncle Rath to keep the ship running top form and I need Auntie Keira to keep an eye on Hawk."

"Hawk. Is that the name he gave you? Doesn't really matter, nobody knows what his real name is, but he is the most loyal man King Borad has. Hawk is completely dedicated to the Arcalian Alliance. The fact Borad sent him to you tells me how badly he truly needs us to keep the Gap closed."

"Fair enough, Poppa, but I still want to keep an eye on him." She hugged her mother then left for her ship. Both Keira and Rathbone were already aboard with their travel gear.

Michella hopped aboard and closed the hatch. A moment later the small fighter dropped out of the Ravage and headed for the Freedom. They had barely left the ship when Rathbone spoke. "Chella, Keira and I are crew members now. Tell us what you need from us. We're not here to interfere or to judge."

"I need your experience and your eyes," she replied. "I also need Hawk to realize there's more than just a crew of kids running this ship. I know Pally would much rather be Engineer than First Man, and I know I need a lot of guidance. I need you to be my first man and I need Aunt Keira to make doubly sure my crew is armed and battle ready. I have no idea at all what we'll be facing, but I want to be ready for it."

"Understood," sang Keira. "Orders?"

"As soon as we're aboard, you two inspect the ship and make note of what we need and what has to happen. When you're ready we'll all meet on the bridge and get organized."

Getting Organized

Michella was on her way back to the bridge when Deann stepped out of the infirmary and called to her. "Chella, got a minute?"

"I'm rather busy now, Deann..."

"Of course you are."

Deann spun on her heel and marched away. Michella was by her side in an instant. "You know you aren't fast enough to get away from me, so why not stop and let me suck up. Deann, I'm sorry, I messed up and you're right to be annoyed with me. Will you give me another chance?"

Deann stopped and faced Michella, her eyes dancing with mischief. "Chella, got a minute?"

"For you, my love, always. What's on your mind?"

"We are, Chella. Are we ever going to have five minutes alone again? We've been on this ship for weeks and I've barely seen you."

"You're right, Sweetheart, and that has to change. The question is, how much change can you handle?"

"What do you mean?"

"Deann, I hate not having you with me more. I want you on my crew. More, I want you to swear the oath with me."

"Chella, what did you just say? Did you just ask me to be your companion?"

"Yes, I did, girl," sighed Michella, as she folded Deann into her arms. Some people came along and squeezed by then they were alone again for a moment.

"Oh, Chella, do you really mean that?"

"Yes, I do. I want you, more, I need you, but the choice is yours."

"Yes, oh gods, yes..." Deann got no further as someone else came along and squeezed past them. "When?" she asked, as soon as they were alone.

"Would right now be too soon?"

"Now? Wait, no, now would be perfect. What are you up to?"

"Come with me to the bridge. I'm going to get a few things organized and I'm going to get some personal time back. Deann, I'm going to make life tough for you for a while, but I need you and I need this to happen. Will you trust me?"

"I'll do whatever you want me to, Chella, you know that."

"Now that holds real promise..."

"Shut up," blushed Deann, as she slapped Michella on the shoulder. "All right, you saucy thing, but be warned. Once you swear the bond, I'll have expectations."

"Be still my heart," laughed Michella, as she took Deann's hand and led her towards the bridge.

They arrived hand in hand on the bridge; all was quiet. "Report," Michella grinned at Pally.

"All's quiet here, Boss. Old Hawk behaved himself."

"Good to know." She grinned as she took the captain's chair Pally had just vacated. Deann stood behind her and put a hand on her shoulder. "Comms."

"Comms, aye," giggled Ellie, as she mimicked Hawk's military jargon. He gave her a sloppy grin and a wink.

"Ship-wide."

"Ship-wide, aye."

"Attention, all ship's crew to the bridge." She gestured with her hand and Ellie flipped the switch to off. "Pally, you still want to be ship's engineer?"

"Yep, I'm just not first man material."

"Yes, you are, but we'll let that pass. Uncle Rath is on board, and he will be First Man for a while until you're ready."

"Dad's on board? Tell me Momma isn't here too." Just then Keira entered the bridge. Rathbone and Allore were right behind her. A moment later and Nellie showed up with the brothers. Palentine's shoulders sagged and he gave Michella a reproachful look.

"Okay people, it's time for us to get organized," said Michella, ignoring Pally. She was nervous, but it didn't show. "Here's what I think should happen. Uncle Rath is now First Man; Pally is ship's engineer. Tarah and Barah, you guys are our main pilots, you'll have to practice with the fighter ships every chance you get. Allore is our medic; the infirmary is her territory. Nellie, you're on comms, sensors, as well as anything else you can learn about this ship.

"Ellie, since I just tried to kill the procurer Poppa sent over, that'll be your job." Ellie was fairly bouncing with delight. This was right up her alley; she loved nothing more than finding ways and means to accomplish what others couldn't. She'd always been their go-to girl when they needed things for a project; this was the same on a bigger scale.

"Deann is now officially a member of this crew. She'll be assisting Allore in the infirmary for the most part, but she'll also be learning everything she can about running the ship. Hawk, since you're the man with the Gap experience and spying know-how, you'll be our specialist. Auntie Keira, you're in charge of weapons, weapons training, and readiness assessment. I need you to make sure we're ready for whatever comes at us." Keira nodded and winked at her.

"Okay, those are the basics, but I want every one of us to get really good at every job. We all have special talents and experiences, but we all need to know every job this crew has, and every job involved with running this ship.

"Now, one last piece of business. Deann and I have agreed to swear the bond of companionship right here, right now with all of you as witness." She stood and gently pulled Deann to her side.

Rathbone stepped up to them with a serious look on his face. "Deann," he rumbled in that deep voice, "do you swear this bond of your own free will?"

"Yes, I do," she nodded shyly.

"Michella, do you swear this bond of your own free will?"

"Yes, I do," she smiled, as she squeezed Deann's hand.

"Objections?" There were none.

"Sworn and witnessed," grinned Rathbone. "Congratulations, ladies."

There was a further round of congratulations from the rest of the crew then, Michella held up her hand for silence. "First Man, the ship is yours. We'll be in the captain's cabin." Deann was blushing furiously as Michella took her hand and led her away to the sound of cat calls and whistles.

The captain's cabin was luxurious by Deann's standards. She'd spent the last few weeks sleeping on a small cot in the infirmary, and before that she had shared a room with her two brothers. The cabin had a bed that was big enough for two people, a desk, two comfortable chairs, a big footlocker and an actual closet for extra clothing. There was also a private shower, sink with mirror above, and toilet.

"Like it?" asked Michella, as she lovingly watch Deann taking it all in.

"Chella, we get to live here? Just us?"

"Yep, just us. It's a bit more than I'm used to."

"Wow, me too. Chella, wha..." Deann got no further as Michella stopped her with a kiss. She moaned softly and melted into Michella's embrace. Knees shaking from the magic of the kiss, Chella held Deann tightly to her. Their tongues danced and their hands began to explore, but the sudden blare of the claxon followed by Rathbone's deep booming voice over the comms spoiled the mood.

"Battle stations. Battle stations. All hands to battle stations. Captain to the bridge."

Deann, raced away towards the infirmary while Michella, face still flushed from the kiss, burst onto the bridge. "Report," she barked, sounding so much like her father Keira actually chuckled.

"Five ships incoming. Fast," replied Rathbone. "They've ignored all comms. Probably pirates. We've been ordered to drop back behind the Ravage."

Michella's eyes swept the bridge, noting each person and their station. "That's not going to happen. Ellie, has the Ravage deployed fighters?"

"Only two, Boss."

"Uncle Rath, prep and launch two more fighters, you in one and Auntie Keira in the other. Take who you need with you. Hawk, get us up beside the Ravage, now."

"Aye, Boss," grinned the tall man, as he easily moved the ship back into position on the Ravage's flank.

Rathbone took Barah and Nellie with him, Keira had taken Pally and Tarah. "Comms."

"Comms, aye," said Ellie.

"Deann and Allore to the bridge." Just then the comms came alive. It was Micha.

"Rath, what the nine hells are you doing? I told you to get your people back."

"Chella here. This is my crew; Uncle Rath is in a fighter ready to launch. Poppa, if we hide behind you they'll think I'm the one with all the precious cargo. They'll see one war ship and one cargo ship. This way they see two warships."

Micha was silent for only a moment. "Good thinking. I agree; two warships it is."

"This better not be another test, Father."

"It wasn't until now, Michella. You're in command; what are your orders?"

"What?"

"We're headed for the Gap, Chella. Things will be a lot worse there. This is your idea and I think I like it. You're in command. What are your orders?"

Michella muttered for a moment then, her mind racing, she accepted. "Understood. Stand ready. If it comes to a fight you take the left flank and I'll take the right."

"Understood."

Allore and Deann were already on the bridge. Allore started to speak, but Michella held up her hand. "You have no wounded yet, Allore. I need you here on sensors. Deann, you're on comms. Hawk, take weapons. Ellie, you're the pilot. Keep us in the air, Little Witch."

Ellie's eyes were wide as she settled into the pilot's seat and readjusted all the settings for her tiny frame.

"Hawk, I assume you're familiar with our weapons."

"Oh, yeah."

"Can you take out the lead ship in one shot?"

"Take out?"

"Destroy utterly."

"One salvo, sure."

"Stand ready. Allore, have they launched any fighters?"

"Not yet. I'm getting funny readings, Chella."

"Explain."

"Three ships are heavily armed, but the other two look like cargo ships."

"Definitely a pirate group," chuckled Hawk.

"All right, people, we're ready. Comms, ship-wide and ship-to-ship, I want everybody on our side to hear this."

Deann frantically searched the panel in front of her then Hawk reached over and flipped two switches for her. He winked and turned back to his own controls, his big hands spread across the firing switches. Deann nodded to Chella that she was ready.

Michella drew a deep breath then leaned back in her captain's chair. "Give me visual, Deann." Deann waved her delicate fingers over the panel until then she found it and, with a grin of delight, flipped the switch.

"Attention, five approaching ships, this is the Freedom of Nova Crew. Respond and identify, failure to comply will be considered an act of aggression." Michella's posture and her voice gave the impression of someone who was completely bored. She got no response.

She indicated with her hand that Deann should leave the visual on. "Launch fighters. Approaching ships, respond and identify." The only response she got was from Allore.

"Fighters launched, Captain."

"Hawk." His big fingers hit the panel instantly. The lead ship started to turn, but it was too late; three missiles streaked across the void and slammed into it. The ship exploded.

"Attention four approaching ships, respond and identify."

"Don't shoot, don't shoot, this is the Almack, escort ship to a trader's convoy. We didn't know you were Nova Crew."

"Lying to me makes me angry," replied Michella, as she lazily sat up in her seat, still facing the camera. "You knew who we are because the Ravage already tried to contact you. Now, my gunner has already targeted your ship. You even flinch and he'll fire." Michella leaned her elbows on her knees and smiled at the camera. "He likes blowing things up.

"You're pirates. Here's how you survive today. You abandon your ship and put all personnel onto the other battleship. You then leave here as fast as you can leaving the two freighters and one battleship empty of people."

"Now wait, you can't..."

"Hawk..."

"Wait! All right, don't shoot. We don't want any trouble with Nova Crew. That was all Exal's doing. Just give us some time."

"You have fifteen minutes to get clear before we blow up your ship, then start on the rest. Clock's moving. Oh, before you go, what's your name?"

"Me?"

"Yes, you."

"I'm Captain Jenkara of the Almack."

"Captain Jenkara, I'm Michella of Nova Crew, the Hound of Nova is my father. I tell you this so you'll believe me when I say to you; if any of my people comes to harm while we loot your two cargo ships, I'll come for you." She jerked her hand and Deann cut off the comm signals.

"Hawk, watch them closely. If they even flinch, fire."

"Understood." They all watched as the pirate ships scrambled together then a few moments later one fighter ship moved away.

"Hawk, we're in Arcalian space aren't we?"

"We are."

"You might want to let the authorities know where they can collect a few pirates."

"Already done, Boss."

Michella turned her full attention on him. "How do you do that so quickly?"

"Sorry, Boss, trade secret," chuckled the big man.

"So, what do you think? Did they booby trap the ships? Have they set a self-destruct? What do you think, Hawk? You're our specialist, do we check out those ships or keep going?"

"Well, Boss, passing them by would be the safest thing to do, but I'd sure like to see what is in those ships. I doubt it is anything major though. If it was they'd have passed us by. The fact they planned to attack us means they were still looking for more plunder."

"Hmmm. I didn't know pirates operated this far into Arcalian space," mused Michella.

"Arcalia's forces are spread way too thin trying to watch the Gap and the borders with Sega. A lot goes by unnoticed."

"So that's why you're really here. If we plug the Gap, Arcalia can defend her borders and keep the peace within those borders."

"That's right. I'm a bit surprised at your grasp of the situation. Impressive."

"I grew up on interstellar politics," sighed Michella. "All right, we'll check it out. Comms, ship-to-ship."

"Comms, aye," giggled Deann as she threw the proper switch.

"They're moving off, people. Uncle Rath, drop back and pick up Hawk. He wants to see what they were carrying. Ravage."

"Ravage here. Well done, Chella. I'm proud of you. That 'I'm just bored' act of yours probably did more to scare them than anything else."

"Thanks Poppa. We're checking out the two ships now. I'd like the Ravage to keep an eye out in case they try to come at us from behind."

"Understood." The Ravage swung easily around to face the direction the pirates had fled.

Michella slumped in her chair, trembling. "The first one is the toughest, Boss," grinned Hawk. "You did just fine." He gave her a sloppy grin and left the bridge.

"Chella, are you okay?" asked Deann, as she rose and stepped to Michella's side.

"I'm good," sighed Michella, as she tried to hide the trembling in her hands.

Deann took her shaking hands and held them steady. "Can I say something?"

"Of course, Sweetie."

"Chella, there are nearly two dozen extra people on this ship. You think of them as passengers, but they're not. They came with you expecting danger and the unknown. We could have used the extra people today."

"She's right, Chella," said Allore.

"Yes, she is," sighed Michella. "Okay, let's get a few more recruits. Comms, ship-wide."

"Comms, ship-wide, aye," laughed Deann, as she slid back into the seat at the station and flipped the switch.

"Attention all personnel, this is Michella. As you know we have just had an encounter with pirates. It has been pointed out to me that you all had as much at stake here as the rest of us. Your lives. From now on every man woman and child aboard this ship will learn as much as they can about the operation of the ship and its weapons. You will also learn how to operate the small fighter ships.

"The next time we have such an encounter you'll all be expected to take an active part. I truly am sorry, but this is what life is likely to be like from now on. If anyone doesn't want to continue with us, we'll be at Arcalia Prime very soon and you can depart there with no hard feelings. Michella out."

"Way to go, Chella," sighed Allore. "Poppa wants you to take on two more crew, you take three, and then you take on two dozen more. What's next, take over your own country, or a whole planet?"

"Shut up, Lore," laughed Michella. "Shut up or I'll get you your own crew."

"It's the right thing to do, Allore, you know that," smiled Deann.

"Yeah, I know. So, now that you're the Boss's companion are you going to take over the world too?"

"Me? Not a chance," smiled Deann. "I'll still be hanging around the infirmary driving you nuts."

Michella saw the relief in Allore's eyes. She really did need Deann as helper. Allore was a great healer, but she was only thirteen years old. Her confidence still needed a lot of building and Deann seemed to have developed a bond of friendship with her. Michella was thrilled that Deann was finding so many ways to fit in.

On to the Gap

Michella lay quietly floating on the euphoria of her spent passions. Deann sighed with contentment and smiled as Michella lightly traced the outline of her arm with delicate fingers and a feather touch. "Chella?"

"Mmmm?"

"Was I... are you... I mean..."

"You were, and still are, absolutely perfect, my love. I'm keeping you."

"Good, because I do want you to keep me, Chella."

"Hey now, none of that. We're a we, a team, a bonded pair, an us, together as one, equals..."

"No, not truly equals, Chella, but I promise we will be if I can survive it."

Michella propped herself up on one elbow to smile directly into her lover's eyes. "My sweet delicious Deann, whatever are you talking about?"

"You, Chella, and me, and this life we're facing. I'm not really equipped to handle what's coming..."

"Oh, but you've found so many ways to fit in already. Allore needs you; I need you,"

"That's not what I mean, Chella. What happens if we're on a planet and things get out of hand? I don't want you distracted trying to protect me when I should be helping you protect the crew. I need to learn, and I have to do it fast. Do you think Keira would teach me?"

"So that's it," sighed Michella as she relaxed back into the soft bed. "Well, she taught my momma; I'm sure she'll help. Do you want me to ask her?"

"No, I'll do it. I need to learn her language and I need her to understand that I want to learn. I'll talk to her."

"All right, sweetheart, but not right now. Right now I want..." She got no further as Nellie's soft voice came over the speaker.

"Shift change, Captain's shift in twenty minutes. Shift change, Captain's shift in twenty minutes."

"Oh, blast," sighed Michella. "I guess we'd better get on the move if we want anything to eat before shift."

"On it," laughed Deann, as she tossed the blanket over Michella's head and leaped toward the shower room.

"Brat," laughed Michella, as she followed her in. As Deann sat on the toilet Michella stepped closer and cradled her head against her belly. "My sweet brat, I'm keeping you."

———◉———

MICHELLA STEPPED ONTO the bridge to find five people gathered around the sensors while Rathbone explained how they worked. Ellie was in the pilot's seat and Hawk was in the Captain's chair. "Anything exciting going on, Hawk?" she asked, waving him back into the chair.

"All's quiet, Boss. We're a couple of days out of Arcalia Prime."

"Does the king know where we are?"

"Sure. Oh, they picked up your pirates and the cargo ships. Thing is, it looked like someone had already looted the cargo ships."

"Really? Dang, you can't leave anything unguarded these days."

"It's a sad truth," chuckled the big fellow.

"How's our new pilot doing?" she asked.

"Great," replied Hawk. "Ellie's a natural." Ellie turned and shook her finger at him then turned back to the controls.

Barah and Nellie wandered in together. Michella faced them with her hands on her hips. "So tell me, is every announcement on this ship got Nellie's voice, or is it just my compartment?"

"All of them," grinned Nellie. "Didn't you like it?"

Michella just rolled her eyes then pointed to the comms station. "Comms, Nellie." Nellie giggled and danced over to the station. "Barah, pilot."

"Aye, Boss," he grinned, as he relieved Ellie at pilot.

"Hawk, are you comfortable there for a little while? I want to take a look at the whole ship."

"I'm good, Michella. Take your time."

"We don't need a babysitter, Chella," said Barah.

"He's not your babysitter," rumbled Rathbone's deep voice, "he's in command of the bridge. That means he has the responsibility of making the decisions, you have the responsibility of carrying out those decisions instantly without argument. Tomorrow or an hour from now it might be me in that chair, or Chella, or Shoban here. It doesn't matter who it is. One day very soon, all our lives might well depend on how fast you can follow the orders from that chair."

"Understood, Sir."

"Barah, if you give me a hard time I'll send for your mother to come sit in that chair for a few shifts."

"Sorry, Uncle Rath. That won't be necessary," sighed Barah, the color rising to his face. He sat still, facing the panel and not moving. A few moments later he heard Rathbone take his pupils off the bridge. A hand fell on his shoulder making him jump.

"Things are pretty quiet, Barah," said Hawk. "Read this while you can; I'll let you know if anything is happening."

"What's this?" asked Barah, his tone surly and defiant as he looked at the reading tablet Hawk had passed to him.

"Fighter pilot's guide to the new ships we're picking up on Arcalia Prime," replied Hawk, as he resumed the Captain's seat. "Got some great stuff in there."

Barah looked at the tablet again then back at Hawk. "Thanks'" Hawk just sprawled loosely in the chair and winked at him.

Ellie had followed Michella on her tour of the ship. They were making a list of things that might be needed, everything from parts and fuel for the ship to clothing and food for the whole crew.

"Looks like you'll have a busy shopping day in the city," grinned Michella.

"Oh, I'll get started long before we land," laughed Ellie. "Hawk gave me a few folks to connect with; he says they can find anything and in a hurry."

"Oh really?"

"Ah-huh, and we have a ton of money we took off that pirate ship."

"Well in that case, you can get something special for me."

"Name it Chella; what do you need?"

"New clothes for Deann. I guess her mother and brothers will need some too. We did just scoop them up, after all."

"Already on my list, Boss." Ellie was grinning with delight.

"Ellie, what's your take on Hawk?"

"I'm still not completely sure, Chella, but I instinctively trust the big slob. I know that's all his years of practice making folks like and trust him, but I still do."

"Keep an eye on him for me."

"I will. Does that mean I can take him with me when I go shopping?"

"Sure thing, take Deann and take Allore with you too. We should all be more than safe on Arcalia Prime."

IN THE END, THEY SPENT a week on Arcalia Prime. It was a week of hard training for all the crews as the Arcalians drilled them on the operations of the new, more advanced ships. The new ships were slightly larger, designed for a crew of ten with room to carry sixty more people and eight small fighters.

After taking a look at the new ships Micha decided to decommission the Ravage and the Freedom in favor of the new ships. The king gave them six in all, fully stocked with fighters and provisions.

In spite of the tight training schedule, Ellie managed to slip away shopping several times, always with Hawk in tow. The day before departure she returned with Hawk carrying a bundle of containers as usual, but her eyes were wild, and her hands were shaking.

Michella was conferring with Micha when Ellie arrived back at the ships. She spotted the eyes instantly. "Ellie, what is it?" Ellie just shook her head as though she didn't trust her voice. "Hawk, report."

"We met a few unhappy people in town," replied the giant as he eased his burden to the deck of the ship.

"So, what happened?"

"We discussed the issue, and they went away even more unhappy," he grinned.

"A little more detail would be nice," sighed Michella. "Don't make me beat it out of you."

"Okay, Boss," chuckled Hawk. "It was a street gang and they had us targeted from the minute we reached the great mall. I saw them moving through the crowds, converging on us. I warned Ellie, but she'd already seen them herself. We moved away to a more open space and they attacked. We convinced them it was a bad idea and they left."

"Convinced them how?" grinned Micha. He could see that all was well and that young Ellie had gotten her first taste of battle, but had been well protected.

"Convinced?" exclaimed Ellie, as she regained her voice. "You killed three people before I could say a word."

"They weren't there to talk, Ellie," replied Hawk.

"Are you so sure?" she asked softly.

"One had a knife within inches of your back, and another was aiming a weapon. Hey, while we're at it, you blew two through a concrete wall and set three more on fire. You should have seen her, Boss. Ellie was amazing. She can watch my back any day."

"Oh, shut up and carry the packages to the Captain's cabin for me." Ellie slapped his arm and walked away.

"Hawk?" Micha's face looked concerned.

"They knew we were coming and exactly where we'd be," he replied evenly. "I think the king has a few rats in his garden and it is time to root them out. I've already made a report and there are men working on it right now."

"Ellie blew two through a wall?" asked Michella. "Hawk, never let her lose control of her temper; bad things could happen if she ever loses her temper."

"No, Boss, Ellie was ice cold all the way through. She just stepped in front of me and did her witchy thing. She showed no emotion at all until it was over, then she got the shakes. I expect that was her first encounter. She'll be fine."

"All right," sighed Michella. "You'd better get going with those packages before she comes back and sets your britches on fire."

"I heard that," he laughed, as he scooped up his load of packages and disappeared into the ship.

"She blew them through a wall," mused Michella, as she watched Hawk's retreating back, "What have you gotten me into, Poppa?"

"Me," chuckled Micha, "Chella, you did this all by yourself. I was more than happy to keep my family together and protect them as I always have, but you got all fired up and demanded changes, big changes. You chose your path Chella, just as I did the day I followed

Lessa off Kora Six. My path has taken me many places I'd rather not go, but we must travel the path we choose. I'll help you all I can, you know that, but..."

"I chose the road so now I have to walk it?"

"Yep, I'm afraid so."

"I think I'm just beginning to understand what your life has been like, Poppa."

"My life hasn't been what I would have chosen, Chella, but it's been good nonetheless. I've spent the years in the company of good friends and I've an amazing family that I'm exceptionally proud of. I chose my road, but I also chose how I walked it."

"Thanks, Poppa. I do understand. Once the road is chosen, it's the way you walk it that defines who you are and the quality of your life."

"You have your mother's wisdom as well as her passion. Go christen your new ship, Chella. We'll be leaving in about two hours. The king has pilots already on the extra ships so we're about as ready as we can be."

"On it, Boss," smiled Michella, as she hugged Micha then disappeared inside. Micha returned to his ship, the newly christened Ravage Two.

Michella made a fast sweep through her new ship, smiling at every turn. This ship was the latest thing the Arcalians had built, and these ships had been developed especially for Nova Clan. It was designed to fight and survive, was extremely fast, and yet had a surprising amount of luxury for the crew and passengers.

She found Deann in the Captain's cabin, sitting on the bed in an array of new clothes. "I said I needed one or two practical outfits, Chella. Look what Ellie brought me, three daily jumpsuits, three skirts with pop tops, a party dress, ... Chella, I've never owned a party dress before. When will I ever get a chance to wear this?"

"Who knows, Sweetheart. Are you pleased?"

"Chella, I'm thrilled and overwhelmed. Oh, there's a message here for you from my mother. I haven't seen her all day, but I found this on the floor when I came in."

"Really, well, let's see what's on her mind." Michella opened the folded paper and read:

"I can't live this way, so I'm leaving. You have stolen my children from me; I hope you treat them well. I don't expect I will ever see them again."

"Well, what does she say?" asked Deann, her curiosity getting the best of her.

Michella pretended to be reading the message. "I have decided to stay on Arcalia Prime. The boys won't leave their sister so I'm leaving them with her. I do hope to see you all well and happy the next time you're here."

"That is not my mamma, Chella," declared Deann, as she rose from the bed and took the paper from Michella's hand. "Yeah, that's Mamma all right," she snarled, as she read the message.

"We've got a couple of hours, maybe Hawk can find her."

"No, Chella, the boys are having a good time on this ship. They're well fed for the first time in their lives, and they've made friends with the other children. They'll be better off here and Mamma will be happier in the city. She made her choice; I'm content to live with it."

"All right, Sweetheart, if you're sure."

"I'm sure."

Michella nodded as she turned towards the door. "Okay, Sweetie. When you're finished putting away your treasure, come up to the bridge. I want you with me when we lift off in this ship for the first time."

"Have you decided on the name for her yet?"

"I think I'll stick with Warbird; what do you think?"

"I like it. The Ravage and the Warbird. That should give the pirates something to think about." Deann was still running her fingers along the fabric of her new clothes as Michella kissed the top of her head then left for the bridge.

"Are we ready for liftoff?" asked Michella, as she strode onto the bridge in her new fatigues. Ellie was on comms and she gave Michella the nod of approval. Chella noticed that everyone was wearing new clothes. "Well, this is a prosperous looking crew," she grinned. Are we ready?"

Rathbone started to rise from the captain's chair, but she patted his shoulder and he sank back. "Comms, ship-wide," he said, and Ellie grinned as she flipped the switch.

"Comms, ship-wide, aye."

"Attention, all stations, we are preparing for lift off. Report."

Pally was the first to respond. "All fighter ships and cargo secure. Engineering secure."

Allore was next. "Infirmary stocked and secure."

"Kitchen secure and ready," came a woman's voice.

Keira's singsong voice was next. Rathbone translated. "Weapons secure and stocked, aye."

As soon as every station had reported in, Chella asked for ship-to-ship with the Ravage. "Ravage, this is the Warbird, ready for orders."

"Well done, Warbird," came Micha's voice. "Tower contacted, lift off in ten. Flight path being transmitted to you now."

Hawk glanced at his panel then nodded to Michella. "Flight path received, Ravage. Lift off in ten. Warbird out."

The new ships were fast and over the next week they had plenty of time to test them. Rathbone and Keira drilled them mercilessly and they were all tired, but confident in their new ship and themselves as crew.

DEANN LAY SLEEPING on Michella's shoulder. Chella ran her finger lightly through her lover's hair and smiled tenderly at her. "You push yourself too hard, Sweetheart," she breathed softly.

"Keira's mean," Deann giggled softly.

"So, you're awake."

"Barely, but I'm awake enough for this. Today's the day Keira and Rathbone go back to the Ravage. She's taught me all she could; now it's up to me to practice. Hawk said he'd spar with me."

"Hawk?"

"He knows a few tricks and he's big and strong enough to make me work without teenage hormones getting in the way."

"Makes sense to me, Sweetheart, but you're not allowed to practice today, today is transition day. Today we reach the Gap; the journey's over and the new life begins."

"I hope it's exciting," smiled Deann, as she rose from the bed and stretched.

"Now you sound like Uncle Zartah," said Michella, smiling as she stretched languidly and relaxed back into the comfort of the bed. The claxon sounded and they felt the ship decelerating swiftly. "Captain to the bridge," purred Nellie's voice.

"I am so going to smack Barah if he doesn't change that," sighed Michella, as she hopped out of bed and began pulling on her jumpsuit. She paused to watch Deann. The girl was checking and concealing several bladed weapons on her person as well as strapping on a blaster and a projectile weapon. She handled all of them with a practised ease. Deann's time with Keira had not been wasted. "Ready?"

Deann nodded and they left for the bridge together. "Report," grinned Michella, as they strode onto the overcrowded bridge. It seemed like half the ship's compliment was there.

"Approaching the Gap, Captain," grinned Rathbone, as he rose from the Captain's chair.

Michella settled into the chair with Deann at her shoulder. A few moments later the Ravage called as both ships coasted to a full stop.

"Ravage to all ships. We've arrived at the Gap, welcome home." It was Lady Arlessa's rich voice and everyone smiled to hear it. "You all know we've come here for more than one purpose. We've come to restore order and we've come to claim this territory as our own. We have a difficult task before us.

"There are some things you need to know about this area of space. Things are not always what they appear to be in the Gap. There are pockets of space here where time and distance have no meaning. If you encounter one of these random events you might glimpse the future, the past, or something else altogether.

"Beware of those nebulous areas like that gaseous cloud before us. That swirling mass can transport you to a completely alien realm. Many ships are lost this way each year as the unwary and foolhardy are swallowed up by the unknown.

"There are other dangers as well, but each ship has people on board who have experience with this area. We are Nova Clan, and we're a unique people. It's my belief that we're well equipped to live and prosper here. I will now turn you over to our clan chieftain, Micha."

"Hi folks. Well, we're here. For good or ill this is home now, or I should say these ships are our homes now and this is our territory. As Miriam says, this is our hunting ground. Now it's time to claim it. In a few moments you might detect a large number of ships approaching us. They're the Arcalian Gap Fleet. They'll pass by on their way home to Arcalia Prime then we're on our own.

"There are a few planets along the edge of the Gap that we'll use as supply dumps. From time to time as needed we'll be able to pick up supplies there and actually feel the wind on our faces. The

Arcalian Fleet will pick up our extra pilots. Thank you gentlemen for the assistance. Micha out."

The comms fell silent and everyone quietly began to mull over the messages. "Arcalian Fleet on sensors, Boss," came a voice Michella didn't recognize. She looked up to see a farmer who had lived about three farms over from her father's. He grinned and winked at her.

"On all screens," she smiled in return.

"All screens, aye." The screens came alive, and a fleet of warships could be seen approaching. They stopped and four small fighters dropped out of the Ravage, went to each of the spare ships then dropped the pilots off with their own fleet. The fleet commander broadcast a wish for good luck and a farewell. The fleet moved away at speed, heading for Arcalia Prime.

They watched until the fleet disappeared from sensors, then Micha's voice came over the comms. "Warbird, send two pilots over to those spare ships, one each. The destination coordinates are being broadcast to the ships now."

"Understood," replied Michella. "Barah, Tarah, go and take a co-pilot each with you." grinning, the two young men fled the bridge. Nellie went with Barah and a middle-aged woman joined Tarah.

"Bella's a natural at the controls." Tarah grinned as he saw Michella's raised eyebrow. She smiled and nodded.

As soon as the fighter ships had transferred pilots to the extra ships, Micha's voice came over the comms again. "We're forming up, Warbird. You fly the right flank; the Ravage will fly the left. Our task is to make certain the four ships are protected."

"Understood, Ravage," replied Michella. She nodded and Hawk moved the Warbird around to the right flank of the small convoy. "All right people, the show's over. Everybody return to their duty station. There was a sudden flurry of activity while the population of the bridge thinned out. As the Warbird settled into position she was battle ready, fighter crews were standing by, and the ship's guns were manned as well.

The group moved out at full speed. It was exciting at first, but the crews soon became bored as nothing at all happened. It was several hours later that the nebulous area appeared on sensors. The claxon sounded, but none of the ships slowed down. Micha's voice came over the comms. "I knew this was here, people. Normally, we avoid these phenomena like the plague, but not this one. This one will batter your senses a bit, but it's hollow. We'll be inside in seconds."

He had barely finished speaking when they were enfolded by the strange gasses floating in space. There was a moment of dizziness where images flashed in their minds and the sound of murmuring voices were heard, and then they were inside. "Fleet; full stop," came Micha's voice.

The ships slowed swiftly and came to a stop in orbit around a dead planet. The comms came to life again. "This planet is from somewhere else," said Micha. "The cities are empty and there's no atmosphere. However, we discovered it by accident and decided it would make a perfect place to hide if we needed to. We'll leave the four extra ships here, fully locked up and witch trapped. No one but us will be able to get inside them, even if they do stumble on them.

"We also have some supplies and weapons in that large hangar near where we'll put the ships. If life goes sideways you can always retreat back here for supplies and a new ship."

Landing coordinates were sent to the four ships and they settled to the surface. They opened up and the fighters brought back the pilots to their respective ships. Once the pilots were safely on board, Lessa and Norlene took a small ship down and sealed the spare ships before returning to the Ravage. Once they were back, Micha addressed the fleet again.

"All right, people, now we go to work. There are three main routes through the Gap. Two are fairly safe except for pirates, and one is unstable. Even so, fools will always try to run it. So, here's the plan. We'll run a blockade on the two main routes first. We're quite well known, so there should be no problems. The Ravage will fly point with the Warbird flying rear guard. Coordinates being sent now." A moment later both ships turned and blasted through the barrier again, headed for the nearest trade route through their territory. Once outside the anomaly, they cut their speed to half and proceeded into the Gap.

Gap seemed like such an inadequate word to describe this section of space. It was vast. So vast it could easily have been impossible for Nara Clan to defend and patrol if not for the anomalies. *How could two ships and less than fifty people hope to control it all?* Michella wondered. It wasn't long before she had her answer.

A few hours in, the ships suddenly swerved to the left. For just a moment their instruments scrambled wildly and the power flickered, then everything stabilized. "Fleet all stop," came Zartah's voice over the comms.

"All stop, aye," responded Ellie, as she grinned at Michella.

"What just happened, Ravage?" asked Michella.

"Forget your sensors, Warbird. Use your eyes. Look back, what do you see?"

Michella rose and stepped forward until she was almost touching the rear veiwscreen. "It looks a bit hazy, rippled or something, but it's hard to see."

"It's a gateway, Michella," came Lessa's voice. "It'll throw you halfway across the Universe to another galaxy. Norlene and I tried to penetrate it with our senses, but only found derelict ships of strange design floating helplessly. It seems there's nothing there and no way back."

Micha came on next. "Have you got those coordinates logged, Chella."

"Logged, aye," nodded Tarah, who was at pilot.

"On we go then, Ravage out."

The Ravage moved off and the Warbird followed in its wake. "I know my father well, people," sighed Michella. "He brought us close to that so we would see for ourselves and believe. We must heed the warning and stay alert. Just because nothing's happening doesn't mean it's safe. Let's all stay sharp."

They travelled the route for several days more. Each time they neared any danger it was pointed out and logged. The Warbird had already downloaded the voyage logs of the Freedom and the original Ravage, but Micha wanted them to see everything first hand. "Experience is the best teacher," he had often said over the years. Michella was now beginning to believe in that saying. You could skim over the logs and miss a lot, a dangerous thing when missing a little could get your crew killed.

They encountered a few pirate groups, but they all fled at the approach of the Ravage. Three days from the Imperial side of the Gap they encountered a group of ten ships. The claxon sounded just as Deann and Michella were leaving their cabin to begin their shift. "Battle stations. Battle stations. All hands to battle stations. Captain to the bridge." That wasn't Nellie's sexy purr; that was Pally's deep rumble that sounded just like his father's. It commanded attention and action.

"Report," barked Michella, as she entered the bridge. Deann had gone to the infirmary to assist Allore.

"Ten ships incoming," said Hawk, as he rose from the chair, "Imperials by the looks of them. I expect they'll fight, as they never come this far in with ships of the line." He moved his tall, loose, frame easily into the main gunner's chair that a woman had just vacated. She stepped to rear sensors. "All stations report ready and standing by, Boss."

"Fighter ships ready?"

"Ready," he grinned, "and the new harnesses are in place."

"Are you sure those harnesses will work, Pally?"

He turned slightly from his panel to grin at her. "They'll work, Chella. A normal will be able to take the accelerations and turns as well as any of us when they're strapped in."

"As long as they can keep their stomachs down," chuckled Hawk. He'd been one of the early test cases.

"Let's all hope they can," muttered Michella. "Ellie, I want everything on comms that you can pick up from those ships."

"They're hailing the Ravage now, Chella. I'll get visual too." Ellie flipped the switches and the voices filled the bridge.

"Attention approaching ships, this is Commander Helsig of the Imperial ship, Intruder. You have entered Imperial space. Stand down and prepare to be boarded."

"My, that's a pretty uniform you're wearing there, Helsig," replied Micha's voice. "Now let me explain a few things to you. Pay close attention for I'll only do this once. My name is Micha. I'm chieftain of Nova Clan. I'm also the man who killed your last emperor and we're the people who destroyed the entire Imperial Fleet. This area of space known as The Gap is now Nova Clan space and you're trespassing. Turn your ships around and go home."

The Imperial commander just laughed. "All you bloody pirates are alike. You think everyone will run and hide at the mention of the Hellhound's name. Prepare to be boarded. You have two minutes."

"You don't," replied Micha. The Ravage opened fire and the lead Imperial ship was nearly cut in half before any of them could respond. Michella had been watching her father's hands on the visuals and knew her orders. The Warbird instantly opened fire on the second ship, crippling it. The Warbird banked hard right and easily avoided a hail of weapons fire from the Imperials.

The Ravage had rolled left at the same time with her six fighters spilling out as she went. The small fighter ships swept in, blazing away at the hangar bay doors of the enemy. They managed to prevent four of the ships from launching fighters, but the remaining ships did launch. The area was suddenly filled with buzzing fighters.

It didn't take long for the Imperials to realize they faced something new. These pirate ships were much faster than the Imperial ships. Their fighters were faster, more manoeuvrable, and more heavily armed. The Imperial fighters were getting cut to ribbons.

The Imperial cruisers weren't doing any better. They'd managed to score a few hits on the larger ships, but they seemed to have little effect. These had to be Arcalian ships. None of them had ever actually seen one, but the Arcalian ships were legendary. The small fighters began to surrender, and the larger ships soon followed.

"I believe you truly must be the Hellhound, pirate," gasped the commander's voice, as the comms crackled back to life. "What are your terms?"

"Stand down," ordered Micha. The Imperials ceased fighting instantly. "Turn around and go home. Carry this message to the Emperor: The Gap is ours. We created it and we'll keep it for ourselves. Stay out and we have no problems. From this day forward any Imperial ship entering Nova Clan territory will be destroyed."

"That's very generous of you, Sir. We will withdraw."

The Imperial ships did a bit of juggling of personnel then four of the original ten moved off towards the Imperial side. The six battered derelicts hung in space for a few moments then witchfire lanced out from the Ravage and all six of them exploded into fragments. The Imperials ships were still close enough to see what had happened. They began to accelerate.

"Ravage to Warbird, report."

"Two of our fighters are in bad shape and we have a number of injuries, but no casualties. The Warbird took a few hits, but no real damage as far as I know. Pally is going out for a look right now. We still have full power and hull integrity."

"You and your crew did well, Chella. I'm proud of you."

"Thanks, Poppa. Why did we let them go?"

"I wanted to send a message. In future we'll run and lure them deeper into the Gap and lose them in the anomalies. We took a big risk here, but we had no choice. See to your people now then we'll turn back and head for the next trade route."

"Understood. Warbird out."

"Ellie, you've got the chair. Leave old Hawk on guns, he seems to like it there."

Hawk chuckled as Michella left the bridge and Ellie eased herself into the command seat. Ellie carefully ran her fingers lightly over the controls of the Captain's chair. "Orders, Captain Ellie?" grinned Hawk.

"Shut up, Hawk," she hissed at him, her face turning red as she nervously clung to the arms of the chair.

"Shutting up, aye."

She shot him a glare, but he was grinning and studying his targeting system. "I know what you're doing," she muttered to herself. "You're trying to make me mad so I'll forget about being nervous. It's not working." She continued to sit very still in the chair until Michella returned.

Claiming the Territory

The infirmary was full when Michella entered. There were a lot of bruises and strained muscles. Allore was working swiftly and efficiently as she patched up the injured. Michella heard one woman gasp with pain as Allore pushed her dislocated shoulder back into place while Deann held her.

"Happy, Chella?"

"Ally, don't even start," said Michella. "I had no choices here at all. People, I'm truly sorry for every injury, I am; but we faced ten Imperial Battleships. These were well manned ships with trained crews, not pirates on old rusty ships. I'm truly sorry, but we're alive."

"That old bull of my father's beat me up worse than this," grinned one young fellow. "Did we win?"

"Yeah, we did," grinned Michella. "Ally, how bad is it?"

"Not really that bad, Chella. There are lots of bruises from being tossed around, a couple of dislocated shoulders from hanging on when the ship moved too quickly, and one broken leg. I'm just stressed, that's all."

"This is what you wanted, Lore."

"I know, be careful what you wish for, right?"

"Absolutely."

"Go do your boss thing, Chella. We've got this."

Michella nodded and left the infirmary. In the mess hall she found the cook swearing like a trooper while she tried to salvage as much of her stores as possible from what had gotten thrown around. Chella quietly backed out and headed for the fighter bay.

"How's it look, Pally?" she asked, as she entered to find him crawling out from under a fighter ship.

"Four of our fighters are good, Chella, but two need a lot of work."

"We'll work with four for now; I need you and your inventive genius on another project."

"What's up, Chella?"

"A lot of our people got hurt, Pally."

"Humans are soft, Chella. You've said so yourself many times."

"Yes, they are, Pally, but these are our humans. Our crew. Our clan. Our friends. We need to do something about this."

"Chella, if we go slower in a battle we're going to get our butts handed to us and you know it. Our ability to withstand the speeds and fast turns is an awesome advantage."

"I know, and I want that for them too."

"You want to enhance them; I'm not a witch. I can't do that."

"No, Lady Arlessa explained why she won't; can't do that anymore. I want you to modify the artificial gravity units on all our ships, the Warbird and the fighters."

"Modify, how?"

"The grav needs to react fast enough to allow the humans to take the speeds and turns."

"It can't be done, Chella."

"Why not?"

"I don't know," he laughed. "I guess because no one has ever done it before, I just assumed it can't be done. Can I get Nellie and Barah to help me?"

"Sure, but why Barah? He's as mechanically minded as I am."

"I need him because Nellie will focus a lot better with him here than if she's mooning over where he might be. Also, if he's here he won't beat me up for spending so much time with Nellie."

"Good thinking, Pally," laughed Michella. She reached for the comm on her shoulder. "Barah and Nellie to Engineering. Pally will meet you there."

"Engineering, aye," replied Nellie's sexy purr. Michella rolled her eyes and headed for the bridge.

———◆———

THE CLAN TURNED BACK after that claiming battle and things were uneventful as the days passed and they returned to Sector Nine space. Several days' cruise put them at the next route through the Gap. They had just barely headed in when five ships appeared on screen closing fast.

The claxon was still blaring for battle stations when Michella reached the bridge. Hawk was already on the guns as she entered. Ellie leaped from the Captain's chair; relief clear on her face. "Report," said Michella, as she eased herself into the chair.

"All stations report battle ready, Chella," sighed Ellie, as she flipped the switches at comms. The screens came alive with the image of the ships bearing down on them. Ellie flicked another switch just as Micha hailed the newcomers from the Ravage. She grinned as she listened to the exchange.

"Ravage to five approaching ships. Reduce speed and identify yourselves or be destroyed."

The ships cut their speed instantly. A moment later Micha got a response. "Micha, sorry about that; I didn't recognize you with that shadow. We'll just be about our business and leave you to yours." The speaker was a grizzled old woman with a nasty scar down her left cheek.

"Hold your position, Zemma," said Micha. "I was looking for you."

Michella leaned forward in her chair, resting her elbows on her knees. At first glance it would be easy to underestimate this woman, but her eyes were shrewd and intelligent. This was going to be interesting.

"Micha, I don't know what you've heard, but it's all lies. I haven't touched a Guild convoy."

"That's not why I wanted to see you, Zemma," smiled Micha. "I have a small favor to ask of you."

The woman's eyes lit up with suspicion. "A favor? Well sure, sweetie, anything for a good looking young fella. Your ship or mine?"

"Zemma, you know a few folks in, shall we say, certain circles on the planets near the Gap. I want you to spread the word for me. Nova Clan has moved into the Gap. The Gap is our territory now; folk here will abide by Nova Clan rules or die; there are no other options. If anyone attacks one of my ships, I'll take it as a personal affront.

"There are six ships in all, the Ravage, the Thunder, the Lance, the Raptor, the Warbird, and the Shield. That shadow of mine is the Warbird. We'll be patrolling the Gap at all times.

"The rules are simple: The Guild is under my protection, anyone else is fair game. There will be no slave raiding along the border planets."

"A lot of people aren't going to like this, Micha."

"Understood. Tell them, Zemma, the Gap is off limits."

"So, how is a girl supposed to make a living out here now, Micha?"

"Same way as always, Zemma. If they enter the Gap you can have them. If they're coming through without Guild signals, you can have them. We're only six ships, Zemma; we can't be everywhere at once."

With that Micha cut the connection and the Ravage moved off into the Gap with the Warbird following. "Chella, I have your father on a secure channel."

"Put him on screen, Ellie."

"Chella, you follow all of that back there?"

"Yes, Poppa. Who is that woman?"

"Zemma is one of the worst pirates in the area. She's an escaped slave; that's where her scars come from. Zemma's as smart as any three people rolled together and completely ruthless."

"Do you trust her?"

"I trust her to be Zemma. She won't risk crossing me, but she won't stop hunting either. I expect she'll start preying on some of the other pirates; at least I hope she will. Never turn your back on her, Chella."

"Understood, Poppa. Understood."

EMPEROR LORAN WAS IN a special room he'd had built for exercise. He had been assured he didn't need to exercise and that it would have no effect on his body at all, but he did it anyway. He needed to train his mind for hand-to-hand combat. He intended to face the Hound again; with different results. A number of shattered targets lay scattered on the floor and another exploded in the air as he shot it down. A slight pinging sound alerted him that someone had entered the outer door.

"I'll be right out, Lizera. Wait there." He put his weapon back on the wall rack, then activated the cleaning bots before exiting the target area. He found her waiting by the window. "I assume this is a private report? Is it about our special project?"

"Yes," she nodded. "I sent ten ships of the line into the Gap to probe the Hound's abilities."

"Results?"

"It took them a while to find him, but they did. His two ships destroyed our ten with ease. Only four returned and then only because he let them go. He sent you a message."

"A message? For me? Does he know who I am?"

"I don't believe so, Sire. The message was generic. He says Nova Clan has claimed the Gap for themselves. If we keep out there are no problems; if we enter none will return. You know; that sort of bluster."

"Don't be too sure of yourself, Lizera. If it were anyone else I might agree, but the Hound doesn't bluster. He never bluffs. He means what he says, and he's quite capable of backing up his position."

"Forgive me, Sire, but the Hound has only two ships with a dozen fighters at most. He has another four ships hidden somewhere in the Gap, but doesn't have the personnel to man them. Why not just send in fifty ships and clean him out?"

"That was tried twenty years ago. Thousands were sent. It failed. No, Lizera, we must take the Hound by subterfuge. He's trying to control the entire region of space with only two ships?"

"Apparently so, Sire."

"Interesting. What else do we know about this new development?"

"He seems to be throwing his weight around with the pirates. He's given them free reign to attack any ship except the Guild, but they aren't allowed to raid into Arcalian space. The Arcalians appear to have withdrawn from the Gap and reinforced their borders with Sega Clan."

"It is difficult to single-handedly patrol such a large area, isn't it? See if you can stir up some mischief in several places at once. Avoid the pirates, we don't need the excess loss, but let's give the Hound plenty to keep him busy. We need to draw them apart. The child will be the weakest link. If we can catch her alone we can have him. He used my daughter against me, now I will use his against him."

"Sire?"

"If we have her in restraints with electrodes attached to sensitive parts of her body, her screams will bring the Hound running to the rescue. We can take him and that accursed Rathbone at the same time.

"We'll set our traps carefully, Lizera. Patience will be our ally. Patience and subterfuge."

———◉———

THE REST OF THE TRIP was uneventful until they reached the Imperial side. As they reached the far rim they detected a large fleet of Imperial ships. The fleet detected them at the same time. "Reverse course, full burn," came Micha's voice over the comms, as the Ravage turned tightly and fled with the Warbird close behind.

For nearly half an hour the Imperials pursued them until, suddenly, two of their ships disappeared from the screens and another bucked wildly and went dark. The Imperial fleet came to a full stop and so did the Novans. Michella noticed that they had veered off considerably from the original path through the Gap. She kept her ship to the Ravage's course, not daring to wander even slightly.

When the Imperials came to a full stop, the Novans turned and faced them across the emptiness. Michella shivered as her father's voice came over the comms. It was colder than the space that the ships floated in. "Attention Imperial ships, this is Micha of Nova Clan. You have invaded our territory when I sent word that this would mean certain death. Why did you come?"

"Attention pirate ships. This is Captain Gerra of the Imperial fleet. Stand down and prepare to be boarded."

"In case you hadn't noticed, Gerra, we've travelled in a tight turn deep into the Gap. We're a long way from the safe path and I'm now between you and the comfort of the Empire. My condolences to all your families."

"Enough of this," snarled the Imperial commander, "ahead full, attack formation Beta." The comms went silent and Michella held her breath. No orders came from the Ravage.

The Imperials were barely halfway to the Ravage when all but three of their ships were seized by an unknown force and ripped apart. Micha's voice returned on a secure channel. "Left thrusters at max. Thrusters only Chella."

"Understood. Left Max thrusters."

The two ships began to move slowly to the right, a movement that went unnoticed by the remaining Imperial ships. Those ships started forward again but didn't get far. The one on the left flank began to buckle. They stopped again, the affected ship sending out small fighters which sped to the lead ship and disappeared inside.

The comms came alive on again. "This is Commander Gerra." The man was ashen and his face registered the horror of what had just happened to his fleet. "We are prepared to surrender. Name your terms."

"This is Micha of Nova Clan, good luck Commander. Warbird, new course laid in?"

"Warbird responding. Course received and laid in." replied Ellie's sweet voice.

"Engage, full burn."

The two Nova ships suddenly blasted away from the Imperials, seeming to rise then fall from the sensors. An hour later they were back where they'd first encountered the Imperials. Micha sat brooding in the captain's chair. Edie stepped in behind him and laid a gentle hand on his shoulder.

"I never get used to it, Edie. I just deliberately wiped out dozens of lives. Gods, how many have I killed in my lifetime." Edie squeezed his shoulder and Lessa spoke.

"They chose their own fate, Micha," Lessa said gently. "There're no innocents in the military. There may be good people, but no innocents. The very nature of the job dictates a loss of innocence. These people chose to obey orders that they knew would place them in danger.

"What else could you do? Have us run away and let them through? Where would it stop?"

"I know, Lessa, I know. The more you give in to the bullies and fanatics the more they want and the worse things get. I just sometimes wish it could be different."

"We all do, Micha; we all do. Now, I know full well that it's Michella and the other kids that are truly on your mind. I'm sorry, dear friend; this is the life they must live. My own daughter is with them, and I can't protect her any more than you can protect Michella. They were born into this just as you were born to farm slaves."

"You're right, Lessa. I was younger than most of them when you trusted me, all of you did. I guess it's my turn."

"Honey, you saw Chella's crew take down those pirates. You know she's as ready as she can be," said Edie, patting his shoulder again. "You know what you have to do."

"I know. I just don't want to do it yet."

"I agree, Love, but the Imperials have taken away that option. Like it or not, if we're going to control the Gap we have to trust our children to handle one of the trade routes."

"Yeah, I just wish I could spare someone for their crew that Chella would accept, but I know the kids don't want their parents watching over their shoulders all the time..."

"Boss, I think I have the answer for you on comms," said Gorda, as he flipped a switch. An old man's voice came over the comms, he sounded bored.

"Mayday, mayday, all passing ships. We've been marooned on this blasted rock for months now. I've been building weapons and will shoot you down if you don't stop to pick us up. Mayday, mayday, all passing ships..."

Rathbone leaped at the comms. "Poppa, is that you? It's Rath. Poppa..."

"Rath? Grandson, is that really you or has Deke been spiking my water again?"

"Poppa, it's me, us, the crew. Where are you?"

"Damned if I know, Rath. We were looking for you when we hit this tiny nebula. Deke thought we could just fly through, but that didn't work."

"Poppa, you disappeared eight years ago. We thought you were dead."

"Eight years? Eight weeks is more like it."

"You hit a time displacement, Poppa Rathbone," said Lessa, as she leaned over Rath's shoulder. "Keep broadcasting, we'll locate and pick you up. Micha has a job for you."

"Well, he'd dang well better feed me first. Our supplies are nearly gone. Deke eats like a pig."

Deke's voice came on from behind old Rathbone. "For the love of all that's holy, Lady Arlessa, save me from being nursemaid to this senile old coot," he chuckled.

"I've got them on sensors," sang Keira. "The Warbird is closer."

"Oh yeah," grinned Micha, "some days it's way better to be lucky than good. Get me the Warbird."

A moment later Michella answered. "Warbird here."

"Chella, I have a task for you. There's a damaged ship close by; I need you to pick up the survivors. Do what you want with them; we're blasting out of here."

"Poppa?"

"I need you to patrol this trade route for now. I'll make a pass through the first one, check the third then come back for you. Good luck, Captain Michella."

"Thank you, Chieftain... I think," came the reply, as the Ravage blasted off at full burn.

"Now what the heck is he up to?" muttered Michella, as she watched the Ravage speed away.

"Who knows," chuckled Nellie. "Comms?"

"Comms. Warbird to the stranded, we'll be right there to pick you up."

Michella was trying to sound official, but the old man's response irritated her. "You'd better move it, girl. That anomaly is coming back, and you don't want to get caught in it. It'll tear your pretty ship apart and us with it."

"Then perhaps I should just leave you there," she retorted. "Stand by. Tarah, get us in there now."

"Hang on," he replied, as his hands danced across the controls.

Michella felt the ship lurch at the sudden acceleration. The Warbird danced around a few free floating asteroids and one small gas cloud as it closed swiftly on the stranded ship's position. Everyone was hanging on tightly as she bore down on a planet-sized hunk of rock and swept gracefully to a landing. The air lock door opened as she touched down.

Three space suited figures were already moving from the downed ship to the Warbird and were soon inside the airlock. As they entered Pally slammed his hand down on the control that shut the door. "They're in," he shouted into the comms, as his hand hit the control.

"Hit it, Tarah," barked Michella, but the Warbird was already rising.

Something seemed to grab the ship and try to drag it back as she rose into space again. The big bird was struggling. "Chella, the hull is under serious stress," said Deann, as she leaned over her sensor panel.

"It's the damned anomaly," growled Tarah. "Come on, Warbird, get us out of here. All right, we're gaining speed, aaaaaaand we're clear." The Warbird streaked back to her original position.

"Chella to infirmary, how are our passengers doing?"

"Pally here, Boss. You'll never guess who we just picked up. Chella, you've got to come down here."

"On my way," she replied, rising from the captain's chair. "Hawk, keep the chair warm. Ellie, make sure he doesn't fall asleep."

The excitement in Pally's voice had her curiosity up and Michella hurried down the corridor to the infirmary. As she approached she thought she heard a familiar voice and she definitely heard Allore giggling as she bantered with an old man. She stepped through the door to see a vaguely familiar face. It took a moment for her to recognize him.

"Grandpoppa Rathbone," she squealed, as she leaped into the old man's arms and hugged him tightly.

"Put me down, girl," he grumbled as he returned her hug, "you're killing me. Besides, this is no way for the captain of a warship to act."

"It is too," she laughed, as she released him and hugged the silver haired woman beside him. "Auntie Nina."

"Little Chella all grown up," said Nina as she returned the hug. "We just saw you a few weeks ago and now you're all grown up, all of you."

"It's been over eight years, Auntie."

"So Allore has been telling us. This is your ship?"

"Yes, the Warbird is our ship. Are they okay, Lore?"

"They're fine, Chella, but Grand Poppa thinks he's starving." Allore shrieked and danced away as Old Rath made a grab for her.

"Then let's go to the kitchen," said Michella. "We've all got stories to tell."

They entered the kitchen to find food waiting for them. The cook knew the stranded would end up in her kitchen and she was ready. Michella called for Deann to join them, then she got a tray of food for them both. As she reached the table Pally was regaling Old Rathbone with the tale of Kon's kidnapping and rescue.

"Looks like Poppa got his way after all," said Allore, as Michella sat beside her.

"Looks like, all right," grinned Michella, as she sat down. Noticing Old Rath's inquisitive glance, she went on to explain. "Grandpoppa Rath, ever since our father gave us this ship he's been trying to get more experienced people onto my crew. I took old Hawk, although I wasn't sure if I should use him or blow him out the air lock. I nearly did blow that other one out the lock."

"Other one?"

"Poppa sent two people over," laughed Allore. "One was supposed to make Chella mad to see what she'd do. That was a bad idea."

"It's not funny, Lore," sighed Michella. "She did rub my fur the wrong way, so I sent her back to Poppa. He called me over to his ship to explain, but the woman was still giving me attitude. I tried to see if I could throw her through a bulkhead, but it didn't work. Poppa wasn't happy so he sent Uncle Rath and Auntie Keira over for a few weeks."

"So you think he engineered this whole rescue?" asked Deke.

"Didn't he, Uncle Deke?"

"Not unless he planned this over eight years ago, Chella," grinned Deke. "We were caught in that time displacement rift for over eight years, or so your people tell me. It must be true because the last time we saw you, you were barely twelve years old and bossy as can be."

"That hasn't changed," giggled Allore.

"Shut up, Lore," laughed Michella. "Okay, but did Poppa know who you folks were before he ordered me to pick you up and then took off at full burn?"

"Yes he did, the sneaky pup," chuckled Old Rath.

"Well, in truth I'd be thrilled and honored if you all would join the crew, but I'll leave that up to you. If you want I'll get you out of the Gap and someplace safe."

"There is no place safe, Chella," sighed Old Rath. "We could see the Gap was becoming a big problem. So after we left your farm the last time we thought we'd swing by for a look before we headed home."

"Poppa's crew went to look for you when you were reported missing in space, but they couldn't find you. How about it, Grandpoppa Rath, the Arlens have elected another guy to your old job, you're between contracts."

"Are you offering me a contract?"

"I am, you and your crew."

"My crew? Oh, yes, my crew. All right, young miss, what are the terms?"

"This is my crew and my ship. Your crew joins my crew, and you get the job of First Man. It'll be up to you to fit the rest of your crew into this one. The job never ends; it just goes on and on. The pay is terrible, but we all share in whatever we can find."

"Come on, Sweetie," grinned Nina. "They're all the family we've got. The rest of the galaxy thinks we're dead anyway; let's stay here and play with the grand kids."

"Deke?"

"I've been out of work for eight years, Rath. I need the job."

"All right, Chella, we accept the contract. When do we start?"

"Right now." She grinned as she reached to her shoulder for her comm unit. "Bridge, ship-wide comms please."

"Ship-wide, aye," sang Ellie. "Go ahead."

"Attention all hands. The Warbird has a new First Man. He is the former governor of the Arlen Alliance, Rathbone of Urn. He'll make himself known to you in his own time." They could hear a few cheers from various parts of the ship.

⟼⊙⟻

THE WARBIRD MADE HER pass through the Gap without incident and turned back. They took their time, exploring, learning as much about the Gap as they could.

It was an off-shift day that found Deann in the small exercise area that Pally had created in the hangar bay. She was practising her hand-to-hand combat forms when she heard the old man's voice behind her. She turned at lightning speed ending in a defensive posture, but he was sitting on the floor, resting his back against the wall.

"Girl, you're all bruised up," he observed.

"I know," she sighed.

"Hurts, doesn't it?"

"Yeah, it does, but it can't be helped," she replied, as she sank to the floor beside him. "Are you really Pally's great grandfather?"

"That I am, girl. I'm older than dirt. Forgive me for saying this, but you don't seem to be having any fun here."

"I'm not," she sighed, "but what else can I do?"

"Just what are you doing, Deann? I mean, why are you doing it?"

"I need to do this for Chella."

"Michella makes you do this?"

"No, no, no, it's not that. She's one of the enhanced; I'm not. If we get into a battle, as I'm sure we will eventually, I need to be ready."

"So she doesn't get distracted trying to protect you?"

"Exactly."

"Keira teach you?"

"Yes, you can tell?"

"I recognized her style; crude but effective. You practice with Hawk, why?"

"Because he's big and strong, like what I'm likely to face."

"I was a small boy when my father began to teach me. I learned how to overcome and kill a much larger and stronger opponent without taking a lot of damage myself. You've learned the strike points and ways to attack them most effectively, but against an experienced opponent you're getting hit with blocks and counter moves. Every time you get hit it takes a toll on you. In a long battle you become less and less effective and you get hit more often. It's a downhill spiral."

"So what do I do?"

"I taught Rathbone what I could, but he's built like a battleship and enjoys getting into the tough stuff. Young Pally is like his father and Rath has taught him well. You're smaller, like me. We have to do things a bit differently. Deann, I have a lot of skills and experience in this area and nobody to teach it to. I'm getting old now and I don't want these skills to die with me. I'll teach you if you promise to pass the skills to another before you die of old age."

"You mean that? You'd teach me?"

"It's a contract, Deann, you know your part."

"Yes, oh gods yes. When can we start?"

"Right now if you want."

"Let's go," she said, as she leaped to her feet. She looked puzzled as he just patted the floor beside him. Bemused, Deann sat back down.

"Lesson one," he grinned. "How to look small and helpless. People always underestimate the small and weaker looking opponent. We need to encourage that habit. Always look helpless. The key is to get from helpless to a defensive stance so fast the opponent doesn't know it's happened until it is too late. Understand that what a person first sees is what they expect. Show them helpless first so their brain expects that."

Deann was ecstatic. She always seemed to have a smile on her face that says, "I have a secret." Michella asked about it, but she would only say that she would reveal all soon. Deann was also surprised that her sessions with Old Rath were always started sitting against the wall. They talked, she practised forms and he corrected, then they talked some more. Then came the day she tried it all out on Hawk for the first time.

They were in the practice area and Deann seemed to be a bit distracted. "Pay attention, girl. You can't go all dreamy eyed in a fight." He leaped at her to grab her in a pinning hold, but she wasn't there. Like water in high wind, she was everywhere and nowhere. Hawk felt her fists hit every vital point on his body as she melted away from his grasp. Her legs entangled his and he toppled over like a tree.

Hawk broke his fall and rolled onto his back, laughing. "You've been training with Old Rath, haven't you?"

"How could you tell?"

"The last time I was put down that easily was twenty years ago. He's the man who did it. All right, Deann, it looks like you've got your equalizer. Wha..." he got no further as the claxon sounded.

"Battle stations, battle stations, all hands to battle stations."

A moment later Chella's voice sounded over the comms. Deann and Hawk were already racing for the bridge. "Fighter crews to your ships, launch when ready. Repeat, fighter crews to your ships, launch when ready."

They reached the bridge and Hawk slid into the main weapon's chair, his huge fingers flying over the console as he readied the guns. Deann leaped to sensors to replace the man who was already halfway to the fighter launch bay. Deke was at pilot and Ellie was at comms. "We're being hailed," said Ellie.

"Ship-wide, all screens."

"Ship-wide, all screens. Aye captain."

"This is the Warbird," said Michella as she rose from the captain's chair and faced the screen. "You're trespassing on Nova Clan territory. Reduce your speed and identify yourself."

"This is the Gap, you stupid little cow. Nobody owns the Gap. Stand down your ship and prepare to be boarded. If you're nice to me I might just keep you for myself." The dirty scraggly bearded man facing her on the screen leered at her as his crew laughed. "Stand down, I say. We have three ships to your one."

"Hawk," Michella said quietly. The big man's fingers flew and the missiles launched. A moment later the lead ship was cut apart. The remaining two ships kept coming, but they didn't get far. Four fighter ships streaked from the Warbird's launch bay and straight at the attackers. Michella watched the battle on the main screen in amazement, her face grim.

The four fighters split apart and attacked. Their twists and turns were so wild and sharp that Michella was certain none of the humans could survive. The inertia would have them pulverized by the hull before they could operate the weapons. However that wasn't the case. The four fighters opened fire and cut apart the two remaining pirate ships with ease. Their twists and turns so fast the sensors had trouble following them.

The four fighters were barely back inside the Warbird when Michella's voice came over the comms. "What in the nine hells are you fools doing? Are you trying to kill our own people? Allore, how many are still alive?" The answer shocked her.

"All of them Chella," replied Allore. "There's not even a scratch for me to bandage."

"Chella, it worked, it worked," shouted Pally.

"All fighter personnel unharmed and accounted for, Captain," came a man's voice.

"Nobody move. I'm coming down there," growled Michella. She rose from the chair and strode swiftly through the door.

As she entered the hangar bay she found a celebration going on. "It works, Chella, it works," laughed Nellie, as she leaped into Michella's arms and hugged her.

"What works, Nellie? What the heck is going on?"

"You told us to find a way to keep everybody safe inside the ships. Harnesses didn't work so we tried something else, a blocking field."

"A blocking field? What's that?"

"The problem was the inertia," said Pally, grinning broadly. "We'd been playing around with inertia blockers at school, remember?"

"Yes, but that only works in tiny spaces, like a child's toy."

"Not anymore," said Barah proudly. "Pally figured out a way to generate a field around each small ship."

"Pally? Why didn't you tell me?"

"I was going to, but we ran into these pirates before I had a chance to test them. Everybody was willing to give it a try, so we gave them a field test today. Chella, they work. Our ships can turn on a pinhead and nobody inside feels a thing."

"How did you ever get that to work? I thought it was impossible."

"It is," laughed Pally, "unless you have a witch to help you modify a few of the smaller chips."

"This is amazing, guys," said Michella, the delight clear in her voice. "Can you do it for the whole ship?"

"I think so," replied Palentine, "But I'd only use it in emergencies."

"Make it happen, you guys. This is amazing."

The claxon sounded again. "Attention all hands, we have a distress call from the Ravage. Captain to the bridge."

"Get those fighters reloaded and ready," shouted Michella, as she ran from the fighter bay towards the bridge.

Planetside

"It's going to pull us apart, Boss," shouted Gorda.

"Turn into it," replied Micha, "Everybody hang on. Miriam, can you tell where it's coming from?"

"It's from that planet, Micha," she replied. "There's a lot of life forms there, but I have no idea what they are."

"Gorda, land her someplace clear of them if you can."

"Working on it, Boss. We're going in."

"Lessa, send out a message to the kids warning them away."

"Already done, Micha. We don't need them getting caught in this too."

Flying into the tractor beam seemed to confuse it and Gorda was able to break free just before they hit the planet's surface. A mass of creatures was waiting for them and a howl of frustration went up as the Ravage veered off at the last minute and landed on a mountain nearby.

The crew poured out of the ship to secure the area, but there was no threat there. The plateau they had landed on was just big enough for a couple of ships the size of the Ravage. The mountain rose behind it in a sheer cliff, offering protection from behind.

"Nice call, Gorda," grinned Rathbone. "We can defend this easily."

"Hope so," said Micha as he gazed out at the mass of creatures heading for the foot of the mountain. "They're coming."

"What are they, Boss?" asked one of the men.

"Really bad news," sighed Micha. "I've seen them before."

"You have?"

"In a vision Lady Norlene once showed me," he replied. "Everybody load up and make every shot count. These things won't stop coming until the last one is dead."

<hr />

"ELLIE, PLAY THAT DISTRESS call for me," said Michella, as she appeared on the bridge and took her seat. Ellie nodded and flipped a switch. Lady Arlessa's voice came over the speakers.

"Warbird, this is the Ravage. We're caught in a beam of some kind, and it's pulling us down to the planet. Stay away, Warbird. Repeat, stay away. The game has changed now. Take your people into hiding; you must survive at all cost. Warn everyone to stay clear of this area. Here are the coordinates."

"It keeps repeating, Chella."

"That's not a distress call, Ellie; it's a warning."

"That's our parents in trouble, Chella."

"You're right, Ellie; it is a distress call. Punch in those coordinates and let's get moving."

"We're already on our way, Boss," replied Deke.

"Who gave the order?"

"I did," replied Ellie.

"See, Ellie, you can take command when you have to. Well done," grinned Michella. "How long until we get there?"

"About two days," replied Ellie. "There's a planet just on the edge of the Gap. I'm guessing the whole star system has been encased by the Gap and something new has come through a rift."

"Then we should be prepared for anything. Comms, ship-wide."

"Ship-wide, aye."

"Attention crew, relax. We're about two days out from the action so get some rest while you can. First man, specialist, meet me in the kitchen." Hawk grinned as he stepped away from the gunner's chair and stretched before following Michella to the mess hall.

When they had all sat down with a snack, Michella called for Pally. While they waited she turned to Old Rath. "Are you going to tell me what is going on between you two or is he?"

"Haven't you told her yet?" asked Hawk.

"Your story to tell, unless you jeopardize the ship or her crew, and I don't see that happening."

"Tell me what, Hawk? 'Fess up now or I'll get Nellie down here to rip it out of your head."

"You already know I'm a spy for the King."

"What else?"

"Nothing important," he sighed.

"He's the king's older brother," said Old Rath. "When their father died he refused the crown saying he could serve Arcalia in better ways."

"Can I trust him Poppa Rath?"

"I would."

"That's good enough for me. Ah, here's Pally."

"What's up, Chella?"

"That inertial blocker field of yours, can you put one around the Warbird?"

"Oh yeah, love to, but you can't use it all the time. Things tend to free float a bit inside it."

"Free float?"

"Yeah, well it blocks inertia of motion, but it also blocks inertia of rest. You get the idea."

"Got it. Can you have it ready by the time we get to the Ravage?"

"Working," he laughed, as he turned and trotted back towards engineering.

"All right, gentlemen, what are we facing here?"

"I have no idea," said Hawk. "You, Governor?"

"None at all," grinned Old Rath. Michella smiled to see the tension between the two men fade away.

"Suggestions? Options?"

"Options? We could just turn around like we were ordered to," said Hawk, "but I don't like that option."

"That's not an option I'm willing to consider. Try harder," replied Michella.

"I suggest we get as battle ready as we can," said Old Rathbone. "Once we get there and that thing grabs us, I say we turn into the pull, follow it down."

"And then blow whatever is generating it to the nine hells and back," grinned Hawk.

"I like it," said Michella. "It's obviously a work of technology or they wouldn't have told us to run. I expect that whoever owns that tech won't be happy to see us blow it up. I'm thinking all fighters should be in the air when we hit atmosphere."

"Agreed," grinned both men.

"Now for a back-up plan," sighed Michella. "I'd like to send someone back to the hideout for another ship, just in case. We should be able to knock out the tractor beam or whatever it is, but we could take a lot of damage in the process. I'd hate to be completely stranded on a planet of unfriendly folk."

"Micha taught you well," chuckled Old Rath. "I'll send Deke with a few of the older folk and the youngest of the kids. We'll only keep a fighting force on the Warbird."

"Agreed," said Michella. "That works for me. Any reason you chose Uncle Deke?"

"You know how he feels about combat and why, Chella."

"I do, Poppa Rath; he's the right choice. Talk to Nellie. She can give him a witch key so he can deactivate the locks on the ship. Auntie Lessa and lady Norlene have them locked up tight."

"What about Allore? Will I send her with them?"

"You can try, Poppa, but you'll lose. That's not a battle I want to fight right now. I'd like you to send Deann, though."

"That's not a battle you want to fight either, Chella."

"Is your protégé ready?"

"She'll do you proud. Now, you spoke of rest for the old and battle weary."

"Yes, I did," she laughed. "Get Uncle Deke on his way then catch ten hours or so of sleep." She rose, gathered the trays, and headed for the kitchen.

"Keep an eye on her, Governor," Hawk said quietly. "She's tough as they come and her father's daughter, but..."

"I know, I know; it can pile up on you. I'll watch her, but we've got to let her fly with her own wings."

"Understood. I'm just the chief gunner on this ship."

"And I'm the chief cook on a pleasure barge," grumbled Old Rath, as he rose from the chair. "Relax, this job should be interesting enough, even for you."

———◦———

"THEY'VE PULLED BACK again, Boss; they've taken heavy casualties. Maybe they'll give it up this time."

"I doubt that, Brenna," said Micha. "Gorda, what do you think?"

"I think those things are too stupid to have organized this. I'd say that whoever is in charge is sending them at us to use up all our ammo."

"Yeah," sighed Micha, as he slumped to the ground and set his back against the cliff, "that was my thought too. How are we doing?"

"We've taken a few wounds from spears and arrows and one dead."

"One dead?"

"Oriel, poor woman panicked and ran off the edge of the slope, fell right into them. They tore her apart."

Micha closed his eyes and shook his head sadly. He didn't speak for long moments. When he looked up there was a tear in his eye. "Rath and Miriam back yet?" he asked softly.

"Miriam's in," replied Gorda. "She's getting a bite to eat. Ah, here she comes now."

"I found it, Boss," she said, as she sat down beside Micha. "It's not much of a trail, but we can get around them and escape deeper into the forest. I heard Rath's big long-range weapon fire a few times. I wonder how the hunting's been."

"Here he comes," chuckled Gorda. "Hey Rath, Miriam wants to know how the hunting is going."

"Hunting was good," grinned Rathbone as he joined them, "lots of game. I managed to peg off a few of the ones in fancy armor, but the two big guys are wearing some sort of shielding. If..."

"Incoming," bawled Zartah. "All hands to the battle line."

"Skeeter," sighed Micha, as he levered himself erect.

"We're starting to run a bit low on ammo, Boss," grunted Rathbone, as he dropped the last case of bullets beside Micha. "I've got the last of the blasters charging up in the ship now, but it's about time for a new plan."

"You're right, Rath," agreed Micha, as they watched Miriam slip over the side of the cliff and disappear again. "We need to get away from here, but I've been waiting for Lady Norlene to recover."

"Then your wait is over, Micha," said Norlene from behind him.

"Norlene," exclaimed Gorda, as he leaped to his feet and gathered her into his arms.

"Easy, easy, big fella," she laughed, as she returned his hug enthusiastically, "I'm still a little shaky. I was too intent on shielding the ship. I should have been watching for a magic user."

"Where's Lessa?"

"Sleeping. It took the good out of her trying to put me back together again. Micha, we've got a problem here."

"Understood. I remember what you showed me about these green buggers. Keira has been scouting them and we're pretty sure they're alone here. They had a big bad magic user with them and two big bosses wearing shielding of some kind. Lessa took out the magician and Rath has managed to peg off most of the leaders, but the two big guys are still functional and driving the others on.

"We need to get out of here to a place of safety for a while. Once we've rested up and devised a plan of action we have to come back and finish the lot of them. I will not have them loose in this galaxy if I can help it."

"Sorry, Boss," sighed Murtah, "the Ravage is done. She'll never fly again. We can probably get everybody aboard the small fighters, but first we have to knock out that machine or they'll just tear us apart."

"Load everybody into five of the six ships. Leave me the sixth. I'll make a run right at them. The rest of you can slip away."

"A noble sacrifice, Micha, but quite unnecessary," said Lessa as she joined them. She sank heavily to the ground and rested her back against Micha's shoulder. "Norlene and I just need two more days to rest then we'll deal with this. Their magic user is dead so he's no problem. Just let us rest up a bit then we'll finish this lot off."

"We don't have that luxury, Lessa," he replied. "We're nearly out of ammo and they aren't going to give us two days' rest."

"Incoming scouts," sang Brenna, as Keira and Miriam glided into the camp on silent feet. Micha had no idea at all how the two women managed to get up and down the cliff so easily, but they did.

"Brace up the line," sang Keira, as her hands danced to the sound of her voice. "They're massing for a final push. The big guys are coming too."

"Aw, skeeter," grumbled Micha, as he rose heavily to his feet. "Rath, you sure we can't use the ship's missiles?"

"Wrong angle, Boss. If we could turn her around a bit we might get in a shot or two from the rear guns, but as she sits..."

"Understood. Everybody make sure you're packing lots of bladed weapons. This could get up close and nasty. We'll need..."

"Micha, Micha," shouted Ena, as she leaped from the ship. "The kids are here."

"Warn them off," he shouted, "send them away."

"I tried, but Chella said to hang on, she's coming in."

"Blast it, why won't that girl ever do as she's told?" he muttered.

"She's too much like that young fellow who followed me to Borealis Prime," grinned Lessa.

Micha just chuckled and shook his head. That's when he heard the thunderous clap as Michella's crew blasted into the atmosphere. They hadn't tried to fight the tractor beam; they raced right at it, forward guns blazing. The machine was shattered into a zillion fragments as missile after missile slammed into it.

The four fighter ships that had followed the Warbird in swept down on the mass of savage creatures charging at Micha's position. Three made a close pass over their heads, strafing the horde with weapons fire and sending the creatures into disarray. One ship dipped right into the mass of bodies, cutting a wide swath through them before coming to a halt right at the feet of the big Bosses.

The remaining three attacked the two giants at terrifying speeds, twisting and turning so tightly the ships should have been ripped apart and the humans inside killed instantly. The Warbird joined in and soon one of the giants lost his shielding. He was cut to ribbons instantly.

The second one suddenly stopped fighting and began to swat at his back, twisting and turning as he did, his leathery wings flapping feebly. Slowly but surely he slowed down then stopped moving. His shields failed completely and he fell, face first, into the dirt with a lone figure attached to his back. It was Deann.

Deann wiped her blades on the giant's tunic then turned her attention to the green monsters running about. They had fled too far apart now, and the fighting was hand to hand. Micha's crew had already descended from their perch and were wading into the fray. Deann faded back into the edge of the scrubby trees and disappeared from sight.

The green monsters were big, strong, and they fought with desperation. They knew there would be no mercy. Keira and Rathbone waded into the battle like a wrecking machine and soon their enemies were fleeing from the two savage warriors.

Michella's young warriors were having a bit more trouble, but they were learning fast. Pally was holding his own, and surprisingly, Hawk was being quite efficient. He was shooting with a projectile weapon in each hand and Ellie was right at his back, zapping any who got too close with witch fire.

Barah and Nellie quickly saw the efficiency of that tactic and she passed Barah her blaster. Michella and Tarah fought side by side and managed to stay alive until Zartah and Murtah waded in to join them.

Micha just stopped and stared at the humans from Michella's crew. They'd leaped from the ships and formed two lines. The front line carried blasters and knelt on one knee, keeping everything from getting close. The second line carried long range projectile weapons; they were firing over the heads of their companions.

Within moments the battlefield was empty of living enemies. Michella was calling for Deann. She'd seen her bring down the giant and several more after that. Somehow Deann always seemed to be behind the enemy. "Right here, Sweetie," said Deann, as she stepped out from behind a bush.

"Deann," shouted Michella, as she swept her lover into a bear hug. "You took way too many chances," she whispered. She was trembling as she hugged Deann tightly.

"No more than you," replied Deann. "Come on; I'm okay, you're fine, now you have to be the captain. Here comes your father."

"Why aren't you people all dead in a pile of twisted metal and crashed ships?" demanded Micha as he reached them.

"Excuse me, Poppa?"

"Chella, even Arcalian ships can't move like that without tearing themselves apart and killing the passengers. Was that the girls?"

"Nope, that was Pally's invention. He calls it an inertia blocker. The whole ship is inside the field and doesn't feel a thing. I'll let him explain it."

Micha put his arms around his daughter and held her gently. "Chella, we told you to stay away."

"Did you really think we would?"

"I'd hoped. I guess you're too much like me. Come on, girls, let's go to that ship of yours and find something to eat." Micha stepped between them and put an arm around each one's shoulder. "Deann, that was something, the way you brought down that giant. I assume you've been training with Old Rath."

"Yeah. Keira taught me what she could, but I just don't have the hurt she did to drive me. Poppa Rath said I needed a different approach, one more like his."

"Well, it's sure working for you."

"Yeah, and I don't get half as many bruises in training."

"What are those things, Poppa?"

"They're from another realm," sighed Micha. "We were on our way to the third passage when we spotted a small star with a planet where they shouldn't be. It appears to be an erratic system, moving around within the Gap. We flew in close for a look and got caught in that tractor beam. At first we fought it and it damn near pulled the ship apart. We managed to get on the ground when they came at us.

"Lessa and Norlene stepped up to have a go at them when Norlene got hit by something and went down hard. Lessa spotted their big bad magic user and blew his buttocks out past Exile, then turned her attention to healing Norlene. We fought the rest as best we could, but they had the numbers, and we were wearing down. Your timing was perfect."

As they reached the Warbird Allore came on the comms. "Chella, you there?"

"Here, Lore."

"Is it over?"

"It's over for now."

"Good, I really need Deann's help in the infirmary."

"On my way, Allore. Be right there." Deann slipped out from under Micha's arm and ran up the hatchway and into the ship.

Michella hugged her father again then stepped back. "Bring all your people over to the Warbird, Poppa. We'll go into orbit to rest and recuperate while we wait for your new ship."

"My new ship?"

"Uncle Deke went to get one of the spares from the hideout. I see now why you wanted to have a few extras handy."

"That was good thinking, Captain Chella," grinned Micha. "I'll go organize my crew."

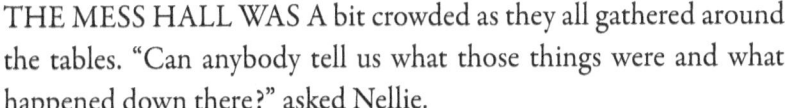

THE MESS HALL WAS A bit crowded as they all gathered around the tables. "Can anybody tell us what those things were and what happened down there?" asked Nellie.

"I don't know what they call themselves, Nellie," responded Norlene. "They're one of several races from another realm of existence. In my day, a high priestess was taken through to their world where she learned the full use of her powers or perished.

"Their world has several species of sentient creatures and a few different races within each one. They're all constantly at war with one another. They have some technology, and plenty of magic users, but have managed to avoid engines of true mass destruction. As soon as one faction begins to develop such a thing the agents of another will shorten the inventor's life very quickly.

"Lessa and I took a terrible risk when we created the Gap to save our people. We knew this could be a possibility. Obviously, the rift appears on both sides. A strong enough magic user could pierce the barrier. They probably came here looking for new worlds to conquer or to escape from a more powerful enemy.

"What's the story of that planet, does anyone know?"

"It was a mining world," said Hawk. "It was abandoned over a thousand years ago or more. Nothing much grows there, but the atmosphere seems to have held. It might recover in time. Now it is mostly used as a hideout for pirates. It is an erratic system, disappearing and reappearing in different places along the edge of the Gap."

"Well, now it has become a bigger problem," said Micha. "As soon as Deke gets here with a ship for us, we'll look her over, preach the gospel of Nova Clan to any pirates we find, clean out any greenies we find, and then set up a beacon warning others away."

"Why wait," grinned Michella, reaching for her comm unit. "Bridge."

"Bridge here."

"Poppa Rath, we need to do a full sensor sweep of the planet. We're looking for life forms, both pirate and alien."

"Started about ten minutes ago, Captain. All clear so far."

"Great," laughed Michella. "So, who's flying this ship? Everybody seems to be in the kitchen."

"Rath is on pilot and Keira's on weapons. Nina is working the sensors. Relax and enjoy some rest. We've got this."

"Thanks, Poppa Rath. Chella out."

"I see everything is well in hand, Chella. Got someplace for us to rest?" asked Edie.

"Take the captain's quarters," replied Deann. "Get some sleep, all of you."

Ambush

Several hours later the claxon sounded. A pirate haven had been found on the southern continent. Micha was still rubbing the sleep from his eyes as he reached the bridge. Michella was in the captain's chair and he grinned with pride as he watched his daughter in action. They were being hailed from the ground. At Michella's nod Nellie put the hail on speakers and flicked on the visual screens.

A fierce looking man appeared on the screen and Hawk moved aside to remain unseen. Michella raised an eyebrow at him, but said nothing. She turned her attention back to the screen. "Attention, incoming ship. Identify and prepare to pay the tax."

"This is the Warbird," said Michella as she leaned forward, resting her elbows on her knees. "What tax would we be discussing?"

"Don't play coy with me, child, or I'll have you in the brothel pens so quick it'll blind you. You know the rules. You hide here; you pay half your cargo in tax. You stay no more than a month, and then you go."

Michella stood and faced the screen, her face grim. "There are new rules, now, pirate. The Gap has been claimed by Nova Clan."

"Well, well, well, you must be the Hound's daughter," he replied in an oily voice, madly gesturing with his hands at someone off screen.

"I'm Michella, Captain of the Warbird, ship of Nova Clan. Hawk, you on guns?"

"Aye, Boss."

"Blow up any ship trying to get off the ground."

"Aye, Boss. Two ships rising now."

"Fire."

"Wait, wait," shouted the man on the screen.

Michella held up her hand and Hawk waited. "Bring them back," snarled the man. The two ships slowly settled back to the ground. The man's face was a mask of rage as he glared at the screen. He was obviously not accustomed to being thwarted. She'd just made a bad enemy and she knew it.

Michella showed no emotion at all as she continued. "Listen carefully while I explain the rules as laid down by the chieftain of Nova Clan. You can raid anyone coming out of the Gap except the Guild or Clan. You can venture as far into the Gap as you choose, but at your own peril. You may not raid into Arcalian space.

"I'll be patrolling this planet for the next few days. Keep your ships on the ground or lose them. Warbird out." Michella gestured with her hand and Ellie cut the comms. Chella sank back into her chair, hands trembling, and swallowed hard.

"Does it ever get easier, Poppa?" she asked.

"I hope not, Chella. Otherwise we become like them."

"Hawk, who was that man and why didn't you want him to see you?" asked Michella.

"He's an Arcalian nobleman, or he was before the king exiled him. His name is Lord Marlon of Mar'lor. The crown was still fresh on Borad's head when he led a rebellion to seize it. He failed and was exiled."

"Not executed?" asked Michella.

"No, well, he is a cousin, after all. Marlon and Borad were best friends since they were small."

"Why didn't you want him to see you?"

"Because, within hours every pirate and smuggler with a grudge would know I'm on your ship."

"I appreciate that, Hawk," sighed Michella. "So, tell me what he's likely to do now that I've slapped his ears."

"Right now he'll be loading up his ships with weapons and men. As soon as you disappear around the planet he'll put everything he's got in the air. He'll hunt you down and you'll be facing a dozen or more ships."

"Skeeter," she muttered. "Ellie, hold her steady above his hideaway."

"Holding steady, aye."

"Sensors, watch him carefully and watch out for anything sneaking up behind us."

"Aye, Captain," sang Keira, as she kept her gaze on the sensors.

"Poppa, what do we do now? I don't want that piece of misery sneaking up behind me."

"Now we check with our specialists," grinned Micha. "Gorda, what do you think?"

"Well, Boss, if we hurry we can get back to the Ravage and pick up the fighters. There's a small moon on that side of the planet we could hide behind. Governor?"

"I like it, Gorda," replied the elder Rathbone. "Between us we can put ten fighters in hiding and another two to flank the Warbird for show. I'm with Michella on this one; never leave a live and vengeful enemy behind."

"All right, we have a plan," said Micha. "What's our back-up plan, Captain Chella?"

"If this goes wrong," she sighed, "every fighter takes off in a different direction and meets back at the hideout to get a new ship. He might be able to follow one or two, but he won't have enough resources left to chase down everybody."

"It's desperate, but I like it, Chella," said Micha. "This is your ship; make it happen."

She nodded then pointed to Nellie who was on comms. "Ship-wide?' Michella nodded. "Ship-wide, aye," grinned Nellie.

"Relax, Mother Hen," came Nellie's soft voice in Chella's mind, "it'll all be fine. Relax."

Michella gave Nellie an appreciative look then spoke to the ship. "Attention everybody, attention. We're preparing for an attack. We'll return to the Ravage to collect her fighter ships. All Warbird fighter crews man your ships and report to Micha when we reach the Ravage."

Michella repeated the message twice more than relaxed back in her chair. "Ellie, to the Ravage, all possible speed."

"To the Ravage, aye."

Micha felt the slightest tug, but nothing more as the Warbird spun one hundred eighty degrees and hit full thrust. On the ground the sensor tech blinked then reported. "They're gone. They just disappeared from the screen."

On the other side of the planet the Warbird dropped through the atmosphere and settled to the ground beside the crippled Ravage. Micha and his crew poured out of the ship then the big bird rose swiftly back into orbit, deploying her own fighter ships. It took about an hour to get the fighters out of the Ravage, but they were finally in orbit.

Micha led the fighters to the small moon and they landed so they wouldn't show up on sensors until it was too late. As the last one settled to the dusty rock, Pally's voice came over the comms.

"Uncle Micha, since your ships are a lot slower than ours, you should keep your crew behind us as much as possible for safety reasons."

"Keira, talk to your son," grumbled Micha. Everyone had a good chuckle and the tension eased out of group. Micha grinned and shook his head. "Young pup," he muttered. Less than an hour later the comms came alive again. It was Michella.

"We've got eighteen ships inbound on sensors. They refuse to answer hails. Make ready, people."

On the Warbird, Michella was preparing for battle, trying to hide her nervousness from her crew. She glanced around and noticed many of her friends were missing; they were on the fighters. "Where's Deann?"

"She's on number three fighter," replied Old Rath. "It was her shift."

"Understood," replied Michella in a soft worried voice. She drew a deep breath and sat up straight in her chair. "All right, people, let's do this. Ellie, see if you can manoeuvre them so our fighters are at their backs."

"Working," sang Ellie.

"Gunners ready?"

"We're ready," replied Hawk, as he winked at the woman who was manning the rear weapons.

"All right, Bim, give me ship-to-ship comms," she said, as she nodded to the teenage boy at the console.

The boy looked terrified, but he was quick. "Ship-to-ship, aye," he replied as he flipped the switch.

"Attention inbound ships, this is the Warbird of Nova Clan. Cut your speed and identify yourselves or be destroyed." Michella stood facing the screen, her face and voice registering no emotion at all. This time she got a reply.

"Found you," came the angry voice, as the ships continued to approach at top speed. The fierce looking man appeared on the screen. "I'll have you stripped and bound in the brothel slave pens before nightfall," he exulted. "I'll be your first then my crew will get a turn. You'll beg me for death before the end, but I promise you a long career in the pens before the sweetness of death claims you."

Michella didn't even flinch. "Attention all inbound ships accompanying this man, break off and flee; I will not pursue you. Continue on course and you'll be destroyed."

The leader laughed and all ships came on. Just as they opened fire the Warbird leaped aside. "So be it," said Michella, as she indicated Bim should cut the connection. Hawk was already firing and two ships had been hit, but the Warbird was moving too fast for the enemy to target effectively.

Like a swarm of angry bees the Nova Clan fighters rose from hiding and struck the pirates from behind. The pirates were flying disguised fighter ships that were fast and well-armed, but the Arcalian fighters were faster and better armed, especially the enhanced ships from the Warbird. They twisted and turned through the enemy ships with ease. More by good luck than anything else the pirates managed to hit two of the fighters and damage them badly. That, however, was the extent of their success.

The last three ships suddenly spewed out escape pods as the ships began to break up. The Nova fighters followed the pods to the ground while the Warbird finished destroying the pirate ships and gathered in the two crippled Nova fighters. Once they had all their people back on board the Warbird dropped down to the surface and began repairs.

Michella spent a long time on comms trying to follow her father's people as they rounded up the surviving pirates. All her people had survived, but she knew there were injuries. Suddenly she realized Deann hadn't joined her on the bridge. She reached for her personal comm unit. "Chella to Deann, where are you? Are you okay?"

It was Allore's voice that replied on Deann's comm. "Chella, it's Lore. You'd better get down here."

Michella bolted from the chair and raced to the infirmary. She found Allore, tears streaming down her face, and Deann lying on a bed, one side of her face bandaged completely. "Lore, is she...?"

"She's alive, Chella," sobbed Allore, as she threw herself into her sister's arms. "Chella, I'm so sorry. I tried to reach Auntie Lessa, but the comms are wonky and I couldn't. I did the best I could, Chella, I tried..."

"Lore, is she alive?"

"Yes," sniffed Allore, as she tried to get her emotions under control.

"Is she going to be all right?"

"I don't know. She lost a lot of blood, and her eye. Oh Chella, her eye was completely gone. I tried to reach Auntie Lessa..."

"Allore, take a deep breath and talk to me. Tell me what you did?"

"I had no choice, Chella. I got the bleeding stopped, and the wound on her face sealed, but the eye was gone. I knew I had some strange things in storage so I looked and found a pair of replacement eyes. You know, the cyborg ones they're using on rich people now. You just put them in and they're supposed to attach themselves."

"I've never heard of anything like that."

"It was in one of the journals I read. They're supposed to be foolproof. Old rich people are using then so they can still see, but they're meant for emergency use like this. When we were on Arcalia, Ellie said I could have anything I wanted, so I asked for a set of these just in case."

"My magic little sister," sighed Michella as she hugged Allore again. "You always run on instinct, and you always come up lucky. Thank you for saving my Deann."

"Chella, I don't know if..."

"Allore, someone said you were looking for me?" asked Lessa, as she appeared in the doorway. Allore flew into her arms and sobbed out the whole story. "Let me see her now," Lessa said gently, as she disentangled herself from Allore's arms.

Lessa stepped to the sleeping Deann and began to run her hands lightly over the girl's body then very delicately inspected her head.

She sang a high sweet note as she held her hands above the bandages. "You did a wonderful job, Allore."

"Did the eye work?"

"It was having trouble because of the extra damage to the socket and surrounding tissue. You did a wonderful job, and she'll recover fully because of it. I've fixed the problem with the eye and it will heal fine. I've erased any scaring around the eye that might form and sped up the healing, but I fear there'll be a scar on her face, the wound was too deep. I may be able to erase most of it later once the healing is complete.

"Just let her rest until she wakes up on her own. She'll need to take it easy for a few days, but I've improved her healing system, so she'll recover faster.

"I have to leave now, but I'll check back on her later." She left with the girls' heartfelt thanks. She smiled and patted Allore's shoulder as she stepped out the door.

"You've got other patients, Lore," sighed Michella, as she sank into a chair beside the sleeping Deann. "I'll stay here with her." Allore nodded and stepped away. A scruffy looking pirate had just been brought in under guard. His arm was bleeding through a poorly wrapped bandage. Allore squared her shoulders and went to him.

DEANN AWAKENED TWO days later, healed in body, but not in spirit. One look at her maimed face and she burst into tears. She fled to the captain's quarters and locked herself in. no matter what Michella said, she would only wail from the other side.

Great wracking sobs shook Deann's body as she slowly raised the huge knife to her chest. She knew right where to place the blade for a quick kill. Her muscles tensed for the thrust when the door suddenly opened, and she was swept into Michella's arms. Ellie gently took the knife from her hand then sent a wave of healing energy through her. She left the lovers alone, softly closing the door behind her.

"Chella, please let me die. I'm ruined. I don't want you to spend the rest of your life trying to protect an invalid."

"Never happen, Sweetheart," Michella breathed softly, as she lightly brushed her lips along Deann's neck just below her ear.

"Chella, what the nine hells are you doing?"

"Huh? Oh nothing, dear, just reminding myself of why I can't ever let you go. Okay, there was a spot right about here..." Deann groaned with desire as the rising passion in her body dispelled the depression and fear from her mind. "Then there is this one over here," breathed Michella, as her lips lightly grazed Deann's jaw line then trailed down to her throat.

"Chella, stop that," moaned Deann, "I'm trying to be serious here..." Michella just giggled as she lowered the zipper of Deann's jumpsuit with her teeth, exposing the naked woman inside. She began nibbling gently at the valley between Deann's breasts.

"Chella, stop that right now." Deann breathed softly as she shrugged off the jumpsuit to give her lover greater access to her body.

"Yes dear, just as soon as I remember my name. Gods woman, you are so delicious."

"Chella, can you truly want me like this?"

"Naked and aroused? You bet I can," she giggled.

Deann's laughter was full and rich as she threw herself backwards onto the bed. "Then stop fooling around and get naked."

"Yes Ma'am, I hear and obey," said Michella, as she swiftly shrugged out of her clothes.

Back on the bridge, Nellie turned away from the others, her face crimson. "Deann will be fine now; Chella has everything under control. They'll be out in a little while." There was a general sigh of relief and a few giggles as Nellie studied a sensor panel that wasn't even turned on.

WHILE MICHELLA TRIED to convince Deann she was still beautiful, loved, and wanted, Micha was overseeing the emptying out of the Ravage and the rounding up of the pirates. He was searching for the leader.

"Zartah to Micha."

"Go ahead."

"Miriam can't find any trace of more, Boss. I think we probably have them all from this area."

"All right, come back in. We'll call it done."

"What are you going to do with the captives, Honey?" asked Edie as she laid her head on his shoulder.

Micha slipped his arm around her waist and gently pulled her closer. "I'll turn them over to the Arcalian Authorities. Hawk says a military ship and a salvage crew are on their way. They should be here soon. Deke will be here in a few more hours. We can spend some time getting our new ship ready."

"Murtah to Micha."

"Go ahead, Murtah."

"One of these captives wants to talk to you, Boss. He says he has valuable information."

"Let me guess, he'll talk in exchange for his freedom."

"Good guess, Micha," laughed Murtah.

"Ena there with you?"

"I'm here, Micha."

"Okay, I'm coming. Micha out. All right, let's go see what sort of mischief this pirate is trying to stir up." He and Edie linked arms and strolled to the makeshift prison compound at the edge of the cliff. There was no way down from there; the path down was near the two ships.

As Micha approached one man stood up and waited. Murtah nodded at him, and he stepped forward. "Who are you?" asked Micha.

"I'm Baka of Arcalia, or I was until we were exiled. Now I'm just Baka."

"All right, Baka, what's on your mind?"

"I know your reputation, Micha. They say you're a hard man, but a fair one. I have information you should have. I want freedom for myself and these people in return."

"He's speak truly," Ena said softly, as Micha gave her a questioning glance. He nodded his thanks.

"Speak up, Baka. If I'm satisfied, I'll let you go, provided you're willing to live by my rules."

"Marlon was the one with a problem, not me. I tried to talk him out of coming at you, but he wouldn't listen."

"He's telling the truth, Micha."

"Thanks, Ena," smiled Micha. "All right, Baka, spill it, all of it."

"Marlon's alive. He had a speeder on his ship and he ran when he had the chance. I believe he'll be back at the hideout by now. He was trying to build a network in the Arcalian Alliance, but he kept getting blocked. About a month ago he sent an assassin after the king. I have no idea what happened with that."

"The man failed. The king is alive and well. What else have you got?"

"Marlon was trying to make an alliance with those things that were set up here. He helped them build the tractor beam."

"An alliance with the greenies?"

"No, the greens are slaves, peasant farmers on their home world, or so I believe. It's the tall ones with the wings that are the masters, the arrogant bastards. Marlon kept a green one in a cage at the hideout. He liked to torture it. The whole key is the big grey one who works the magic. He came through by accident. The rest could only get here with his help."

"That's good to know. Lessa killed that one. At least no more can come through."

"Unless another one like the first finds his way here and brings them," sighed Baka. "I don't like those things. They'd have the lot of us in chains in a heartbeat. I tried to tell him, but Marlon wouldn't listen."

"Let them go, Murtah," sighed Micha, as he leaned back against the cliff wall. "Tell me, Baka, what was your position with Marlon?"

"I was his first man."

"You say he's still alive. Are you still his man?"

"No. Over two hundred men and women died in that battle. Some were right bastards and others were just descent people trying to survive. There was no good reason for any of it. From here I see only nine of us left. They've all agreed to follow me if I can keep them alive. I'm my own man now."

"Ena?"

"Truth, Micha."

"Baka, can your people survive on this planet?"

"It'll be tough, but I think we can make it."

"All right, I've got a deal for you. I'll see if I can get you a ship. In return you play by our rules, and you keep an eye on this planet. At the first sign of any more unnaturals appearing here, you come to me."

"That's a deal. Micha, you'll really give us a ship?"

"If we can find or salvage one. Remember, no raiding in Arcalian space."

"There'll be no raiding at all," sighed Baka. "Running the sanctuary was always more profitable anyway."

"And not half as dangerous," said an older woman with a badly scarred face. "Take the deal, Baka. It's the best chance we've had in years."

"I agree," he said, as he offered Micha his hand.

Hawk arrived in time to see the handshake. Baka recognized him and started to kneel, but a slight shake of the head from Hawk and he caught himself. "Hawk," grinned Micha, "Baka here has just agreed to keep an eye on this planet for us. He could probably use a ship, what do you think?"

"He'll need something, that's for sure," replied Hawk, as he sank to the ground and sat with his back to the cliff face. "I'd want one if it was me," he grinned and winked at Baka, who nodded his thanks. Perhaps one day he might get to go home, after all.

Micha pushed himself away from the rock face and sighed as he gazed out over the former battlefield. "You might want to keep your folks here for a while, Baka. "At least until I've had a chance to inform all my people not to shoot you."

"Sounds good to me," chuckled Baka, as he sank to the ground near Hawk.

"I'll just leave old Hawk here to pretend to be guarding you," grinned Micha, as he led his crew away.

A while later Hawk returned to the main campsite alone. "Everything under control?" asked Micha. Hawk just grinned and nodded as he headed for the Warbird's ramp.

------- ◉ -------

DEANN LAY BASKING IN the afterglow of their love making. She lovingly stroked the mass of dark hair that spilled across her abdomen. Michella giggled and tickled Deann's belly to make her laugh. "Chella, behave, I want to be serious now."

"All right, but no more nonsense about leaving me, got it?"

"Chella, what's going to become of me?"

"What do you mean, Sweetie? You're all better now, same as before."

"No, I'm not the same as before. Forget the scar for now, there's a bigger problem."

"Oh?"

"Chella, I bumped into the wall a dozen times just trying to get here."

"There's something wrong with the new eye?"

"Not wrong, it's actually too good."

Michella propped herself up on one elbow to give Deann her full attention. "What do you mean, Sweetheart?"

"The new eye sees things. It sees through clothes, thin walls, and it can see far away objects. It is disconcerting as hell, and I kept bumping into things."

"Can you see okay with that eye closed?"

"I don't know; let me try." She rose from the bed with a liquid grace that made Michella catch her breath. Old Rath's training had made a big difference in Deann. She began moving about the small room with one eye closed, reaching out to touch different objects. "That's better, but I don't have much depth perception. Maybe I can be the cook's helper or something..."

"Maybe you should talk to Allore or Auntie Lessa."

With a sigh of resignation Deann sat on the edge of the bed. "I guess you're right. Maybe they can fix this. Should I put on clothes first?"

"Absolutely not. If you're going to be looking through everybody's clothes they should be able to see you too," Michella replied, trying to keep the laughter out of her voice. She failed. She burst into a fit of giggles when Deann poked her in the ribs with a finger.

"All right, Chella, you've got captain stuff to do. I'll go see what can be done to get me fixed up." Deann was tucking away hidden weapons as she spoke. It was now a habit, and she was barely aware of what she was doing. Glancing up she saw the look of concern on her lover's face. "I'll be all right, Sweetheart. You fixed my fears. Now I have to find a way to function again. You go to work. I'll be fine."

"Promise?"

"I promise. I'll go straight to the infirmary." She didn't make it. Halfway there she met Rathbone coming the other way.

"Greetings, fellow cyborg," he grinned at her.

"Hi," she replied, unsure. This giant of a man had never actually spoken directly to her before. His very nearness and his fearsome reputation were intimidating, to say the least.

"Can I see it?" he asked. "Allore says they can do some amazing things."

"Uh, okay, I guess," she replied as she took her hand away from her eye. She was momentarily rocked by a wave visual stimulation that threw off her balance and depth perception. She quickly closed her good eye and the world settled down a bit.

Rathbone's huge hands had caught her as she tottered. As soon as she steadied he released her. "It takes a while for the rest of the body to get used to working with the machine," he rumbled kindly. "I tripped over my own shadow for days until I got used to the new leg parts. So, what can it do?"

"Well," she said, as she carefully managed her balance, "I can see through stuff, and I can see far away really well. I'm hoping Allore can adjust the blasted thing down to normal."

"I wouldn't," he said. "Those things can be useful. Can you demonstrate?"

"Sure." She glanced at him then grinned. "You have a tattoo over the scar on your left arm and you have a six inch throwing knife up your right sleeve. It has Keira's name scratched on the handle."

"What color is the handle?"

"The handle is flesh tone and the blade is a Damascus, they don't reflect the light the same; easier to hide."

"Well, I'll be damned," he laughed. "Girl, I wouldn't mess that up if I had it."

"But it messes me up."

"Hmmm, may I make a suggestion?"

"Sure."

"I get the impression you've been trying to find a way to prove your worth to the enhanced crew. You need an edge to show that you're an equal. Am I right?"

"Yeah, you're right," she sighed, as she leaned her back against the wall. "Poppa Rath tell you he's been teaching me?"

"He did."

"He ask you to talk to me about this?"

"Busted," laughed Rathbone. "Deann, you've got your edge. You already have the admiration of all the crews. Woman, you brought down old leather wings by yourself. That's earned you your place, never doubt that. Now you have a chance for something more."

"Oh?"

"Now you have enhanced tools. You also have a reputation. Play up the rep, then you can drop back and disappear at will."

"I don't understand."

"Listen, everybody knows you as a giant killer now. Play the part. Wear a patch over the new eye, carry weapons openly, and carry yourself like a dangerous woman. If a need for stealth comes up you can ditch the weapons, hide the eye patch, pop on a peasant dress and nobody would give you a second look. They'd be looking for Deann the Giant Killer, not the pretty little miss carrying packages down the street."

"You mean give people one thing to expect then show them something very different. By the time they figure it out it is too late?"

"Yep, the gospel according to Poppa Rathbone as taught to me when I was a child."

"You know, that's so crazy I like it. I'll do it. Thank you for this, Rathbone."

"For what? I didn't do anything, girl. You'd have figured it out on your own."

"Yes, you did. You helped me see myself in a better light. You also called me cyborg. I guess I'm really that now. Now I truly do belong."

"Yes, with the other guys retiring, it's just you, me, and Jorge now. We'll have to stick together."

Impulsively, she hugged him tightly for a moment. "Thank you."

"My pleasure, Deann. Hang on now, I'll get you some help with the game." He reached for the comm unit at his shoulder. "Rathbone to Keira," he sang.

"Here," she replied.

"Can you meet Deann at the infirmary?"

"Will do."

"She's on her way, Deann."

"I love that language you guys have," smiled Deann. "I have to learn that."

"Work on it," he sang, as he patted her shoulder and walked away.

Deann shook her head, having no idea at all of what he had just said, and continued on to the infirmary. Lessa was there with Allore and she explained the problem to them and the idea that Rathbone had given her. They both loved it.

"Sorry," sighed Allore. "They're designed to be used in pairs."

"It's okay, Lore, you saved my life and patched me up really well. Now we need to figure out what to do about the eye so I can walk without bumping into things or walking off cliffs."

"I have the answer for you, Deann," smiled Lessa. "Wait here, I'll be right back." She slipped out the door and disappeared. She was gone for a while, so Deann did her best to help Allore while she waited. Keira arrived and Deann explained Rathbone's idea and what she wanted to do. Keira laughed with delight and indicated she'd be happy to help. She left again just as Lessa returned.

"Deann, check this out," grinned Lessa as she passed Deann a small pouch.

Deann opened it to find a black eye patch with a design in silver thread worked around it. The black leather strap was adjustable. She put it on, and it seemed to mold itself to her face. It was so comfortable it felt like she wasn't actually wearing it.

"Now open both eyes, Deann," said Lessa.

Deann opened the mechanical eye and squealed with delight. "I can see normal," she gasped. This is amazing."

"I worked a bit of magic on it," laughed Lessa. "Now lift the patch and close the good eye."

"I've still got the enhancements," said Deann, as she followed Lessa's instructions. "Oh Lady Arlessa, this is amazing. How can I ever thank you?"

"No thanks are necessary, Deann," laughed Lessa, as she hugged the excited girl. "There are two spares in the pouch, and I'll give Ellie the instructions for making new ones if you ever need them. Now, I think Keira wants you. Go play."

With a giggle in her voice and a dance in her step, Deann fled the infirmary and followed Keira, who led her to the Ravage. When they re-emerged, the new Deann was ready. The few newly freed pirates who saw her shrank away from her path and Deann grinned as Keira winked at her.

As they headed back to the Warbird, Micha saw them out of the corner of his eye. With a diving roll that was too fast for the eye to follow he came up with a blaster aimed at each of them before he realized who it was. "Deann? Dammit woman, you frightened five years out of me," he exclaimed, as he holstered his weapons again. "Girl, you look dangerous. Has Chella seen this yet?"

"Not yet," she grinned.

"She'll love it," he laughed. "Go on."

Deann was still grinning as she entered the Warbird. Everyone she encountered moved out of her way with a look of concern. She stopped at the door of the bridge and took a deep breath before she entered.

"Reporting for duty, Captain," she said, as she strode onto the bridge.

Several gasps and shocked looks from her crew caused Michella to turn. She sucked in her breath, and then gave a long slow wolf whistle as she took in the dangerous woman before her.

Deann tried to hold the dangerous look, but couldn't. Her huge grin spoiled it somewhat. She was wearing heavy combat boots with a large knife sticking out the top of each one. Her snug fitting cut off fatigues were hanging just above her knees with a blaster strapped to her left hip and a projectile weapon to the right. The belt was lined with the handles of throwing knives.

Her light jacket was opened and a tight fitting tank top was underneath. The pockets of the jacket were bulging with ammunition and there were other small throwing weapons strapped to her forearms. She'd rolled up the sleeves to make sure the weapons could be seen. The design on her eye patch made it look like steel bolts attached to her skull.

Deann had added a leather choker with studs on it and she'd used make up to enhance the scar on her face. Her long hair was braided at the back to complete the look. The final weapon was a long bladed dagger that was strapped to her back with the hilt within easy reach.

"Oh my dear gods, I am so in lust," sighed Michella. "Nobody tell Deann or I'll be in trouble." There was a round of laughter at that.

"So, Captain, got room for one more warrior on your crew?" Deann asked, with mischief in her eyes.

"Indeed I do, Lady Blade, indeed I do. You can finish this duty shift on weapons. You are familiar with the weapons system of this type of ship aren't you?"

"Intimately," purred Deann, as she slid gracefully into the chief gunner's seat.

"Deann, you're one scary sexy woman and I almost wish you were single," laughed Pally, as he turned back to his control panel.

"Only almost?" she teased. "Hmmm, I guess I'll have to work on it a bit."

"Deann, if you ramp it up any more none of us will get any work done," laughed Ellie. "Chella, control your woman."

"Oh Ellie, I really don't want to," purred Chella. There was another round of laughter as Deann blushed to her roots. Just then the comms began to squawk.

———— ◉ ————

"WE SHOULD MOVE EVERYBODY and the Bird down off the ledge, Poppa," sang Michella, as she emerged from the ship to find her father. "We've got lots of company coming."

"Oh?" asked Micha, as he looked up from the rough map in the dirt he was studying.

"Uncle Deke is a few hours out and the Arcalian military will be here about the same time."

"All right, people," called Micha, "let's move down below, we've got incoming." Everybody set to work lowering supplies down on cables and the Warbird carried as much as she could as she lifted off slightly then settled to the ground below the ridge. About an hour later the Arcalians arrived.

"This is Captain Orcan of the Reacher; calling the Novans."

"This is Micha aboard the Warbird. Welcome, Captain."

"I hear you have some captive pirates for me, Micha."

"Actually, none survived so far, but there's another nest of them I want to clear out. Want to tag along and look for passengers?"

"Love to," he laughed. "Is that the salvage ship on that ledge?"

"Yep, that's my poor Ravage. We've cleaned out everything we want or can use. Your boys can take her away."

"They're not going to meet anything unusual are they?"

"Nope, we've dealt with that. It's clear."

"Good to know, Micha. When do you want to go hunting?"

"I have a new ship inbound, Captain. As soon as she lands we'll get loaded up and move out."

"All right, Micha. We'll just hang out in orbit here and relax for a while. Orcan out."

Deke arrived shortly after and the crews set to work. As soon as they were ready the new ship lifted off, followed by the Warbird.

"This is the Lance, Micha of Nova commanding. Acknowledge."

"Reacher here, Orcan commanding. Orders, Micha?"

"Nova Clan will do the nasty if there is any to be done, Captain. Your job is to hang in orbit and make sure none escape."

"It'll be our very great pleasure to do so, Micha."

"You expected me to send you in first and save my own people, right?"

"Anybody else would have, Micha."

"I'm not anybody else, Captain. This is our territory, and we police it. Here we go; the Warbird will lead us in. Micha out."

"Micha, why are you sending Chella in first?" asked Edie, as she looked up from the sensor panel.

"Because Marlon has a big hate on for her, Edie. If he's down there he won't be able to resist telling her what he plans to do to her."

"And that'll tell us where he is."

"Exactly. With luck I can slip in and break his neck while he's still running off at the mouth on comms."

"I like it, Micha, honey. I like it."

Captive

The three ships hung in space above the pirate haven. "This is the Warbird calling Haven," said Chella, as she stood impassively before the screens. She got no response. "This is the Warbird. I'll count to ten then I'll start pounding the ground with missile fire. If there's anyone alive down there I suggest you respond or run for cover." This time she got a response.

Marlon appeared on the screen, his face a mask of rage. "So you think you've won do you? I have news for you, girlie. You can send all the missiles you want and I won't care one whit. You'd better watch that pretty belly of yours though." His hand slapped down hard and several missiles leaped into the sky.

The missiles were barely halfway to their destination when the Warbird passed them going the other way. "Dammit, Chella," cursed Micha, as he saw her ship dive towards the ground, "gunners, knock down those missiles." His command came a bit late as Keira and Brenna had already opened fire. All the missiles exploded harmlessly in space. By then the Warbird was on the ground. "Jorge, get us down there." The Lance dropped swiftly towards the ground.

As the Warbird dropped towards the planet Michella was barking orders. "Everybody arm themselves. We go out in two's. We have no friends here, people. Take no chances. Nellie and Barah, Hawk and Ellie, Pally and Tarah, Deann, you're with me."

"No girl for me," sighed Palentine, as he guided the ship to the ground. "I guess I'll just have to make do with Tarah; he's pretty close anyway."

"Ha, ha, ha, just for that you're on your own tonight, buddy boy," laughed Tarah.

"Save the domestic dispute for later, boys," growled Michella. "Keep your eyes open and take no chances. Poppa Rath, seal up the Bird and make sure I have a home to come back to."

"Aye, Boss," grinned the elder Rathbone, as he checked his blaster. "Ground troops are at the cargo ramp. All is secure. That bugger will be in a bunker somewhere, Chella. Watch for traps. Deann, remember your training."

Deann saluted him as they left the ship and fanned out. What they had was a small town. The landing site was empty of ships and humans. They searched the two hangars but found no one. By the time they'd secured the landing site, the Lance was on the ground. Micha and his crew came pouring out. "Report," he barked, as he spotted Michella and Deann emerging from a hangar.

"The landing site and hangars are clear, Poppa," replied Michella. "There appears to be a bit of a town here. How do you want to do this?"

"We'll go left, you go right. There's only one street, so they can't be far. Check every building thoroughly. Keep an eye out for bunkers; he'll be in one if it's here."

"There's a bunker under every building," said Baka, as he joined them. "They're all connected by tunnels."

"You know your way around down there?" asked Micha.

"I do," replied Baka. "I'll guide you, but I leave the rest of my people on the ship."

"Agreed," replied Micha. "Chella, you and your crew clear the buildings; we'll go below and clear out the bunkers."

"Understood, Poppa. All right, people; in pairs, one group to a building. We leap frog our way up the street on the right then back on the other side. Deann and I get the first building."

They approached first building cautiously. As they neared the door, Deann flipped up her eye patch and looked the building over.

"I can't see anything," she said, as she lowered the patch again. "The first room is clear for sure."

"Awesome," grinned Michella. She spun and lashed out with her foot. The door exploded inward and Deann dashed inside, weapons drawn. A short while later they re-emerged. "Building's clear. We found the hatch to the underground and put a heavy crate on it."

"All right," grinned Micha. "That'll be our point of entry. Let's go, crew."

As Micha's crew vanished inside that building, Pally and Tarah checked the next one. It was clear as were the next two. Michella and Deann found two teenage girls chained to a wall in the next one. Both had been badly abused. They brought them out wrapped in blankets and sent them to the ships. Allore was waiting when they arrived.

Ellie and Hawk hit resistance in the next one, but it took only moments to put it down. When they emerged Ellie looked annoyed. "You didn't have to kill them all," she growled at Hawk.

"Yes, I did," he replied.

"I don't understand why," snarled Ellie, as she stalked angrily away.

Pally and Tarah cleared out the next one. Pally came out first. "Don't shoot, folks, these people are no threat."

"What have you got there, Pally?" asked Michella.

"Brothel slave pen inside, Chella. We took the guards down and set these ladies free. They need some clothes and a good meal. Should we take them to the ship?" She nodded and he led the eight battered women away. Tarah followed, covered in blood. His big grin said it wasn't his.

Ellie swallowed hard as she watched the women being led away. "That's why," said a soft voice beside her. She turned to see Hawk walk away.

Hawk had taken only a few steps when he froze in place, his muscles locked, unable to move. Slowly he was lifted up and set back down facing the young witch. Suddenly he was released and she was in his arms, beating his chest with her tiny fist as tears ran down her face. "The next time you walk away from me, I'll set your britches on fire," she threatened. The tall man just held her gently until the emotion passed.

"Last one's ours," said Deann, as she flipped up her eye patch for a moment. "There are two guards standing by a large crate, but I can't see what's inside it."

"Let's have a closer look," Michella said grimly. The brothel slaves had set a burning rage in her heart. That was the fate the pirate Marlon had in store for her.

She was about to kick in the door when Deann stepped up and fired her blaster. The door blew inwards and sailed across the room, knocking down one of the guards. The other guard fell to her projectile weapon. The first one looked at her and tried to crawl away. "Who are you?" he stammered, as she advanced on him.

"I am Death," she replied, as she aimed her weapon.

"No, please," he cowered, as he threw away his blaster.

"Hands in the air, outside now," said Michella, as she stepped between them. "One false move and I'll let her have you." The man scurried around them and fled outside, his arms high over his head and begging for mercy.

"The place is clear except for this crate," said Deann, as she lowered her eye patch.

"So, let's see what's in it," grinned Michella, as she jerked the cover off the crate. She gasped and stepped back.

The crate was actually a cage with steel bars. It contained one of the green creatures. The cage was far too small for the beast to stand, so it was forced to remain in a squatting position. It was bleeding from several wounds and there were scabs where other wounds had healed poorly. It seemed to be conscious, but barely.

"What should we do with it?" asked Deann.

"Kill me, woman named Death," groaned a gravelly voice, "grant me peace."

"I might be able to get that lock," muttered Michella. "Keep a weapon on him."

"Chella?"

"He's been tortured enough, Deann. That's not our way. We'll kill him if we have to, but not like this."

"You be careful, girl," said Deann, as her weapons spun easily in her hands and pointed at the monster in the cage.

"Hang on, big fella, we'll get you out of there, but you'd better behave."

"Krak'sul will not harm you," it replied. "Strength gone, life fading. Great pain, just want to rest."

Michella worked at the lock for a few more minutes then gave up. She couldn't break the lock, nor could she tear the door from the hinges. "Skeeter," she muttered, as she reached for her comm. "Is there anybody out there who can pick a lock for me?"

"Coming," replied Ellie. She and Hawk arrived in moments. Michella pointed to the locked cage. Ellie gasped and took a step back, but Hawk showed no emotion at all as he knelt at the cage door. He inspected the lock for a moment then stood up.

"You can't pick it, Boss. It's rigged to explode if you open it. You need the codes."

"We've got to get him out of there," replied Michella.

"Pick it, Hawk," sighed Ellie. "I'll contain the explosion."

"Are you sure?"

"It'll be the easiest thing I've had to do in weeks," she replied. "Give me a minute then pick the lock." She focused her will for a moment then nodded to Hawk. He took out a small pouch of tools and set to work.

As Ellie focused, Deann took off her armored vest. "Cover your face with this," she said, as she pushed it through the bars of the cage. The creature met her eyes for a moment then nodded his thanks as he painfully worked the vest up over his head for protection.

There was a sudden explosion and the fragments of the shattered lock hung in the air, no bigger than a ball. Ellie released the spell and the broken bits fell to the floor with a clatter. Hawk looked at the tip of his lock pick which had been sheared off in the blast. He looked up at Ellie and she winked at him mischievously.

"Let's get him out of there," said Deann, as she swung the cage door wide open. "Easy now, big fella."

"Too many days in cage," gasped the green creature, "muscles locked."

"Just relax and let us get you out," said Ellie, as she suddenly glared at the cage. With a groan of protest the metal welds popped apart and the cage walls fell outwards. The creature grunted as the cage lid fell on his head. "Sorry," she giggled. The big beast actually chuckled as Michella lifted the lid off of him and Hawk tried to help him stand. They failed. He fell sideways knocking Hawk flat in the process.

"Shut up, Ellie," grumbled Hawk, as he climbed to his feet again. She just giggled harder.

"Michella to Allore."

"I'm a bit busy now, Chella."

"You're going to be busier. Get your buttocks down here and bring Pally with you. We need some extra muscle. Pally will know where we are."

"On our way, Captain Cruel," replied Allore, as the comm went silent.

"Was I that bad as a teenager?" sighed Michella.

"Worse," giggled Ellie. Michella made a face at her then grinned. A moment later Allore arrived with Pally in tow.

"What the..." gasped Allore, as she saw the huge green creature lying on the floor curled up in a squat position.

"He's hurt, Lore," said Michella.

"I can see that," she replied. "Stop trying to stand him up. Get back and let me look at him."

"Be careful, Lore," said Pally, as he stared at one of the creatures he had so recently fought.

"Pally, what harm can he do in the shape he's in?" Allore crouched beside him and began to gently feel the tightly knotted muscles. "Can you speak?" she asked.

"I can," he replied.

"What happened to you? Was it poison?"

"Torture," he replied.

"Marlon had him in a small cage, Lore," said Deann. "He couldn't stand up or stretch out."

"Okay, I have a cure for that," said Allore, "but I have no idea if it will work on you or not. Are you willing to try it?"

"Yes."

"I know nothing about your kind. It might be a poison to you."

"And it might be delicious," he chuckled in reply.

"No, it won't," said Pally. "All of Lore's remedies taste bad."

"Shut up, Pally," said Allore, laughing. "Shut up all of you. If this works, big fella, you'll have to protect me from all these savages."

"If you can ease the pain in my body and restore me, gentle healer, I will protect you from the gods themselves for the rest of my days."

"Hang on, big guy. It should work pretty quickly, but if it does you'll be like a bowl of soup for an hour or so."

Allore injected something into his arm then began to gently massage his huge muscles. After a few moments, he groaned and began to straighten out his limbs. He sighed deeply as his body relaxed. He rolled onto his back and began flexing his huge hands then the arms and legs.

"You'll be pretty weak for an hour or so," smiled Allore, then she shrieked and leaped back as he surged to his feet.

Instantly there were weapon pointed at him, but he stood as still as death. "You're an honorable people," he said in that gravelly voice. "I thank you for restoring me so I might stand and face death with honor. I'm ready."

"Oh, you can forget that, Mister Green," said Allore, as she stepped closer to him again. "You mentioned honor. Are you an honorable man who keeps his word?"

"Krak'sul's word is law unto him."

"Then you will not die this day or any other for a very long time."

"I don't understand."

"You swore to protect me from the gods themselves if needs be. You're my bodyguard and you need to be alive to do your job."

The big creature just blinked at her in bemusement.

"Allore..."

"No, Chella, forget that. I'm keeping him. Everybody back off and put away those weapons."

"Lore, we don't know anything at all about this creature," said Tarah, as he tried to reason with her.

"Creature, Tarah? Your mother was a mutant on Exile. How much did your father know about her before he trusted her?"

"I don't like that M word, Allore..."

"Neither do I, Tarah," she sighed. "I don't like the word Spawn or creature either. Krak'sul?"

"Yes?"

"What are your people called?"

"Korim."

"There, he's Kark'sul of the Korim. You're Tarah, son of a Devan woman, and I'm Allore, daughter of an enhanced man and woman. We're all the same here."

"No, we're not," growled Tarah, as he accepted his defeat. "He's green."

"You're short," said Krak'sul.

With wide eyes, Tarah turned to him, making eye contact for the first time. "You're ugly."

The big creature looked thoughtful for a moment then nodded his head sadly. "You win," he grunted.

Everyone burst out laughing. Tarah just shook his head then extended his hand. "You're as crazy as the rest of us. You'll fit right in." Chuckling, the big green man gripped Tarah's arm just above the wrist for a moment, then released him.

"Come on," said Allore, "I want to get you back to the infirmary where I can tend those wounds." She led the way out the door to find a blood-spattered Micha and crew outside with several captives.

As soon as they saw Krak'sul, several weapons came to bear, but Allore stood in front of him protectively. "Stop it. Do you people always have to shoot everything that moves?"

"Allore, step aside," said Micha.

"No. I won't let you hurt Krak'sul. He's been hurt enough already. I'm taking him to the infirmary to clean his wounds."

"That's a brilliant idea, child," snarled Marlon, "heal the animal so he can rip out your throat." He turned to glare at Micha. "Get on with it, Micha. Call down the military to arrest me. Send me home to Arcalia. I'll be back here in a month with a better ship and bigger crew. I'll have those daughters of yours in..."

He got no further. Krak'sul's ham-sized fist cracked against his skull killing him instantly. The body lay on the ground twitching.

No one spoke for a moment, then Baka knelt beside the body. "After what you did to this poor beast you had that coming." He sighed and closed the dead man's eyes. "He wasn't always like this, Micha, but the exile made him crazy. He just got worse as time went by." He dropped his ragged jacket over the dead man's face then stood up, being careful to stay well out of Krak'sul's reach.

The big green creature was standing still as stone with Allore right in front of him. She slowly turned to glare at him. "Why did you do that?"

"He threatened you. He tortured me, so I knew he meant the threat. Now he can never bring you harm. It makes my task much easier."

"Just what task would that be?" asked Micha.

"He's my bodyguard, Poppa," sighed Allore. "Listen carefully, Krak'sul. You just can't go killing people because they might harm me one day. You have to wait until they actually try. Do you understand?"

"I understand," he chuckled. "Great healer, I killed this one because of what was done to me for his amusement. It was more an act of revenge than an act of prevention."

Micha stood looking the green man over. He was about six feet tall and easily 300 pounds of body weight. His skin was green and fairly rippled with the play of the massive muscles underneath. A ragged loincloth covered him at the waist, but that was his only clothing. There were three fingers and a wide thumb on each hand, but only two toes on the large feet. His brow ridge was thick, his jaws heavy with a short tusk jutting up from each side. His jet black hair was shaved back and pulled into a scalp lock. He carried a lot of scars.

Dark eyes, almost black, met Micha's gaze steadily. "Since you are here and have captured this place, I assume you have defeated my people and the batwings."

"We did," Micha replied. "Some of your people escaped, but not more than three or four. The batwings, as you call them, are dead; as is the grey thing that used the magic."

"That is welcome news."

"Deann killed a batwing all by herself," said Tarah, as he grinned at her.

"Which one did you kill?" asked Krak'sul, as he turned very slowly to face Deann. "Did it have jagged red scars down its chest and neck?"

"Yes," she nodded.

"I owe you a great debt, warrior. That one forced me to watch as it tortured my companion and child to death. My companion gave it those scars before she died."

"Why would it do that?" asked Allore.

"It was to show me and my people our utter defeat, and to make certain we knew how they dealt with rebellious slaves. We were farmers and hunters, but the wars came as they always do. The batwings defeated and enslaved us, forcing us to fight their wars for them. There was trouble among them. Our masters joined with a grey cleric who brought us here to this place.

"Once here with only two of them, I tried to lead a rebellion. I failed. I was captured and put in that small cage where your people found me. They freed me and Healer Allore restored me. I swore an oath to protect her from the gods themselves if she could do it. She did and I will hold to that vow. You are war leader here; will you permit this?"

"There's a lot I need to know first before I let you live," sighed Micha.

"Father..."

"Be quiet, Allore. I have to think this through." Allore blushed with embarrassment, but she remained silent. She recognized the *tone of doom,* as she called it, in his voice.

"You need to rest, War Leader," said Krak'sul. "Tired leaders make mistakes fatal to many. I will remain here, or you can put me in a cage until you're rested."

"Ena?"

"I sense no deceit or aggression from him, Micha."

"Lessa?"

"I agree with Ena. I sense no danger from this man."

"Fair enough. Come with me, I'll put you in the brig for the night then we'll talk in the morning." Micha turned and headed back towards the landing strip and the two ships. The rest followed, Krak'sul first among them with Micha's crew watching him carefully.

They entered the Lance and Micha led Krak'sul to the brig. "Nice big cage," grinned the green creature. "Lots of room to stretch out; hard for torturers to get at you. I like it."

"There'll be no torture aboard my ship," growled Micha. "Get some rest."

"You forgot to lock the cage," said Krak'sul, as Micha walked away.

"Did I? I must be more tired than I thought." Krak'sul chuckled then stretched out on the bunk. He sighed with contentment, free of pain for the first time in many days.

Micha emerged from the brig to find Keira watching the door. "I'll take first watch," she signalled with her hands. Micha grinned, then kissed her cheek before heading to the captain's quarters for some rest.

Micha awoke several hours later. Edie was still sleeping, and he decided not to wake her. He dressed quietly then slipped out the door. He picked up a snack at the mess hall then headed for the brig; it was empty. Keira was sleeping on Krak'sul's bunk. She stirred as he entered.

"Rath and Green have gone to find his clothes," she signalled sleepily. He grinned and quietly slipped out the door. He found Rathbone, Zartah, Miriam, and Krak'sul, now fully dressed in heavy leather armor nearby. The green man was scratching a design in the dirt. He stood up as Micha approached.

"Tell me your kind actually sleep," grinned Micha.

"We do, war leader," replied Krak'sul. "However, the young healer's magic is powerful; I didn't need much rest. I found Rath asleep on watch, so I went to find my gear."

Rathbone just chuckled at that.

"Right," grinned Micha. "My guess is Rath found your gear while Keira was on watch. You woke up and got dressed, then he took you for some food while Keira got some sleep on your bunk."

"Good guess, Boss," grinned Rathbone.

"So, what are you guys up to?"

"This is a map of the place you fought the batwings," said Krak'sul. "Here is the altar where the cleric came through. The stone of magic is in a cave beneath. That's where the portal can be created. Shatter the stone and collapse the cavern. That's how to stop more coming through.

"Most of my clan were farmers. Those you fought, those you destroyed. You say some escaped into the hills and you tracked them. A few are still free. There were three hunters with us. I expect those are the ones who eluded you. I, too, was once a hunter. I can show Tracker Miriam what to look for and we can find them. If I can find them, will you spare them?"

"That depends on them," replied Micha. "Baka is staying here to keep an eye on this planet. Your hunters would make better allies than enemies. What do you think?"

"This land is poor of soil and sparse of game, but we have lived in worse. They could prosper here. The hunters are not docile slaves; without their families as hostage it'll be hard to control them."

"There are no slaves in Nova Clan territory. All are free folk; yours will be too. Zartah, what do you think?"

"I like it, Boss. Krak'sul can show the witches where the spot is, then he can come with us to find his folk."

"All right, crew, let's get something to eat then warm up the ships," said Micha. "Are those Krak'sul's weapons?" He was pointing to a small pile of bladed weapons attached to a leather harness. Zartah grinned and passed them to the big green man.

It took a while for everyone to get a meal and ready to go. Baka and his people stayed behind to tidy up and get the station ready again. Several of the abused women agreed to stay with them. The two teenagers Chella and Deann had set free wanted to come with them, so they were taken aboard the Warbird along with two others.

The two ships rose into the air and leaped toward space, the Lance leading the way. They circled the planet and dropped back down at the place where they had first encountered Krak'sul's people. It was swarming with Korim under the whip of a gigantic batwing. The Ravage had been lifted off, so the two ships landed on that ledge.

The Korim poured towards the ships, howling for blood and waving their weapons. Just as the mass of warriors reached the base of the cliff, Krak'sul showed himself. He held his arms high and wide and roared. The Korim below stopped. He spoke a few words then roared again. All of the Korim raised clenched fists to him and answered his roar. They turned to face the batwing as Krak'sul scrambled down the trail.

"For the Clan," he bellowed, as he raced through his people to lead them in a charge against the batwing. Snarling, the huge creature spread its wings and rose above the ground, spraying the Korim with a magic weapon. They fell by the hundreds.

With a scream of pure rage, Arlessa released the bonds she kept on her temper. Great black bolts of energy flew from her hands to strike the batwinged giant. It withered and fell to the ground dead. The remaining Korim tore it asunder.

More Korim appeared and attacked Krak'sul and his warriors. A blast of pure white light from Norlene's hands exploded the portal, killing those who were too close and closing it completely. As she focused on that a bolt of dark energy struck her and sent her reeling. A tall slender man, grey-skinned and wearing a black robe, arose from the ground and sent another bolt of energy at her. Lessa stepped in front of it and blocked it. She was unharmed.

A scream of rage and challenge burst from her lips as she hurled her malice at the grey man and he faltered. He sent another bolt at her, but she shrugged it off and blasted him again. Terrified he turned to run, but she formed a hound of dark energy and sent it after him. He fought with his magic, but the hound ripped him apart then slowly dissolved into the air.

Another batwing had managed to get through before the portal was closed, but Norlene was back on her feet. She sent a bolt of energy at it and it exploded. All of the Korim stopped fighting and gazed about in confusion.

Krak'sul began to bawl orders. They put away their weapons and formed an orderly series of lines. He spoke to them for a few moments, and they listened then spoke among themselves for a moment before replying to him. He nodded then turned to seek Micha. He found him holding Lessa in his arms. She was trembling and cursing, a snarl on her perfect features.

"Are there more?" she demanded, as Krak'sul reached them.

"I don't know, Sorceress," he said, dropping to one knee. "The root of the portal is in a small cavern below that altar. If there are any more they will be magic users and they will be at that root stone."

"Rise," she demanded. "Can you lead me there?"

"I can."

"Do it. This ends here." He started away with her close behind. Micha and crew started to follow, but Norlene stopped them.

"This is a battle you can't fight, people. Let her go. Let the witch handle this one."

Micha nodded as Lessa followed Krak'sul around behind that altar where so many had poured through. It was nothing but rubble now. They disappeared down a slope, but a moment later, Krak'sul came running back. "Take cover," he shouted; but it was too late.

The ground suddenly exploded upwards, showering dirt, debris, and stones in all direction. Then the ground itself began to boil and a large gout of molten rock burst up to the surface. An angry faced Lessa strode across the flowing lava and onto safe ground. "It's done."

"A useful tool?" asked Rathbone, as she approached.

"Yes, but one difficult to put down." He nodded his understanding as she struggled to regain her composure. She held out her hand and Brenna took it, squeezing it gently.

"Come on, Love. Let's get you something to eat. That always helps." Lessa nodded and allowed Brenna to lead her back to the ship.

Micha watched her go for a moment then turned his attention back to Krak'sul. "What's all that?" He asked as he pointed to the orderly lines of Korim standing stock still.

"These folk are not of my clan, they're warrior clans," replied the big green man. "They want to go back if it's possible."

"I'll see," sighed Micha, as he turned to Norlene. "Any chances for these folks?"

"I can send them back, Micha," she said, as she looked them over, "but it'll be a one way trip. Krak'sul, tell them the doorway will be small. They'll have to go through one at a time and quickly. I won't be able to hold it open for long."

"But the other one destroyed the crystal."

"I don't need it." She grinned as she stepped forward. She closed her eyes and began breathing deeply. "Almost ready, better tell them."

Krak'sul hurried to the group of Korim warriors and spoke briefly. They instantly formed a single line and approached Norlene. As soon as they saw the shining globe they began to run toward it. One by one they vanished into it until they were all gone. She sighed and dispersed the portal.

"All right, they're gone, Micha. The rest of this mess is your problem." She leaned heavily against Gorda's arm.

"Yep, time to work this out, I guess," he agreed as he reached for his comm on his shoulder. "Poppa Rath, Jorge, bring those ships down to the base please. I have tired people down here."

"Coming, Boss," replied Jorge. Both ships lifted off then settled back to the ground at the base of the cliff.

As the ships landed Micha turned back to Krak'sul. "Originally we came back here to find your hunters. See what you can do."

The big hunter nodded and trotted to an open area. Lifting his hands to his mouth he gave a long wild howl that echoed eerily through the canyon. A moment later there was an answering call then three green skinned people came down out of the scrubby forest and approached him. There was a round of laughter and shoulder pounding, then they stood back and saluted Krak'sul, right fist to left shoulder. He nodded then returned to Micha.

"They have accepted me as their leader once again," he said. "We're trapped here in your realm and I've sworn to protect the young healer. I ask again; will you permit this?"

"I'm willing to consider it, but we need to consult Michella. Allore is healer on her crew. There she is now." He raised his arm and she waved back. He signalled her to join him, and she approached, accompanied by Deann, Old Rath, Hawk, and Ellie.

"Are we finished here, Poppa?" she asked, as they reached Micha and Krak'sul.

"Almost, Chella. We just have to decide what to do with Krak'sul and his hunters."

"Well, Allore will skin us both if we try anything with her bodyguard. Ellie, would you be kind enough to..."

"Sure, Boss," giggled Ellie. She closed her eyes for a moment and focused. "I'm not sure, Chella," she said, as she opened her eyes again.

"He's utterly devoted to his oath of protecting Allore, that much I know, but he's also completely devoted to his people, his clan."

"Krak'sul, you say these are the last of your clan. Are your people willing to join our clan?" asked Michella.

The big green man was taken aback. "You would adopt us into your clan?"

"I'll have to clear it with the clan chieftain first. What do you say, Poppa?"

"You're as bad as Allore," sighed Micha. "You get this from your mother, you know."

"I know. So?"

"This is a dangerous gamble, Chella."

"I know that too, Poppa, but I think Krak'sul deserves a chance. You didn't see him in that cage. After what they did to him I think we owe him a chance."

"We'll prove our worth to you, Chieftain."

"All right, Chella, looks like you have new crew members. Welcome to the clan, Krak'sul." For the first time, they actually saw emotion on the green man's face. "Looks like we're done here, Chella. You take the Warbird back to the hideout. I'll go check in with Baka and then join you there. I think we have enough people now to man a third ship, don't you?"

"We are starting to get a bit cramped, Poppa," she laughed, as she reached for her comm unit. "Attention all Warbird crew, return to the ship and prepare for liftoff. Pilot, sound ship's recall.

"Okay, Krak'sul, bring your folk and let's get aboard. We can get to know one another in the kitchen."

"Bonding by sharing food," he grinned. "I like this clan."

Several people were already in the kitchen enjoying a meal when Deann entered, followed by Krak'sul and the three hunters, one grizzled old fellow and two females. The room fell silent, and everyone stared. Sensing the unease of the Korim, Deann spoke up. "What are you all staring at? Is it my eye patch? Is it?"

She turned to Krak'sul. "They're staring at my patch, aren't they?"

"It must be the patch, Lady Warrior. There is nothing else unusual here."

"Maybe it's my scar," she said, as she turned back to the room. "Is that it? Is it my scar?"

"It's not your scar," said Tarah, as he squeezed past the Korim to grab a plate and start filling it, "it's your nipples showing through that shirt. They sure got my attention." There were a few nervous snickers as she put her fists on her hips and glared at him.

Allore pushed her way in next. "Hey, everybody," she sang in a loud cheerful voice, "this big fellow is my bodyguard. His name is Krak'sul. I haven't met the others yet. Like us, these folks are a long way from home. Please make them welcome." She led them to the food line and demonstrated how the system worked.

The Korim nervously held their plates and spoke softly among themselves as they tried to decide what might be good and what not. When the plates were full they all retired to a long table. Some people got up and moved away, a few others didn't. Deann took note, and spoke softly into her comm unit. A moment later, Michella's voice came over the ship's speakers.

"Attention all hands, this is the Captain speaking. We've taken on four new crew members. As you can see their appearance is a bit different from ours. They're Korim and they're the last survivors of their once enslaved clan. Please make them welcome and help them fit in.

"Also, Nova Clan will soon be launching a third ship. We'll be calling for volunteers for that ship's crew. That is all."

"In other words," Deann said a bit loudly, "anyone who no longer wants to be on this ship, for any reason, now's your chance to get a new assignment." Her gaze was hard and several people wouldn't meet her eyes.

———◉———

"GIVE ME THE BAD NEWS, Lizera," sighed Loran, as she entered his office. He was staring out the window once again.

"How did you know it was bad news?" she asked, as she quietly approached.

"It's time for a report on our Sector Nine project. I rarely get good news from that quarter."

"We've lost our base on the inner ring of the Gap. However, we have managed to keep one agent there and now we have one on the daughter's ship. You were correct in your assumption the Hound would knock down that base. However, he hasn't yet learned of the Hub in Arcalian space."

"The ruse worked then?"

"Yes, Sire. As you predicted, the abused brothel slaves got the sympathy of the Hound and his offspring. There is another development as well."

"Oh, do tell?"

"We knew of the green aliens. As you predicted, the Hounds has eradicated them, all except four."

"What's he doing with those four?"

"The daughter has taken them in as part of her crew."

That brought a smile to the emperor's lips. "Excellent. Have your agent cause a few disruptions. A little race war aboard her ship should prove amusing. I also want the location of that hideout of theirs. That too would be useful information."

"I'll get on it at once, Sire. It shouldn't be too difficult. There's one more thing, Sire."

"And that is?"

"One of the young woman's crew has invented an inertial dampening system. With it their ships can do amazing things and those inside feel nothing."

"We need the specs for that, immediately."

"Already working on it, Sire." She smiled as she rose to leave.

Taking the Hard Road

The Warbird was barely through the anomaly at the hideout when Nellie's sexy purr sounded softly in Michella's mind. "Ellie needs to talk to you in private, Mother Hen." Michella nodded slightly, but anyone watching her wouldn't have noticed for she didn't look up from her food. A moment later she leaned over and nibbled on Deann's ear.

"Something's up," she breathed softly, as her lips touched Deann. "Take me to the cabin then we'll call Ellie."

Deann giggled then took Michella by the hand and led her away. "They're at it again," Pally sighed elaborately. Seeing the puzzled look on Krak'sul's face, he explained. "Chella and Deann are newly bonded companions." The big hunter chuckled then spoke to his companions. The older male and female laughed, but the younger female's face seemed to turn a deeper shade of green and she looked down at her plate.

Pally noticed and grinned to himself. The Korim females were built sturdy. They had wide shoulders with muscular arms, large firm breasts, tight waists that were also heavily muscled, wide hips and long powerful looking legs. The older one wore her hair in a long braid down her back with the front of her head shaved clean. The younger one's hair was cut short and the sides of her head shaved to make one thick strip of hair from front to back. It was stained a deep red. Pally was startled to find himself so strongly attracted to her.

As Deann and Chella entered the cabin, Deann grabbed Michella in a hip throw and tossed her on the bed. Chella shrieked as she landed on her back. Deann slowly and deliberately lifted her eye patch and gazed lasciviously as her companion. "Deann, what are you doing?"

"Looking through your clothes and imagining how much fun I'm going to have getting you out of them."

"Darling girl, have you forgotten why we're here?"

"We have to wait a while to keep up the ruse, don't we?"

"Well, yes, I suppose so. Any ideas how we might pass the time?"

"Several," replied Deann, as she licked her lips then suddenly pounced on Michella and blew loud rude noises on her abdomen. Michella shrieked with laughter then caught Deann and pulled her into a kiss.

It was some time later the two women managed to struggle back into their clothes, satisfied smiles on their faces. Michella grinned with delight as she kissed Deann's cheek and reached for her comm unit. "Michella to bridge."

"Bridge here," replied Ellie.

"Ellie, have you got those specs for the inertial dampening fields with you?"

"Right here, Boss. Shall I bring them to you?"

"Yes, bring them to my cabin, please."

"On my way."

A few moments later she tapped on the door then slipped inside as Deann opened the door. "What's up, Ellie?" asked Michella.

"We've got a spy on board, Chella."

"Hawk, so?"

"Hawk's ours, Chella. I trust him. He shows me the stuff he reports to the king, and he showed me how he does it."

"He did?"

"Yeah. So, early this shift he was making his report when he spotted another report going out. It went to somebody on Benda Four. That's a planet in Arcalian space close to the first path through the Gap. There's only a few small towns and a couple of military bases there, as the planet is mostly forest and water. The king keeps it as his personal hunting ground and holiday retreat."

"So the king has two spies on board, big deal," sighed Michella.

"No, Chella. Hawk decoded the report. It was sent by an Imperial spy. A woman reported she had finally infiltrated our ship. Hawk is monitoring the subspace frequency for more reports and any instructions she might receive."

"Is she able to monitor his reports too?"

"Probably."

"Good. That means we can keep an eye on her and feed her misinformation. Imperial, eh? I think I need to talk to Poppa in private. Ellie, we're just sitting around here anyway, take a fighter and go meet Poppa. Say you need to talk to your mother about girl stuff or something. She can let Poppa know and he can be ready when he gets here."

"I'm on it, Chella," grinned Ellie. "You guys just go back to whatever it was you were doing."

"Get out," laughed Michella.

Two days later the Lance arrived and settled into orbit. After a sleep cycle, Micha contacted Michella. "Micha to Warbird."

"Warbird here, Michella speaking."

"Chella, bring your first man and your specialist. We'll meet outside then choose the ship and go aboard. Once we have a chance to look her over we can decide how we'll divide up the crews."

"Understood. Warbird out."

A few moments later a fighter ship dropped out of the Warbird. Old Rath watched as Hawk went over the inside of the fighter carefully. "What's going on, Chella?"

"Are we clear here, Hawk?"

"We are now," he replied as he held up a tiny listening device. He opened a release port and shot it out into space.

"Bring Poppa Rath up to speed on the spy thing." Hawk settled in beside the old man and told him everything.

The old man listened attentively as they waited for the ship from the Lance. "You were right not to say anything on the ship, Chella. What's the plan?"

"The plan is to talk with Poppa and whoever he brings with him. We work out a plan together. I know this is a chance to spread some misinformation to the Imperials, but my first instinct is to find her, interrogate her, and then blow her out the air lock."

"I like that plan," chuckled Old Rath.

A fighter dropped out of the Lance and led them to an empty ship. Once on board Hawk laid it all out for Micha, Zartah, and Gorda. "What frequency was that again?" asked Gorda as Hawk finished. Gorda was sitting at the comms station. Hawk told him. "Well I'll be damned," he sighed after a moment. "That's a neat trick."

"What is it, Gorda?"

"Boss, they're sending out messages mixed in the static of systems bychatter."

"Bychatter?"

"Yeah, all ships systems talk to each other to keep the whole thing running the way it's supposed to. No human could figure out what they're saying because it is machine to machine so we always just ignore it. These bastards are using it to send information to the emperor."

"Bastards, as in more than one?"

"Yes, Chella's is reporting and so is the one on our ship."

"Our ship?"

"Afraid so, Boss."

"Skeeter. Have we any idea who they are?"

"I know who ours is," replied Hawk. "I've got her pegged, but didn't move on her in case she wasn't alone or had sabotaged the ship."

"All right people, options, suggestions?"

"Let's capture the one on our ship," suggested Hawk. "Once we have her, we can interrogate her; maybe learn all sorts of useful stuff. I suggest we go back and Captain Michella announces we're getting a new ship. All hands on her crew report to the boarding area immediately for initial inspection. We grab her as soon as she steps onboard before she has a chance to set any listeners or explosives. Then we can clear the Warbird."

"Chella?"

"I like it, Poppa. Poppa Rath?"

"I like it, Boss. It's a good plan."

"Gorda, Zartah?"

"Let's do it," they grinned in unison.

Michella reached for her comm unit. "Michella to Warbird."

"Warbird here, Captain Chella," purred Nellie.

"Turn it down, Nellie. I have old men with me; we don't want them to have a heart attack or anything."

"Sorry," giggled Nellie. "What's up, Momma Hen?"

"Bring the Warbird over and lock up with us, Nellie. We're getting a new ship. Tell everyone who is staying with us to come on board. Those who are transferring to the new crew stay on the Bird."

"Understood, Boss." A moment later Nellie's soft voice sounded in Michella's mind. "What's up, Chella."

"There's a spy on the Bird, Nellie. This'll let us catch her," Michella replied, forming each word carefully in her mind.

"Understood." Nellie's voice left her, and then the Warbird began to slowly move over to lock up with the new ship.

The ships locked and the doors slowly swung open. The crew began to move across to the new ship, chatting among themselves. Suddenly Hawk moved like a striking panther, but his target was faster. She twisted out of his grasp then lashed out with a kick that sent him sprawling.

Suddenly the woman froze in place, unable to move. "Her jaws," shouted Hawk. "Freeze her jaws, Ellie; don't let her bite down." The woman broke out in sweat from the effort to move or bite, but she couldn't move.

Ellie grinned as she held the woman fast. She signalled with her hand and Nellie approached the captive. "Sleep," she purred, as she caressed the woman's face. The woman went limp and melted into her arms.

Palentine stepped in and scooped her up. "Where do you want her, Chella?"

"Put her in the brig for now, Pally. Nellie, go with him and make sure she stays asleep until we're ready to question her."

"Understood," sang Nellie, as she followed Pally down the corridor.

"Now, folks, let me explain what just happened here," began Michella as she addressed the others who had witnessed the capture. "We've had an Imperial spy on board our ship. This was just a ruse to capture her. Everybody will bunk over here for a few days while Hawk and Pally go over the Bird with a fine toothed comb. Once we're sure there's no sabotage or listening devices on board, we'll go home."

"Poppa Rath, bring the rest of them over so Hawk can get started."

"Boss," grinned Hawk. "I'd really like to interrogate the spy first to get a sense of what she might have done. You know, find out her objectives and things like that."

"All right, Hawk. That makes sense."

"I'll send for Lessa and Ena too," grinned Micha. "Lessa is really good at interrogation and Ena can spot a lie six lightyears away."

THE SPY SLOWLY OPENED her eyes and looked at her surroundings. Her training asserted itself and she lay still, trying to gather as much information as possible. The information her senses relayed wasn't encouraging. She could barely move. Her body was terribly slow to respond to her commands. She'd been drugged. Worse yet, her captors were all watching her, smiling.

"Ellie, that's perfect," smiled the tall, golden-haired, woman. "I'm proud of you. Can you hold her like that?"

"No problem at all, Momma."

"Excellent, shall we begin?"

The captive recognized the woman approaching her and tried desperately to bite down hard. Her jaws worked slowly but they worked. Nothing happened. There was no burning sensation and no swift death. There was just a hole where her tooth had been removed.

The black witch smiled pleasantly as she addressed the spy. "You can relax. We took the precaution of removing the poisoned tooth. You won't die this day, but you will sing. You will sing us a song of treachery and deceit."

She blew a strange powder in the woman's face and the whole world seemed to go fuzzy. There was a voice asking questions, why? Oh, wait, she knew the answers. Oh yes, she could make the voice happy, she knew the answers.

"Who are you working for?" asked the voice.

"I report to Lizera herself," she replied in a dreamy voice.

"Who is Lizera?"

"She's the emperor's chief of information gathering. She's a personal friend of the emperor resurrected."

"The emperor resurrected?"

"The Hound of the Black Witch is a fool," the woman replied dreamily. "He returned the emperor's body to us. The memory shield implanted in the emperor's brain worked perfectly. A new body was built for him, and the brain implanted. He's stronger now and without the weaknesses that caused his death. He will come for the Hound in due time."

"I can hardly wait," growled Micha. Lessa waved him to silence.

"What was your task?"

"We knew the Hound would discover and destroy our agent on Gamma Dex, the exiled Arcalian. I was planted there to infiltrate his ship."

"You were on the wrong ship."

"No, my mission was to find my way onto this ship. When I reported that I was in place, I was instructed to cause as much disruption as possible with a view to the whelp's eventual capture."

"There's more, Lessa," Ena said softly.

"How were you supposed to create disruption?"

"I was to cause racial hatred between the aliens and humans. Also, I was to sabotage the ship and lay blame on the Arcalian spy. If opportunity arose, I was to kill the Hound, but not the whelp. The emperor wants her for himself."

"What does he want me for?" asked Michella.

"The Black Witch took his daughter; the emperor has sworn to kill the Witch's daughter and take the Hound's child for his bride."

"I swear that'll never happen," snarled Michella. "Did you sabotage my ship?"

"I did and you'll never find it."

"Why not?"

"I hid it inside the walls of the fighter bay. The next day Palentine changed the wall, and I couldn't get near enough to retrieve it. I set the timer before I left the ship."

"Was it just the one piece of sabotage?"

"Yes. It was all I had time for. It should have exploded by now."

"You mean this?" said Michella as she tossed a deactivated explosive on the floor. "Nice try."

"Can you still contact Lizera?"

"No."

"A lie," said Ena. "The lies are so deeply conditioned that she actually believes them, but she's still capable of the contact."

"How?" asked Lessa.

"The brain implant that allows her to connect with our comms is inactive right now."

"Yes, I destroyed it."

"No Lady, it has regrown."

"You'll have to kill me to stop it," she said, a lazy chuckle escaping from her lips.

"Don't tempt me," snarled Michella. "Tell us how you got your assignments."

"They come through the Hub on Takon Three."

"Explain the Hub," said Lessa.

"The Hub is central to all operations in Sector Nine," the woman replied dreamily. "All orders come to there and then are relayed to all agents. I was chosen because I'm the best. I report directly to Lizera."

"How did you infiltrate my ship?"

"That was easy. I waited with Marlon until you arrived, then I joined the brothel slaves in the pen. I knew Micha would free the slaves. It would then be a matter of working my way into his confidence and then yours. I got lucky and was taken directly onto your ship."

"One last question," said Lessa. "Are there other Imperial spies among us?"

"There is another on the Hound's ship."

"Name that spy."

"I don't know who it is," she laughed lazily.

"That's truth," sighed Ena. "She has no idea who it is."

"I guess we're done here," sighed Micha.

Hawk had been sitting quietly, watching, listening, judging the responses. Ena could spot the lies, but he could see more. He knew what had to be done and he knew none of these people would do it. As soon as Micha announced the interview was over. Hawk pulled out his weapon and shot the prisoner. She fell to the floor with a bullet in her brain.

Michella turned to him, her eyes blazing. "What the hells did you do that for? Are you insane?"

"She was already starting to make a report. This had to be done and you all know it. Would you have done it? Would any of you? I didn't think so.

"You're being hunted, Michella. Hunted by a man with unlimited resources and endless determination; a complete madman. You must sever every link he's established to you." With that Hawk walked out of the room.

Michella started after him, but Micha caught her arm and stopped her. "Let him go, Chella," he said gently. "The man was right about what had to be done, but he was wrong about none of us doing it."

"You were going to kill her?"

"There was no other way, Chella. You heard her; her connection had already grown back. Her reports would have resumed as soon as Lessa's potion wore off. Chella, I didn't invent this game, nor did I establish the rules. Hawk didn't either. We just do what we have to do to survive.

"Chella, Emperor Loran is the most tenacious man I've ever known. He's decided he wants you and he'll never stop until he gets what he wants. I tried killing him, but it seems that didn't stop him. I need you to be extra careful."

Michella gazed into her father's eyes for a long moment, and then nodded. "All right, Poppa, I'll be on my guard. I can deal with the killing when it's in space and I can't see the faces or if they are fighting me, but just shooting a prisoner..."

"I know, Chella, I know."

"It just seems to me that it makes us no better than they are."

"You're right, Chella; it makes us exactly like them. The only difference here is that we're trying to survive; they're trying to make that stop."

Michella nodded then turned to look at the body on the floor. "This foolishness will be the death of us all," she sighed. "How did this all get started?"

"This sort of thing has been going on as long as there have been people," said Micha. "This particular piece of the chaos was started by a madman's ambitions."

"Emperor Loran?"

"Yes. He was just O'Loran back then when he destroyed Nova. That eventually set Lessa against him. He kept trying harder and she made us to help her keep him and those like him in check. This is what we were made for, Chella. This is what we do."

"I accept that, Poppa. I just wish there was a better way of doing it."

"So do I, honey. Let me know if you find it."

"You'll be the first," she sighed, as she turned away from the body on the floor.

<hr>

THE TALL MAN SAT ALONE in his quarters, staring at the almost empty bottle of intoxicant on the small table. It wasn't going to be nearly enough. A soft knock came at his door. "Go away," he growled. The knock came again. "It's locked for a reason," he sighed heavily. "Go away."

He rolled his eyes and sighed again as he heard the lock snick open. Ellie stepped softly through the now unlocked door and closed it behind her. "Go away, Ellie. Leave me be."

"I will," she said softly, as she laid a gentle hand on his shoulder. "I just wanted to bring you this." She set a full bottle beside the nearly empty one, then patted his shoulder before leaving the room. He stopped her at the door.

"Ellie..."

"It's all right, Hawk. I got a lot of answers and an education today. I'll cover tomorrow's shift for you." She stepped through the door and locked it behind her.

He stared at the door for some time, then opened the new bottle and took a long pull of the fiery liquid. "Working locks without a lock pick; now there's a skill worth the learning," he mused, as he took another drink.

The next day Hawk arrived on the bridge for his regular shift. "Hawk..."

"Ellie, please don't shout."

"Sorry," she whispered with a giggle in her voice. "Are you okay?"

"I will be in a week or two," he replied, as he sank into the chair at comms. That was followed by a round of snickers from the others.

"WE'RE STILL HAVING trouble pinning down the rebels in the Inarr system of Sector Two, Sire," said the admiral, visibly sweating. He knew all too well the emperor did not tolerate failure.

"What's taking so long? You should have suppressed those swine weeks ago."

"It's the planets, Sire. One is all swamp and the other is dense forest. We're..."

"Poison the atmosphere, blow up the planets. I'd don't care how you do it, Admiral. I just want it done. Whatever you do, be swift and merciless. These people are giving other systems ideas. Ideas we cannot afford to ignore. Two weeks, Admiral. In two weeks you will have it done or I'll put a more capable man in your place. Now get out of my sight." Loran crumpled a metal canister in his hand and the admiral fled.

"Sit down, Lizera. Tell me some good news for a change."

"You always know when I sneak up behind you," she smiled, as she sank gracefully into a chair.

"I have eyes in the back of my head. What news of Sector Nine?"

"I believe the trap has been sprung, Sire. As we thought, the spy on the girl's ship was sloppy enough to get caught."

"Are you certain?"

"All reports stopped suddenly. She was entering the new ship when it stopped. Later a garbled phrase or two arrived, but nothing since. I believe she was caught, interrogated then killed. I have a report from the Hound's ship that there's much talk of the Hub. I believe he's taken the bait."

"Finally something is going according to plan. Have you had any luck with the location to that hideout?"

"Sorry, Sire. Our spy on the Hound's ship isn't highly placed and has no access to the bridge. Also, with that walking lie detector on board, she has to be extremely careful."

"Understood. I'll endeavour to curb my impatience, Lizera. We must proceed carefully. I want this done right."

"We'll be cautious, Sire. You'll have your revenge and your bride."

"Soon the Hound will watch me wed his child before he's killed, and then she'll be thrown in prison with an inhibitor on her stupid head. She'll remain there until she rots and dies of old age. Yes, Lizera, revenge is indeed a dish best served cold. Go now and prepare for the journey. We don't want to keep our guest waiting."

"Sire, is it truly necessary for you to go in person? We both know things can, and often do, go awry in Sector Nine. It would be safer for you to remain here and let me bring them to you."

"No, Lizera. I do trust you to get this done, but I want, need, to take a hand personally."

"You want to face the Hound again on a battleground of your own choosing."

"Oh yes, indeed I do. There'll be no forest to hide in this time, no weakness in my back to take advantage of. This time I will personally crush the life out of him. Right after he gives me his daughter's hand in marriage, of course."

A chill actually ran up Lizera's spine at the madness in his laughter. She quietly slipped from the room.

The Hunters

S everal days later, three ships left the hideout and set course for Takon Three. Micha had renamed the Lance the Ravage, Michella kept the Warbird, and Zartah was commanding the Shield. Gorda, Miriam, and Norlene had gone with Zartah.

Michella had sent several of her human crew as well. She'd kept only a chosen few she knew would have no problems working with the Korim. All of her original crew, plus Hawk and the Korim, rounded out the ship's compliment.

All three ships and their fighters were fully equipped with inertia blockers and the crews had practised using them. They were ready for whatever might come along and Micha was determined to clear away as much of Loran's network of spies as he could. He already knew who the spy on his ship was. He was just biding his time.

To Michella's surprise and delight, the Korim had found ways to fit in to the crew very quickly. Their grasp of language was startling in that it took only a few days for them to be able to communicate effectively. They were likable people. Krak'sul and Allore became buddies almost instantly. They spent many hours telling each other all about the farms they had left behind while she taught him what she could about healing.

The male Korim hunter was Dor'cas. He and Old Rath began to spend lots of time together, swapping stories while he learned the ins and outs of the ship. Geela, the older female soon invaded the kitchen and became a cook's favorite. It didn't take long before they were taking turns as cook or working together on creating a new dish.

The young female was different. Alise was quite shy, yet keenly interested in everything new. It wasn't long before her inquisitive nature put her in Palentine's path. For some reason he couldn't name he was drawn to her. Part of it was her powerful build and part of it was her rich feminine voice. The male Korim had deep raspy voices, but the female voices were truly seductive. Tarah mentioned Palentine's fascination one day in the engine room.

"So, Pally, are you planning to ask Alise to swear the oath with you?"

"What????"

"Come on, you drool every time she walks into a room," laughed Tarah.

"Tarah..."

"Hey, I have no problems here. You know that."

"Yeah, I guess. The thing is, Tarah, I don't even know if I can. Do her people choose companions the way we do? Do they mate the way we do? Hells, is she even interested?"

"Yes, to all three questions," said a rich contralto voice behind him.

Palentine spun like a startled cat, his face turning crimson as he looked into her dark eyes. "You knew she was there," he accused, as he rounded on Tarah.

"Yes, I did." He laughed as he slapped Palentine on the shoulder and headed for the door. "You're on your own now. Talk to each other, kiddies."

"Alise..." Pally was still blushing furiously as he turned to face her again, "I... are you certain?"

"No," she sighed in reply. "You and Tarah are special friends, yes?"

"No... Well, yes, sometimes, but we're not sworn companions. We don't... I mean I..."

"It is the same with our people. Some like both, others just like males or females. Tarah likes males, but you like both, yes?"

"Well, yes, but... Alise, it isn't customary to talk about such things with strangers."

"We are not so strange to each other; we have met often before and know our names. We are both of the clan... Oh, yes, I guess I am strange to you at that." She lowered her eyes and turned away.

Palentine gently took her arm and turned her back. "Alise, we're different, but that doesn't matter to me. Is it a problem for you?"

"Well, you are strong like the Korim. I guess I could get used to the brown skin in time, but the lack of tusks... I just don't know..."

Pally's laugh was full and rich. "I can't do much about the brown skin, but maybe I can make a pair of false tusks to put you at ease."

The girl laughed with him then went serious again. "Pally, I'm strange to this realm. I have no way to get back to my world, and even if I did I'd be killed or made slave. I like your people, this clan. I want to be a part of this. I need to find a place here. I believe our two peoples mate the same way..."

"How about we just spend some time together," smiled Pally, as he reached for her hands. "Let's explore being friends first while you get comfortable with being a Novan."

"Special friends?" She was gazing into his eyes and he was getting lost in hers.

"Are you certain?"

"Oh yes."

"Why do I feel like I just got caught in a trap?"

"Because you did. I am a hunter, after all, but I'll do what I can to make the trap comfortable."

"That's what I'm afraid of," he said, as he slipped his arm around her waist and pulled her close.

"I promise I'll be gentle as I tame you," she breathed, as her eyes fluttered closed and her strong arms encircled his neck.

"I can hardly wait," he said, as he brought his lips to hers. The tusks proved to be a problem, but they had fun exploring ways around the obstacle.

Hours later they entered the kitchen hand in hand. Once again there were stares, but they turned to chuckles as the young couple both blushed to their roots. "Are you all right, Alise?" grinned Michella.

"I am full strong, Captain Michella," she replied softly.

"Pally?" asked Chella.

"Chella, you know what happened every time..."

"I know, but not now?"

"Not now, Alise is amazing."

"Stop," hissed Alise, as she gave him a poke in the ribs with her elbow. "Can I ask what happen before or is that another thing you don't talk about with strangers?"

"You're not a stranger now, Alise," smiled Michella, "you're clan. Besides, in a way this is something you should know about our gentle giant."

"Gentle?" exclaimed Alise with feigned surprise.

"Stop," laughed Pally, as he put an arm around her shoulders and hugged her. "Alise my few previous attempts to enjoy other women went badly. I tried not to hurt them, but I'm strong and..."

"You're not that strong," she teased. He laughed and squeezed her shoulders again. "I understand. They were weak and frightened by your passion. On our own world, the Korim rarely mate with other races for the same reason.

"Captain Michella, you command here; will you permit this, or must I now go to another ship?"

"You don't need my permission for this, Alise. Besides, Pally would shoot me if I sent you away."

"Count on it," rumbled the young giant.

In the kitchen Geela and the cook were working side by side. "Am I seeing what I think I'm seeing?" the cook asked softly.

"You are," grunted Geela, as she swiftly diced another huge carrot into the stew. "Ah, the young; they think with their bodies and not their heads. I think I like what I see, Cook. It tells me we few Korim may yet find a home here."

"I don't think that'll be any problem at all," grinned the cook. "You're a strange looking lot to the rest of us, but I imagine it must be considerably harder for you. I can look around and see folk like myself everywhere, but you only have each other."

"We will survive, Cook. It's in our nature to survive."

———— ◉ ————

TWO DAYS OUT FROM THE hideout, Michella suddenly had an idea. Grinning, she sat up straighter in her captain's chair. "Comms."

"Comms, aye," purred Nellie.

"Get me the Ravage."

A moment later her father answered. "Ravage here; what's up Chella?"

"Poppa, would you consider committing a terrible crime against the king of Arcalia?" she grinned wider as she saw Hawk sit up straighter at pilot. She knew this conversation would go straight to the king.

"Sure. What have you got in mind?"

"We're running low on supplies since we helped stock the Shield's larder, and I'll bet you are too. The king's private hunting planet is near. I'd like to stop by and set my hunters loose. Heck, I'd like to go hunting myself."

"I love it, Chella," laughed Micha. I'll bet Miriam would enjoy a chance to run loose for a while too. Tell Hawk to report to Borad that we're going hunting. He'll be lucky if there's any game left when we're finished. I assume Hawk knows the location; you take lead, and we'll follow."

"Hawk..."

"Course correction in three, two, one... New course laid in and transmitted to the fleet, Captain."

"Take us to playland, Hawk; full burn."

"Full burn, aye," chuckled Hawk.

"Comms, ship-wide."

"Ship-wide, aye."

"Attention, all hands, this is the captain. We're taking a detour to top up our supplies. We should arrive in a few hours. All hunters prepare your gear; you'll have work to do."

The Korim hunters gathered in the launch bay as soon as the planet came in sight. They were surprised to find Ellie waiting for them with a huge supply of weapons, blades, rope, clothing, etc. "Take what you need," she said as they looked at her inquisitively. "If there's something else you might need, tell me what it is and I'll see if I can find it. If not, I'll get it the first time we hit a town big enough."

Dor'cas grunted with satisfaction as he chose a sturdy blade. Geela chose a knife as well, and a length rope. Alise chose a tough twine for a spare bowstring. "If I had a forge I could make some spear points," mused Dor'cas.

"Would stone points do?" asked Ellie.

"Stone? Yes, if they're well formed, but we haven't used stone for many generations."

"I'll see if Auntie Miriam has any spares. She hunts with a spear too."

"I'll never understand that," grunted a small man as he entered, a long range weapon over his shoulder.

"The hunt is for food and leather for clothing," said Geela as she turned to him. "You're Owen, yes?" He nodded. "Owen, hunting with that weapon is for enemies and for food for the starving. Food for the strong must be hunted with honor if it's to bring strength and honor to the clan."

Owen nodded slowly. "All right, Geela. Truth is, I'm more of a farmer than a hunter. If you'd rather, I'll stay behind to help with the butchering when you're ready."

"You are not to lead us?"

"Lead you? Hell, no. You folk are hunters, born and raised. You go play in the woods and I'll stay here, out of the flies. Call me on comms when you need me and I'll come with the lads to pick up the meat." He grinned and left the area.

"What is the story of Owen and his long range weapon?" asked Geela.

"Owen was a sniper in the wars," replied Ellie. "They say he was the best."

"Are we to be trusted to hunt alone then?" asked Geela.

"The clan needs food, Geela. You folk are our clan's hunters," replied Ellie.

"Touch down in ten," Nellie purred over the comms. "Hunters to the launch bay."

The ships set down in a large clearing near a slow moving river. The planet was covered with boreal forest for as far as they had been able to see. As the Korim reached the ground they saw a short, but powerfully built, woman walking towards them. As she reached them she dropped to one knee and spoke.

"It is good to see the Korim again. I bring gifts of spear points I made myself. I hope they're sufficient to your needs."

"Thank you, Miriam," replied Dor'cas. "Rise and tell me why you greet us so formally."

"As one who is different yet who has found a home with these generous people, I wanted to show respect for you and your time of newness among us," replied Miriam. "This is how we do that among the people from which I came."

"We're honored, Miriam," said Geela. "Will you hunt with us?"

"I was hoping you'd ask," laughed Miriam as she leaped to her feet. "Let's go; first one to spot a game trail leads the hunt." They all ran to the edge of the forest and disappeared into the trees.

Day was winding down. The folk had spent most of the day just wandering about in the clearing, sipping water from the clear running stream, and enjoying sunshine on their faces. "I had no idea how much I really miss this until right now," sighed Micha, as he and Edie watched the sun setting over the trees.

"A sunset?"

"All of it, Edie, the warmth of the sun on my back, the breeze in your hair, the cool of the water on bare feet, the ground under my feet, all of it. Those are amazing ships, but ships are for getting from one place to another; they make poor homes. We need to find a real home for our people."

"Perhaps we will, my lover," she said, smiling as she snuggled under his arm, "but for now we keep them alive and free. Even if we can come back here once in a while it would help."

"Now that's a wonderful idea, my love. Let's spend a few days here and clear our heads."

Zartah wandered up to them, but didn't speak. He waited for them to notice him. "Miriam staying out under the trees tonight?" asked Micha.

"You guessed it, Boss," chuckled the big man. "She says the Korim are great hunters. They'll be back tomorrow with enough meat to feed us all for months."

"Sounds like she's having fun," smiled Edie. "Wishing you were with her?"

"Not tonight," grinned Zartah. "She can have the rocks and bugs; I'll sleep better in the bunk." He bid them goodnight and walked away.

Michella and Deann walked by and Micha could hear their soft voices. "So, what will it be tonight, Sweetheart, a soft bunk or under the trees?"

"That tall grass smells a lot like the hay loft on your father's farm, Chella. I vote for the grass."

"What about you, Sweetheart, grass or ship?" grinned Micha, as he hugged Edie tighter.

"I vote with Zartah," smiled Edie. "I want my regular bed."

"Bed it is," said Micha, as he took one last deep breath of the cool breeze then took her hand and led her back to the ship.

The next morning Miriam returned alone, all smiles. She and Zartah took a fighter ship and returned to the place where the Korim had the game collected. They loaded what they could onto the ship then returned to the main camp. On the next trip they got the last of it. Miriam and the Korim returned on foot while Zartah ferried the meat to the camp.

When they emerged from the forest, Alise had several fowl strung together and carried across her broad shoulders. She tossed them to Palentine. "I bring meat; prepare it for me."

Everyone stopped and stared. Pally barely moved a muscle for a moment then he leaped at her, scooped her over his shoulder and ran for the stream. Alise squealed in protest, but he headed for the pool and launched her. She grabbed his arm and he was carried into the water with her, as were the fowl.

They surfaced from the water, sputtering, and laughing to the cheers and cat calls of the clan. "Come, Pally, help me dress these." She laughed as they struggled to the shallower water. "I want to roast them over a fire for you tonight."

"Oh by thunder, yes," bellowed a fellow who had overheard. "Open fire tonight."

"Open fire," rang out several more voices.

"I'll start gathering stone," said one man. "I'll find the makings of some spits," declared another. "I'll start digging the main pit," said Zartah. Everyone pitched in and the meat was soon prepared and stored away, the hides scraped, rubbed with sweet grass and stretched out in the sun, the fire pit dug, and dry wood collected for the fire.

As the sun set everyone was gathered around the dying fire, well fed and content. After some good-natured debate, Micha agreed to a one week stay before setting out again.

AN OLD, BATTERED WARSHIP slowly worked her way through the Gap. She had encountered only a single group of pirates and had easily dispatched them. The ship was a disguised Imperial warship, and she was heavily armed. At first glance the crew might look like a band of brigands, but they were too well disciplined, too well armed, and far too numerous.

The captain sat nervously in his chair as the tall man stood just behind him. "I'm sorry, Sire, but the Gap demands patience. If we make one hasty move here it could be the end of us."

"Understood, Captain," came that cold metallic voice behind him.

"Sire, if I may, why have we come this route? The other two paths are more easily traversed and can be done with greater haste."

"I'm far more interested in stealth than speed, Captain, yet I grow impatient. I understand that staring over your shoulder will not diminish the distance so I'll withdraw to my quarters. Please have Lizera sent to me there at once."

The emperor turned and left the bridge. He returned to the Captain's quarters which he had seconded for himself. Lizera was there waiting for him outside the door. "Come in, Lizera. I wish to speak privately." He opened the door and led her inside.

"So, any news from the hub? Do they have my prize yet?"

"All is quiet there, Sire. The Hound has not yet arrived."

"Blast, now what has gone amiss? Could he have puzzled it out? No, I think not. Something has distracted him. Freeing slaves somewhere, most likely." He sighed began to pace slowly about the small cabin. "No matter, he will come. Perhaps I'll have the pleasure of greeting him myself."

"What if he just informs King Borad and lets the Arcalians deal with the Hub?"

"He won't. The Hound will see this Hub as part of his bargain with Borad. He'll take it upon himself to do the job."

"As you say, Sire. There is one bright note though."

"Oh?"

"We've located the Hawk."

"That accursed spy; where is he; have you managed to kill him?"

"Sadly, Sire, he is very much alive. Apparently he's aboard the Warbird. Somehow he's managed to become part of the daughter's crew. He even goes by the name of Hawk."

"Truly? Well, now. Two birds with a single stone; I'm feeling much better already."

The Hub

The fires crackled in the pit, throwing light and warmth to the folk gathered around it, slowly roasting treats Geela and Cook had prepared for them. Micha looked up and smiled as Lessa approached. "Is she sleeping, Lessa?"

"Like a baby, Micha. Our spy won't awaken until time for her next shift."

"Perfect. All right, people, it's time for a council of war. We know there's an Imperial spy network in the free alliance and we know where it's based; at least we believe we do. Since it's on the border of our territory, it's our job to eradicate it. We leave for Takon Three in the morning.

"Since this is going to be an urban operation, I want Rathbone to lead it."

"Which one?" chuckled Old Rath.

"Both of you," grinned Micha.

"Looks like you're up, Poppa," chuckled Rathbone.

"Alright," said the old fellow, as he twisted around a bit to get more comfortable on the ground. "Hawk, I smell a trap. How about you?"

"Trap," agreed the tall man as he eased his elbows forward on his knees. "That spy was way too sloppy. I should never have found her. She said she reports directly to Lizera. I've spent the past fifteen years trying to get someone close to that woman. If she was as highly placed as she thought she was, that name would never have passed her lips, even under the Lady's spell. Besides, the poison in her tooth wasn't fatal."

"It wouldn't have killed her?" asked Lessa.

"No. It would have made her sick enough to wish for death, but it wouldn't have killed her. Somebody wanted us to find her, and they wanted us to know about the Hub. I doubt that it's really the center of operations in this sector. I think it's just an elaborate setup. Somebody wants Nova Clan out of the way."

"Somebody wants revenge," sighed Micha, "and I know just who it is."

"Father," said Brenna, "or what's left of him. I guess my father died long ago. This robot thing that looks like him really isn't."

"No, it isn't, love," soothed Lessa, as she put her arm around Brenna's shoulders.

"Okay, it's a trap," said Micha. "Loran's after my hide and according to that spy, he's going to use Chella to get to me."

"He's got to catch me first," said Michella.

"Don't be so sure," said Old Rath. "Micha has two daughters."

"Allore is just turning fourteen," said Edie indignantly.

"What difference would that make to a madman?" sighed Norlene. "How do we proceed?"

The elder Rathbone thought for a moment before speaking. Finally he looked up and replied. "First we need to know his objectives. He wants revenge on Micha. I believe he plans to use one of the girls as leverage to force Micha into a one-on-one battle in a place of his own choosing. We have to use that against him. That'll be our one chance to take him down."

Michella saw the sadness on Brenna's face and an idea suddenly occurred to her. She reached out and laid a gentle hand on the small woman's shoulder. "Auntie Brenna, I know you wish there was a way to do this without killing him. I think I have an idea how we can do that and still rid ourselves of him forever."

"Chella?"

"I'm all for that if you can figure it out, Chella," said Micha. "I tried killing him and that didn't work. What have you got in mind?"

"We'll need to capture him."

"Okay, and then what?"

"You once showed us an anomaly that shoots you away to another galaxy with no way back. Let's put him on a ship and send him through. That'll get him out of our hair, and he'll still survive. Who knows, he might even conquer that galaxy."

"Oh, Chella, that would be perfect," said Brenna. "Micha, can we do that?"

Micha gazed into her imploring eyes and melted. Lessa was eyeing him eagerly too. This could mend the damage in his clan caused when he'd killed Loran twenty years before. There was only one problem. He'd already given the mission to Old Rath. "I'm game for it, Brenna," he replied gently, "but it's not my call. This is Rathbone of Urn's mission."

"Poppa Rath?" she asked, as she turned to him hopefully.

"I have no problem with it," he replied, "provided we can do it. Hawk?"

"I like it," nodded Hawk. "It gets rid of the madman and leaves no martyr behind. It'll all depend on the Ladies Arlessa and Norlene, though."

"Us?" they asked in unison.

"Someone will have to render him unconscious so we can transport him. If even half the reports are true, none of us is going to be able to do it; he's far too strong."

"I believe there will be no problem at all," replied Lessa.

"All right then," said Old Rath. "We have our objective, now let's put our heads together and see if we can figure out how we can achieve that."

The planning session went on well into the night. In the end they stayed another day to work on it. When the ships finally rose from the surface they had a plan. The spy on the Ravage had no idea how she'd gotten sick or what she had missed over the three days she was out with a high fever.

———◉———

THE BIG SHIP SETTLED to a rest at the space dock of Alton City on Takon Three. A blacked out limo was waiting to take the tall man and his female companion to their destination in the city. "Are you certain of this man and his people, Lizera?"

"Yes, Sire. Tekka's the most feared and respected criminal on three planets. He's sheltered and assisted our operations here for fifteen years and I've never known him to fail. He'll do what's required of him."

"Very good then, I'm anxious to meet this excellent fellow. Perhaps I'll make him governor of Sector Nine when this is all over."

An hour later the emperor, his aide, and a rat faced man were in a plush office waiting for word of Nova Clan's whereabouts. A woman entered, whispered to the rat faced man for a moment then slipped quietly from the room. "All's well, Sire," said Tekka, as he smiled ingratiatingly at the Emperor. "The Novans have been spotted again, as you predicted. They're headed this way. Their ships should be landing in the next few hours."

"You have all your people in place?"

"I do. I have people everywhere. If they're looking for the hub of your operations, my people will know. As soon as they're located, the girl will be taken and brought to you as promised."

———◉———

"JIN, I DON'T THINK this is such a good idea. We're talking about crossing both Nova Crew and Tekka. I know what Tekka would do if he even suspected we thought of a double cross. Besides that, having Micha and his crew on our trail would be worse."

"Bix, my old son, ye've gotta use yer head here. This young'un is one of Micha's cubs. The Emperor will pay more for her than we could make in a lifetime working for Tekka or scratching for rocks on some damned asteroid. We can snatch her up and be halfway through the Gap before Tekka suspects a thing. We'll be richer than kings and lost in Sector Three where Micha will never go."

"I don't know, Jin. They say he went after the emperor right on Elliston Prime. That witch can track us no matter where we go."

"Look, Bix, does ye want to spend the rest of yer life running errands for Tekka or scratching for sparklies out in the 'roid belt? That gal is right there at the bar and a kingdom is in yer hand; all ye have to do is close yer fingers and take it."

"All right, Jin, but I still don't like it."

"Ye worry too much, Bix."

"Tekka isn't going to like being double crossed either."

"Ha, Tekka isn't paying us half what the Imperials will pay. Old Tek set it up, we grab the prize, and we get back everything he stole from us over the years and more besides. Ayra will see us through the Gap then we kill her to keep her mouth shut. It'll be just ye and me, Bix, like always."

Michella had no idea how she'd be captured, but she'd set herself up as bait. There was no other way to do this, and she wasn't going to risk Allore. Emperor Loran wanted a daughter of Micha and she was going to be the only one available, and on her terms. She sighed and ordered another drink.

She had a feeling it would happen soon. Michella had been asking the kinds of questions Hawk said would draw attention. She'd been steered to this rather seedy bar in a more rundown section of the city. Michella felt a slight bump and a sting as the man next to her jostled her arm. He muttered an apology and moved away. A moment later the nausea hit her, and the room began to spin. A wave of dizziness washed over her, and she nearly fell off the bar stool.

"Ye don't look so good, girly," said a rough voice, as hands gripped her arm to steady her. "Here, I'll help ye outside for some fresh air." His arm slipped around her and his hand gripped her breast painfully. Michella tried to fight him, but her trembling knees wouldn't hold her up.

"Help me," she screamed in her mind, but the words didn't come out.

As the man half carried her through the back door, Hawk slipped out of his chair to follow. Hawk stepped through the door and was hit from behind by blaster fire. He was hurled across the alley to lie face down and unconscious on the ground. The man who shot him reached back inside and triggered the fire alarm. In the madness that followed Zartah and Miriam were unable to get to the back door in time. All they found outside was Hawk lying in a heap.

Back at the Ravage, Nellie screamed and fainted.

———◉———

TEKKA EXCLAIMED AND began to swear profusely. His minions fled his wrath and raced for the spaceport. "Find them," he bellowed. "Find them and bring me their eyeless heads."

"What has happened?" asked the cold metallic voice of the emperor. The tall man had been standing in the shadows when the messenger arrived. His voice cut through the rat faced man's rage like a knife. Tekka was visibly shaking as he turned to face the man in the corner.

"We've been double crossed," he said, as he swallowed hard.

"Explain."

That voice carried the promise of pain and death. Tekka swallowed again and began to babble. "It was Jin and Bix who found her. Those scumbags have always been two of the more dependable rogues in my employ. They caught her easily, then they slugged their driver and took off. They went straight to the space port and blasted off. They've headed into the Gap."

"How much did they know?"

"Nothing, nothing, I swear. They were offered a standard fee and told to snatch the girl then bring her to me here. That's all they knew. They didn't know who she was or who she was for."

"Find them. Find them now," snarled Loran. "Kill them and bring me the woman, alive and unharmed." The rat faced man scurried from the room.

"You just can't trust anybody anymore," sighed the woman, as she stepped to the emperor's side.

"Excuse me?"

"These idiots must have recognized the girl and decided to try for bigger profits," replied Lizera. "They've gone into the Gap. My guess is they're headed for Elliston Prime to sell you their prize."

"Bloody morons," growled Loran. "Contact the ship. We're going after them ourselves."

———◉———

ABOARD THE RAVAGE NELLIE was coming around. "Nellie, Nellie, talk to me girl."

"Allore, what's that horrible stench?" Nellie asked groggily, as she sat up with Barah's help.

"Smelling salts," grinned Allore. "Nellie, what happened?"

"Oh my gods, Chella," gasped Nellie, as she struggled to her feet. "They took her, Lore."

"Wasn't that the idea?" asked Barah.

"No, Barah, they took her off world."

"What???" That was Micha.

"They took her off world, Uncle Micha," replied Nellie. "They hurt her then took her off world."

"Skeeter," snarled Micha, as he grabbed his comm unit. "This is Micha, abort. I repeat, abort and return to the Ravage. Now.

"Nellie, can you track her?"

"No, Uncle Micha, I can't. She was sick and he was pawing at her then she was ripped away from me. I blacked out and wasn't able to see which way they took her. Hawk was shot and I don't know what happened to him either."

Before anything else could happen, Deann took command. Grabbing her comm she began to bark orders. "Warbird crew to the ship. Now. Chella's been taken. We're going after her.

"Warbird Bridge."

"Bridge here, Ellie speaking."

"Warm her up, Ellie. Get her ready to blast off. Hawk is down, does anybody know where he is?"

"Hawk here, Deann," came his voice sounding ragged. "I'm on my way home with Zartah and Miriam. Deann, I know who took her and I know where they'll be taking her."

Deann turned to Micha and started to speak, but he cut her off. "Get your ship in the air, Deann. I have an errand to run here, then I'll catch up with you." She gave a curt nod then fled the Ravage for the Warbird.

Micha reached for his comm again. "All enhanced Nova Crew suit up for war; human crew prepare to defend the ships from attack. Ladies Norlene and Lessa, we have work to do. Jorge, bring me that sleeping cook's helper, then suit up."

The Warbird had already lifted off by the time Micha's crew of warriors was ready to go. "What's up, Boss?" asked Zartah.

"It's all gone sideways," said Micha, fully in cold warrior mode now. "They took Michella, but double crossed their boss and went off world with her. The Warbird has gone after them. We'll follow them when we're finished."

"What are we doing?" asked Rathbone.

"We're sending Loran and everybody else a message."

"What message is that, Micha?" asked Brenna.

"If you come after Nova Clan, Nova Clan will come after you. Lessa, please wake up that spy and get a location of the big boss around here. We're going to take this operation apart in an extreme fashion. I'm going to make some bad things happen before I leave here."

"I'll get the grenades," sang Keira, as she raced away.

Into the Gap

"Crew's all aboard, Deann," came Old Rath's voice over the comms.

"Lock her up, Poppa Rath. Tarah, get us into the sky. Somebody find me Hawk." Deann was in the captain's chair, and everybody was content to have her there. She was cold and efficient, just like Micha when the pressure was on.

"Hawk here, Deann," came that deep voice, as he made his way painfully onto the bridge.

"Can you function?"

"I can."

"Take pilot and talk to me. Tarah, on guns." Tarah held the chair steady for Hawk, then moved to weapons. Hawk was at the controls as the ship left atmosphere and hurtled into space. The big bird leaped towards the Gap.

"Talk to me, Hawk."

"I know the men who took her, Deann. It was Jin and Bix. That was the plan, so I didn't interfere; I followed as Jin took her out through the back door. I expected Bix would be driving the getaway speeder, but he was behind me. He shot me with a blaster then triggered the fire alarm. Fortunately my absorb vest soaked up most of the blast or I wouldn't be here.

"I came to with Zartah slapping my face and Miriam trying to pump air into my lungs. They took me back inside where we pieced it together. Those two morons will take Michella straight to Elliston Prime to claim the reward. They obviously didn't know Loran was in town. They've also just double crossed the biggest crime boss in the sector. They're as good as dead no matter what happens now."

"Which path through will they take?"

"The worst is close by. My thought is they have a guide ready. Jin is a nasty piece of work, but he's careful. He'd have thought this through before he took the chance. By taking the bad road they'll hope to shake off or lose any pursuit."

"Have you been through there?"

"Several times."

"Find them for me, Hawk. We have to get her back."

"We will, Deann," said Nellie, as she rose from comms and put her arm around Deann's shoulders. "We will, and then they'll pay for the things they've done."

Everyone was silent then as the big bird streaked towards the twin red stars that marked the entrance to the Gap like warning beacons. Deann sat brooding as Ellie searched the skies with the sensors and Nellie reached out with her mind. Nellie came up empty, but Ellie didn't. "Deann, this is one busy pathway."

"What do you mean, Ellie?"

"They're well out in front of us, but I count at least nine ships going the same way we are."

"Can you identify any of them?"

"Not yet, sorry."

"Comms, engine room."

"Engine room, aye," said Bim. The young fellow was actually pretty darned efficient and had become a stable part of the bridge crew.

"Engines," said Pally's voice.

"More speed," said Deann.

"You can have a bit more for a while, Deann, but we can't keep it up. What we have right now is the best we can maintain long term."

"Can you give me one hard burst then drop back to max?"

"That I can do safely, Captain."

"Do it."

"Aye, Captain."

The comm went silent and she turned to Ellie. "Ellie, I need to know who those ships are as soon as possible."

"Understood." Ellie's concerned glance at Hawk's back caught Deann's attention.

"Go ahead Ellie," she said, as she rose from the chair. "Take a minute to rest your eyes." She glanced meaningfully at Hawk and Ellie gave her a quick hug of gratitude as she stepped past.

Hawk sighed deeply as Ellie's small hands touched his shoulders and a wave of healing energy swept over him. She held it for a moment then stepped away. The sweetness of it lingered and he straightened in his seat.

"Hawk, feeling better?" asked Deann, as she resumed her place in the captain's chair.

"Much."

"I expect we'll soon be in a combat situation. Are you able to function at that level?"

"Yes."

"Good. Poppa Rath, are you on the bridge?"

"Tail gunner right now," grinned the old fellow. "What do you need, Deann?"

"It should be you in this chair; we both know that. Take over."

"Nope."

"Nope? What do you mean, nope?"

"Michella is your companion; this is her ship and therefore your ship right now. I'm first man on this ship, you're the captain."

"You mean this is the test you said I'd have to face one day."

"That's right. Deann, it came to you a lot sooner than I'd have wanted for you, but here it is. Sooner or later everyone has to face the ultimate test if they're to prove their own worth to themselves. You must do this, for you and for Chella. As first man, I can only advise."

"All right, what do you advise?"

"You seem to have a handle on it; just keep doing what you're doing."

"Fat lot of help you are," she grumbled, as she sank back into the Captain's chair.

The old fellow chuckled to himself. "You know," he said, "that's exactly what I told my grandfather when I was your age."

A sleep cycle later they got some action.

"I've got them, Deann," said Ellie. "That burst of speed gained us some distance. The first ship looks like an old warship, but it is heavily armed and has new armor coating. The others farther ahead just look like well-armed pirate ships, you know, no two alike. Also there's a single blip way out ahead. That might be the kidnappers."

"Is there anybody behind us?"

"Two behind us, Deann, but they're not gaining on us," said Nina. She was on aft sensors.

"Message just in, Captain," said young Bim. "Those two behind are the Ravage and the Shield."

"Good to know, thanks, Bim. Tarah, you on guns?"

"Guns, aye," replied Tarah.

"Barah?"

"Secondary gunner on aft guns, Captain Deann," said Barah.

"Tarah, as soon as we're close enough target that first ship's engines. Barah, as soon as we go past them, target and destroy their sensor array."

"Aye, Captain," came both voices.

"Deann?" inquired Old Rath.

"My guess is that ship with all the fancy armor is the emperor after the same prize we are."

"That would be my guess, too," agreed Old Rath.

"Second that," chimed in Hawk.

"I want to cripple his ship and leave him for Micha to deal with," said Deann. "We don't have time to slow down for him. We can't let those scumbags get away with Chella."

"We're being hailed, Captain," grinned Bim.

"Comms and cams," said Deann.

"Comms and cams, aye."

The screen came alive with the image of a middle aged man with iron grey hair. His stiff stance and commanding air said he was military even though he wasn't wearing a uniform. "Approaching ship, reduce speed and identify yourselves."

"This is the Warbird of Nova Clan," said Deann as she rose to face the screen, "Deann of Nova commanding. I know who your passenger is. Tell Emperor Loran I have his granddaughters aboard if he wants to see them." She motioned with her hand and the two young witches stepped up beside her.

"Granddaughters?" said a metallic voice as the emperor stepped in front of the screen. "I knew Brenna had a child, but I didn't know she had two."

Deann stepped away and out of sight as Nellie spoke. "I'm Brenna of Nova's daughter, Emperor Loran. My name is Nellie of Nova Clan. This is my sister/cousin, Ellie. She's Ellie of Nova Clan, daughter of Arlessa with Brenna as DNA donor. Lady Arlessa was the DNA donor for my birth."

Deann was signalling for them to keep him talking. "Tell me, grandfather," said Nellie, "if you knew of my existence, why did you not ever try to contact me or mother?"

"There are extenuating circumstances and family dynamics of which I'm certain you are aware, Nellie. Ask your captain to lock ships so we can meet in person..." comms were cut off as Tarah opened fire. Two missiles slammed into the aft engine area of the disguised warship effectively crippling it.

The Imperials returned fire, but the Warbird avoided with ease and swept past. As she passed, Barah fired. A single missile destroyed the sensor array of the Imperial ship. "Nice shooting, guys," said Deann. "Bim, message the Ravage and let Micha know who's waiting for him back there. Hawk, see what you can do about catching up to that next lot. Ellie, you back at sensors?"

"Sensors, aye," replied Ellie.

"Have you still got that blip out ahead on sensors?"

"Yes, it's a ship, but I can't tell you anything more about it. At the rate we're all going we should catch up with most of those ships and the blip about the same time."

"We've got a new tail, captain Deann," said Nina.

"Can you identify?"

"It appears to be an Imperial fighter. It's falling back slowly."

"Looks like Loran doesn't give up easily," muttered Deann. "Bim, inform the Ravage that a fighter has left the crippled ship and is following us."

"Message away, captain," Bim said a moment later.

"How long until we catch them, Hawk?"

"No more than a day at this speed if we can hold it, Captain."

"In that case, get down to the infirmary to see Allore. You've been in that chair far too long now. Tarah can take over while you get patched up. Ellie, go with him to make sure he gets there in one piece."

With a sheepish grin, Hawk rose and allowed Ellie to lead him off the bridge.

"THEY'RE FIRING," SHOUTED the man at sensors. "We're hit," came another voice as the ship shuddered. "Engines are down."

"Return fire," bellowed the captain, "return fire."

"I can't get a lock, Sir," shouted the gunner. "No ship should be able to twist and turn like that. I can't get a lock."

"Incoming," bawled another voice. Again the ship shuddered. "We're hit. Sensors are down. We're dead in space, Captain."

"Idiots," growled Loran. "This is the best ship in my fleet? They put you down without even slowing their speed." He grabbed the captain and hurled him into the bulkhead. The man fell dead to the floor. "Get a fighter ship ready, man it with two gunners. I'll pilot it myself. Come along Lizera, we're going after them.

"Get this damned ship repaired and catch up as quickly as possible."

"Yes, Sire," replied the next in command, but the emperor was already gone from the bridge. A few moments later a single fighter dropped out of the bay and set out after the Warbird. Both gunners silently prayed they would never catch up.

———— ◉ ————

LESSA DROPPED THE UNCONSCIOUS woman back to the floor. "That should be all we need, Micha. What shall I do with her?"

"Bring her along; we'll drop her in the city someplace. We'll be long gone before she wakes up. Ready, people? All right, let's go."

The launch bay doors opened and two fighter ships swept out. There was a swarm of police vehicles surrounding the bigger ships. They opened fire but were ignored. As the fighters sped away over the city a voice boomed over the external speakers of the Ravage.

"Attention Police, this is the Ravage, Owen of Nova Commanding. We are here on an official mission sanctioned by the King of Arcalia. If you attempt to interfere, you will be destroyed. Bring one ounce of harm to one of our people and your city will be leveled; starting with you. Go back to your normal course of business."

There was a lot of talk and bluster from those outside, but the sight of the Ravage rising into the air and training her weapons on them changed their minds. Tekka wasn't paying them enough to face a warship. They went back to their stations.

The battle was short and brutal. The two fighters landed in the courtyard of the giant building that looked like a warehouse. Their missiles destroyed much of it then the crew hit the ground. All who opposed were killed as they swept through. Tekka was found in his office, a bullet through his brain and a gun in his hand.

Rathbone planted his explosives and they flew off as the rest of Tekka's complex evaporated in the explosion that followed their exit. They sped back to the spaceport and disappeared into their ships. "Get us in the air, Jorge," bawled Micha as he slammed the control to close up the launch bay doors. The Ravage leaped skyward with the Shield close behind.

As the Ravage reached open space Brenna was already searching the skies with the long range sensors. "Brenna, any sign?" asked Micha.

"I've got the Warbird on long range. The message was right; they're taking the hard way through."

"Get after them, Jorge, full burn."

"Full burn, aye."

A few hours later, Lessa grinned and turned from comms. "We have a message from the Warbird, Micha. It appears the Emperor had a warship here and he went after the kidnappers too. Deann caught the ship and disabled it. Loran is now following the Warbird in a fighter, but he's losing ground. We should overtake him long before he has a chance to do any further harm."

"Now that's a piece of good news," sighed Micha. "With a bit of luck the Gap will swallow him up for us. Sorry, Brenna."

"It's all right, Micha. I know that robot isn't really my father, neither was the half man who first became emperor. My father died soon after I first left Elliston Prime. It's just that the machine still holds something of him, and I'd like to see that survive if possible. I like Chella's idea, but if that can't happen we have to find a way to finish him permanently."

"Chella's plan will work, Sweetheart," smiled Lessa. "All I have to do is get close enough to him to use Rathbone's gift. He'll be expecting witchcraft, not a tech attack."

"Won't he have had that chip removed by now?" asked Brenna.

"Remember what happened with the chip in the spy's head?" chuckled Lessa. "I'll bet the same thing has happened this time too."

"I hope you're right, Lessa," sighed Micha. "It would be the best solution; however, I have Rath working on a backup just in case."

"Of course you do," laughed Lessa. "I'd be shocked if you didn't."

Micha smiled and relaxed back in his chair. There was nothing to do now but wait. He didn't have to wait long before Brenna spoke again. "We're coming up on the crippled warship now, Micha. They seem to have regained some engines as they're moving again."

"Edie, you on weapons?"

"Locked and loaded my lover."

"Shut down their engines again for me."

"Coming into range now. Shutting down the engines." Two missiles streaked out from the Ravage and exploded against the crippled ship, destroying the engines completely. "Their engines are down."

"Thank you, Edie," grinned Micha. "Lessa, send a message back to Takon Three. I thought I saw Zemma's ship in that space dock. Let her know where she can salvage an Imperial warship. Oh, tell her it might still have a few Imperials on it."

"Message sent," Lessa said a few moments later. "Micha, what are you up to?"

"Zemma will take that ship and repair it for herself," grinned Micha. "She knows we're flying Arcalian ships so she won't come at us, but she will prey on the other pirates. She will also owe us a big favor, so we'll have little to fear from her for a while. Zemma will make the Clan a far better ally than enemy. That's my goal for the long run."

"One former slave to another?" asked Brenna softly.

"Yes, Brenna," replied Micha. "I'll admit I do have a soft spot for former slaves who've managed to escape and make a life for themselves."

Micha sank back into his chair. There was nothing more he could do now but wait; wait and hope Deann could catch up with the kidnappers. In the few short months since he'd first met her, Micha had seen her go from a shy farm girl to a hardened warrior. If Deann could catch up they'd have Michella back in a heartbeat.

———◉———

HAWK AND ELLIE REACHED the infirmary in time to arrive in the middle of a dispute. It was almost funny to watch the gigantic green warrior arguing and losing to the small, but fierce, Allore.

"No, Allore," Krak'sul sighed in exasperation, "I will not teach you how to use that weapon. You will remain on the ship where a healer belongs. If there's fighting to be done, others will do it."

"Michella's my sister," declared Allore. "I'm going to get her back with or without your help. I know how to use some weapons; they'll just have to do."

"I won't let you leave the ship."

"You can't stop me. You have to do what I say."

"No, I don't. I have to protect you. That means I keep you on the ship. Besides, we may not have to fight off ship anyway."

"We'll have to board their ship," replied Allore. "I'll be going."

"I hate to interrupt this delightful family squabble," grinned Ellie, "but my buddy here needs to be patched up. He took a hit from a blaster a while back."

"Front, back, or side?" asked Allore, as she helped Hawk onto a bed.

"I was hit from behind," he replied.

"Face down then," she said, as she and Krak'sul helped him roll over.

"Hawk, talk some sense into this girl, would you?" asked Krak'sul.

"Hawk, make this big lug nut see reason," urged Allore, as her small fingers expertly poked and prodded along his spine. "Ah, here we are." She placed her hands over a spot on his spine then pushed down firmly. There was a popping sound, then he sighed with relief. A moment later she found another spot and popped it back into place. "That should do it, Hawk. The headache should go away now."

"Hold still for a moment," said Ellie. "I'll give you a shot of the magic to help that along." Once again, Hawk felt the sweetness of the healing energy wash over him as her tiny hands gently touched the last spot on his spine that Allore had adjusted. When she finished he smiled and sat up.

"Well," said Allore, "are you going to talk sense to him or not?"

"How about I talk sense to you both?" Hawk grinned. "Krak'sul, by no choice of our own, we're a people at war. However, we seem to be well suited for it. You won't be able to put Allore in a box and keep her safe. She will face danger and you'll have to face it with her.

"Allore, you want weapons, but you're ignoring the greatest weapon of all, and apparently only you can wield it."

"Excuse me? Which weapon would that be, Sir Spy?" she asked tartly.

"The Korim. Krak'sul has sworn to protect you and he's the Korim leader." He grinned as he stepped out of the infirmary and headed back to the bridge with Ellie. Krak'sul and Allore stood eyeing each other as they thought over what he had said.

Hawk," said Ellie, as they neared the bridge, "I noticed something when you were talking to Allore and Krak'sul."

"Oh? What was that?"

"You said 'we are a people at war'. You don't make mistakes like that. Do you now consider yourself one of us?"

"Yes, I do, Ellie," he sighed, as he stepped aside to let her enter first, "but for the life of me I can't tell you why."

"That part I don't need to know." She grinned as she patted his arm then moved to take over the sensors from Deann who then moved back to the captain's chair.

———— ◉ ————

"SIRE, WE'LL NEVER CATCH them in this fighter."

"I know that, Lizera," snarled Loran. "We're just trying to keep them in sight until they all meet and start fighting among themselves. We'll stand back and watch, then take out whoever is left. With any luck at all, our own ship will catch up to us by then."

Run to Ground

Michella screamed as the realization of intense pain penetrated her foggy brain. "So, you're going to live after all," laughed a woman's harsh voice. That voice seemed vaguely familiar somehow.

Fighting through the pain, Michella forced her eyes open. She was lying on the floor, naked and in restraints. Standing over her, holding an electric prod, was Ayra, the woman she'd thrown off her ship. The woman laughed as she jabbed Michella with the prod again.

"Leave off, Ayra," growled a man's voice. "Stop torturing her and get yer arse back in the pilot's seat. That lot's gaining on us."

"Torturing her? You're the one who raped her, you idiot."

"Didn't hurt her none; she was out cold. Now get yerself up here. All this'll be for naught if they catch us."

"Not so tough now, are you, daddy's girl?" snarled the woman, as she pushed Michela's face with her boot. "Stop your whining, Jin. They'll never catch us. They'll all be swallowed up by the Gap long before they get close."

"They're already close, ye foolish cow. We're ten days or more from Imperial space and they'll have us within a few hours."

"No, they won't," she replied, as she resumed the pilot's chair. "There should be an anomaly showing up on sensors any minute. It's a friendly, but nobody knows that. We'll drop inside and they'll think the Gap ate us. Inside that anomaly is another world. It has a few primitives on it, but we can easily wait there for years if we have to."

"Years?"

"Don't worry so much, Bix," she laughed. "We'll hole up there for a few days, until they stop looking for us, then we slip out and head for Elliston Prime. All we'll lose is a few days."

Michella's face burned with shame and rage as she realized the truth of what Ayra had said; she had been raped. "Stop it, Chella," she railed at herself. "You don't have time for this, and it can't be undone. Now you have to survive, get free, and then kill these vermin so they can never hurt anyone else. Get focused." Just for the slightest moment she thought she felt the touch of Nellie's mind.

———◦———

"THERE'RE TWO SHIPS gaining on us at an alarming rate, Sire."

"I know, and I have a good idea who they are. Brace yourselves for evasive action."

A moment later the comms crackled as the two Arcalian ships closed in. "Imperial fighter ship, this is the Ravage, Micha commanding. I know who you are, and I have a message for you. Your warship is being salvaged by pirates as we speak. You're alone here. Cut your engines and wait; we'll come back for you."

"Open fire," snarled the emperor, but the two bigger ships easily avoided the attack and continued on their way.

"Hmmm," mused Loran as he watched the two ships moving away at a speed he couldn't hope to match. "It seems the Arcalians have come up with something new. Lizera, I want the designs for that ship."

"Yes Sir, as soon as we get back to civilization I'll get right to work on it."

"I wonder how they can manoeuvre like that without killing everyone on board."

"They truly must have figured out how to beat the inertia problem," mused Lizera.

"Indeed," he replied. "You know, I think we should steal one of those ships. It'll be easier to study one than to steal the plans from that paranoid fool, Borad."

——————◉——————

AT NELLIE'S GASP EVERYONE'S attention suddenly focused on her. "Nellie?"

"It was her, Deann. It was just a touch then gone, but it was her. We're getting closer."

"Can you tell me anything at all?"

"She been hurt, Deann," Nellie said gently, "and she's angry. That's all I got. I tried to tell her we're coming, but we're still too far away."

"Keep at it, Nellie," sighed Deann. "Get me Allore on comms."

"I'm right behind you, Dee."

"Lore, did you hear that?"

"I did. When we catch them I'm going with you."

"Damn right you are; she's hurt and will need you. Make sure your kit is packed and ready."

"They're gone," exclaimed Ellie. She was bent over the sensors. "Three of the other ships just exploded and the front ship is gone."

"What in the nine hells," said Deann. Slow us down; find them."

"I know where they are, Deann," said Hawk. "We've got them now. Cutting speed."

"Talk to me, Hawk."

"They'll have gone to Vakay, it's the only answer."

"Explain."

"Right along here," said Hawk, as he eased their speed a bit, "is an anomaly, a big one. You get too close and your ship gets torn apart like the three ahead of us. The thing is, there's a way in. Inside the anomaly is a star system with the sweetest little planet you could imagine. It is mostly forests and oceans with sandy beaches. There's a species of farmers who live there, but they're few and keep to themselves. I call it Vakay because I found it by accident and stayed a couple of weeks just enjoying the fresh air. They must have learned of it somehow."

"The other ships have slowed down and are disappearing from sensors," said Ellie. "Either they were close enough to follow them in or they've been swallowed by the anomaly."

"Ignore them for now," said Deann. "If that's where they've gone then get us in there, Hawk. We'll sort them out when we catch them."

"Aye, Captain. Transmitting course changes to the Ravage and Shield now. Okay, there's that big gas ball on the right, we move up a bit, then a hard left and in we go."

Everyone watched the screens as they passed through the narrow tunnel of space between roiling gasses. There was a slight wisp of fog then they were through. A single star gleamed in the distance. There was no sign of the lone ship, but five of the surviving pursuers were easily spotted.

"It's them," exulted Ellie. "They're heading straight for that planet with two moons."

"That's the only habitable planet in the system," said Hawk. "The rest are too hot or too frozen."

"It's her," exclaimed Nellie. "It's Chella. I've told her to hang on, we're coming."

"Get us after them, Hawk."

———◈———

"HA, THAT SHOULD DO it," exulted Ayra. "We just disappeared from their sensors. As far as they know, we've just been swallowed up by the Gap. We'll give them a day or two to give up and go home, then we'll head out for Elliston Prime. I wish I could see their..."

"They found us," exclaimed Bix. "There's five ships just come through the anomaly. They're headed right for us."

"You festering idiots," spat Ayra, "I told you to make sure there weren't any trackers on the ship."

"We must have missed one" muttered Jin. "Stop yer bawlin' and get us on the ground someplace safe before they can target us. They'll most likely be Tekka's men. They're city rats, we can fool them up easy. The one that was behind them will be Micha. He's the one I'm worried about."

"At least he won't be able to find us here," muttered Ayra, as she circled the planet to get out of sensors on the pursuing ships.

"Yes, he will," declared Bix. "A lone ship broke through just as we got out of sight."

Ayra flinched as a gun was placed to her temple. "Ye'd better have some good tricks up yer sleeve besides that ugly arm," growled Jin. "Otherwise ye'll be the first to die."

"Settle down, Jin," she replied, trying to keep her voice steady. "We're not done yet, not by half. I know just the place to hide out for a few days."

While her captors fought among themselves, Michella lay shivering on the cold metal deck. Her hips ached from whatever abuse had happened while she was unconscious and her breasts burned from the electric prod she'd been hit with. Deep inside something began to grow. Pushing through the shame and pain, it fed on them until her mind was consumed with a single thought. "Kill."

The ship landed tight against a rock wall, scraping the hull on the way down. Jin and Bix were still swearing at Ayra as they picked themselves off the floor from the hard landing.

"Stop your whining and come see where we are," growled Ayra as she threw the switch to open the lower hatch and drop the ramp. She rose and grabbed Michella by the hair, standing her up. She cut the tight bonds from the girl's ankles and shoved her towards the door. "Try anything and I'll shoot your legs off," snarled Ayra. "The bounty is for a live Spawn; nothing was said about how intact they had to be."

"Leave off, Ayra," snarled Bix, as he caught the staggering Michella. "Here girly, I'll lend you an arm while we go see what this stupid cow has done to us." His arm slid around her, his hand grasping at her breast and pinching her nipple. She screamed and tried to fight him.

Bix struck her hard across the mouth, sending her reeling against the bulkhead. "You're a slave now, girl; best you start learning your place. I'll touch you whenever and wherever I want. If you move you'll be punished. You'll do as you're told, when you're told, and you'll do nothing until you are told." He grabbed her nipples again and hauled her away from the bulkhead, squeezing painfully. "Now get moving." He pushed her towards the elevator.

Michella was forced to kneel while the rode down to the hatch and ramp. Outside the ship was a huge cavern with the ship blocking most of the entryway. "See, Jin," crowed Ayra. "They can only get at us one at a time. After we've killed a bunch of them they'll get tired and try to force their way in. we'll fire up the engines and fry the lot of them. Same goes for Micha if he finds us."

"He'll find us," sighed Bix, "you know he will. I warned you about this, Jin."

"Stop yer danged worrying, Bix," growled Jin. "Give me time to think. Take that'un back in the cave and make sure she is tied up good and proper. Don't hurt her too much neither. She won't be worth a jot the way you two are abusing her."

"Aw, Jin, you've already had her..."

"She was out cold, Bix. It didn't hurt her a bit."

"Yeah, well, I like them awake and screaming a lot better."

"I know, old buddy, I know. Once we sell this'un we can buy as many as you can handle, then add one more for good measure. Now put her back in the cave a bit and make sure she's secure."

Grumbling, Bix led Michella back into the cave then made her lie down while he applied new restraints to her ankles and knees. "Don't go away, sweetie," he cackled as he slapped her hard on the rump. Laughing to himself he rose and returned to his companions. They were gathering weapons and preparing a defensive position.

With her ankles, knees, and wrists bound tightly together Michella wasn't able to move much, but she was able to move her fingers. Those questing fingers eventually found a sharp stone and began to work away at her bindings. "Kill," she breathed softly, as she worked, her eyes never leaving the captors nearby. Every time one of them glanced her way she froze, then resumed as they looked away. "Kill them with stone."

<hr />

"WE'RE THROUGH. FULL burn," said Deann.

Pally's voice came over the comms. "Deann, we'll burn out the engines at this rate."

"I don't care," she replied. "They have Chella and they're on the ground. Those other five ships are already landing and we're still an hour out. Full burn."

"Deann, we've run them too hot for too long, full burn and we won't be able to land until we make repairs. We've caught them, Deann. They're not going anywhere."

Deann sighed deeply and stopped pacing. She sank into the captain's chair, brooding. "All right, can we make three quarter speed?"

"Half speed would be better."

"Half speed then, but nudge it a bit, will you?"

"Will do, thanks, Deann."

Deann brooded for a while longer, then sighed and rose to continue her pacing. "Nellie, anything new?"

"No," replied Nellie, "they must be on the other side of the planet. All I get is the word 'kill'."

Deann sank back into the captain's chair. "Sensors to main screen."

"Main screen, aye," replied Ellie, as she flipped the switch. The main screen lit up to watch five blips slowly disappear behind the growing bulk of the planet.

"I'm going to hunt these people," muttered Deann. "When I find them I'm going to make them sorry they messed with us. They'll regret what they've done to her before I let them die. Once I have her back safe and sound I'm going back after that so called emperor. I'll tear that machine apart and ship all the parts into different suns. We'll see if the bastard can come back from that."

A small hand landed on her shoulder. "And I'm going to help you do it, Deann," said Allore from behind her. "We're a team, you and I, and we're going to make sure no one messes with our people ever again." Deann just patted the hand on her shoulder and brooded as they made their way slowly towards the planet.

They finally arrived at the planet and swung around to the back side. Six blips suddenly appeared on sensors. Five were a short space away from the one. As they neared the landing site of the cluster of five, Hawk suddenly panicked. "Noooo, nooo. I'll kill every freaking one of you slimeballs if you've gone anywhere near them."

"Hawk, talk to me."

"There's a village near here, Deann. It looks as though they've landed right on top of it. Those folk won't be expecting trouble; they'll get slaughtered."

"Put us down there, now."

Cursing like a madman Hawk set the ship down at the edge of the village. It was easy to see the damage as soon as they touched the ground. The group of ships had landed too close, destroying crops, and setting fire to buildings. There were bodies of strange creatures lying near burned down buildings.

As they exited the ship a shot rang out and dirt was kicked up at Hawk's feet. He ignored it as he raced to one of the huts still standing, Ellie close behind him. "Take cover," shouted Deann as she ran a zigzag pattern toward the one ship with an open hatch. She was almost to it when another shot rang out; a man screamed and fell out of the target ship.

Deann stopped and looked back. Owen was leaning against the side of the Warbird's gangway, his long-range rifle in his hands. "You go on, Deann," he shouted. "I'll keep them pinned down." She saluted him and ran on. As she reached the ship Owen stopped firing.

That was a fine shot, Owen," said a rich feminine voice close behind him.

"Old Betsy never fails me," he grinned. Geela patted his shoulder and walked back towards the kitchen.

A man poked his head out the hatch of one ship then ducked back inside. When no bullet was forthcoming, he looked out again. He grunted and grasped at the dagger that suddenly appeared in his chest. He looked up to see Deann sprint past him into the ship. As he sank to the floor she ran past firing her blaster. His companion was hurled against the bulkhead. He slid to the floor never to rise again.

Deann prowled through the ship, her eye patch flipped up and her artificial eye checking every room. She killed one more man she found in the engine room then grabbed her comm. "This one's clear; checking the next one." She checked them all, but found no more people.

Deann was just returning to the ship when Allore came on the comm. "Dee, I'm needed here to help these people. I'm sending Krak'sul to you. We're in the village."

Deann headed into the village to find her crew staring nervously at a group of strange creatures holding wicked looking spears and farm implements. The creatures were humanoid, tall and lean of build with a bluish cast to their skin. They had large eyes, tall pointed ears, short bottom tusks like the Korim, long arms with two fingers and a thumb on each hand. Two were barefoot and she could see two large toes to the long feet.

Actually, their faces would be quite pleasant without the scowls and the fear written all over them. All the males seemed a bit stooped forward, but the females stood tall and straight. Deann saw the powder keg ready to explode and knew she had to stop it before things went crazy. She didn't want to hurt these people and she didn't want to waste time.

"Everybody relax," she said, as she lowered her weapon. "Does anyone here speak our language?"

"We can speak the language of Aman-da," said an older fellow, as he stepped forward, leaning on his spear for support. "Are you leader of Aman'da's people?"

"No. Our leader was taken and brought here. We have come to take her back. I lead for now."

"Are you planning to finish what the others started?"

"No. We don't want to harm your people. What happened here?"

"Aman-da has always been a friend, so we thought the ships would bring more interesting folk. They landed in our fields, then when we ran to tell them not to destroy the crops they started killing. They set fire to our homes, barns, then..."

"Okay, I can see the damage," sighed Deann. "We'll help you repair your homes and fields, but first we have to get Michella back."

"They went, that way," he replied, pointing towards the mountains with his spear. "It's growing dark now; you won't be able to follow until morning. We will offer what hospitality we can, but first I must know something. Have you brought the Korim to finish what those others started?"

"What?"

"Our people have been enemies before, Deann," said Dor'cas, as the Korim approached. "It's good to see the Fellie again. In my time I have fought against and beside the Fellie. I would rather fight beside them as friends, but that is for Deann to decide."

"Friends then," said Deann. "So your people are called the Fellie, we're Novans. Those others are humans and we have business with them. Let's go people."

"Darkness is almost upon us," said the old Fellie. "You cannot hunt in the dark. Wait until morning. They won't move at night either."

"Skeeter," snarled Deann, then she caught herself. "Korim hunters, find the trail and get after them. Rest at dark, but get on them at first light. Send someone back for us when you find them."

The Korim hunters sped away as Deann reached for her comms. "Poppa Rath, take the bird up and watch for Micha. Also, make sure nothing gets off world."

"Understood," came his reply.

"Nellie, are you on the ground?"

"We're here, Deann," sang Nellie. She was standing in the doorway of a large hut. "Allore needs the help."

Deann nodded, then turned to Krak'sul. "Since we're resting until morning we might as well help Allore."

"We will watch for enemies," said the old fellow. "You folk rest."

"There are none, my friend," she sighed. "They left and I've killed the rest. The hunters will warn us if there's any danger. Come on, Novans, let's all see what we can do to help Allore before it gets too dark." As she spoke the Warbird lifted off and vanished into the sky.

They entered the long hut to see that Allore had it set up like a field hospital. There were at least a dozen wounded Fellie and she was just bandaging up the last one. She met Deann's eyes and nodded towards the end of the hut. Hawk was there cradling a child in his arms. A pregnant female lay wounded, her hand weakly resting on his arm. "The child's all right, Deann," Allore said softly. "The woman is badly hurt, however, she'll survive and so will the child she carries. They're Hawk's family."

Ellie was looking at Hawk, a strange expression on her face. Nellie put a hand on her shoulder and they pressed their foreheads together for a moment. Finally Ellie sighed and smiled weakly then turned and approached Hawk. She patted his shoulder then sank to her knees beside the wounded woman. Placing her hands on the woman, she sang a soft sweet note and let the healing energy flow. The woman's eyes opened wide for a moment then she sighed deeply and smiled. Her eyes fluttered closed and she went to sleep, her pain gone for the moment.

Hawk's huge hand landed gently on Ellie's shoulder. "Thanks for that, Ellie."

"She's your companion?"

"Yes, but I can't ever take her with me. You can see what would happen the instant some fool saw her."

"Understood. So, who is this little guy?"

"This is Aman-don, my son."

"Lucky boy," grinned Ellie.

"Oh?"

"Yeah, he looks like his mom," she giggled.

"That's going to cost you, kiddo," chuckled Hawk, his mood broken at last.

WHILE THE NOVANS SETTLED down with the villagers for the night, things were about to go crazy inside the cavern. Nellie still couldn't penetrate Michella's mind. The fog of rage and blood lust were too strong. The three kidnappers had prepared their defenses well, and the total darkness of night would keep their pursuers at bay until morning. They'd be well rested and ready.

While they labored to set up a defensive position and fought among themselves, Michella worked steadily at her bonds. Several times she felt Nellie's mind reaching for her, but she brushed it aside. She needed to focus. Just as the defenses were ready, her wrists were freed. Exultation flared in her heart as she sawed at the bonds on her ankles and knees. Once free, she didn't move, she just lay there flexing her muscles. It took some time to get the blood flowing again. A feral grin peeled back her lips as she heard them talking and planning. "Not this time," she snarled silently.

"Well, that's about it," said Bix. "We've got the way blocked and booby trapped. It's dark as space out there now. Let's get some rest while we can."

"All right, ye go on," said Jin. "I'll be along soon."

"Now what the nine hells are you going to do, Jin?" demanded Ayra.

"I'm jist going to have a bit of fun before bed, that's all."

"You're a sick man, Jin," chuckled Ayra.

"Let me go first, Jin," said Bix. "Once you put her to sleep she won't be no fun for me at all."

"You wants a live one kicking and screaming, Bix, grab onto old Ayra there. She'll put up a fight for ye, sure enough."

"Try it, Bix, and you're a dead man," growled Ayra.

"Dammit, Jin, the next one we take is mine first every time," whined Bix.

"That's a promise, Bix," replied Jin. "You two head into the ship for some sleep. I'll be awake for quite a while, but I don't want an audience."

"Just keep her alive," snarled Ayra. "She's worthless to us dead."

Ayra and Bix headed up into the ship and Jin rose, stretched, then turned to where Michella lay on the cold stone. He pulled something out of his pocket as he approached her. "Don't look so scared, girly," he grinned. "Old Jin'll give ye something to help ye sleep. It's far better than letting Bix have a go at ye. He's a hard and cruel boy, my old friend Bix. Just hold out yer arm now, and…"

He got no further as Michella surged to her feet, seizing his wrist in one hand and driving her sharp stone into his belly with the other. The force of her blow lifted him into the air and ripped him open. He fell back to the cavern floor and lay moaning, trying to stuff his entrails back into place. Michella saw the terror in his eyes as she pulled back her arm.

"I am Michella of Nova, daughter of Micha and Edie; I will never be a slave," she snarled, "and I will never submit." She grunted with the effort as she brought the stone down on his skull.

Jin lay dead on the ground, and she stood over him, trembling. Finally she knelt and took off his boots. Naked except for Jin's boots and weapon's belt, Michella slipped past the booby traps at the entrance and out into the pitch black night. Going strictly by feel she worked her way from the ship and across the rocky clearing to the forest. She continued to move slowly through the trees until she found a mossy bank. She lay down and cried herself to sleep.

Deep in the darkness of the starless night, a warm body found her and settled down. A wet tongue caressed her cheek and she buried her face in the soft warm fur. "Oh, Jak," she sobbed, "how did you ever get here, how did you ever find me?" He just licked her again and wagged his tail. Michella went back to sleep, hugging the big dog to her. At last she got some rest.

———————⊳●⊲———————

"SHE'S SLEEPING NOW, Deann," said Nellie, as she sat with Deann by the fire. "She killed one of them and escaped into the forest. Jak is with her. I'm going to try healing her mind through her dreams. You get some rest."

"Jak? He ran off as soon as we landed. I guess he knew more than we did. I'm glad he found her."

High above the planet the Warbird contacted the Ravage and Shield as they appeared through the anomaly. When dawn came Nova Clan was fully gathered on the edge of the Fellie village. The Fellie were getting nervous with all these heavily armed humans in their village.

As Micha reached the ground, Deann came to meet him, the elderly Fellie beside her. Micha didn't even flick an eye at the strange appearance of Deann's companion. "Deann, report."

"We followed Chella's captors here and found these folks all shot up. Hawk has a family here, so he knew the way in. I promised to help these folks rebuild when our work is done.

"Allore has a field hospital set up in that long hut. She could use a few more skilled healers." Edie and Lessa nodded and headed for the hut. Deann went on with her report.

"According to Nellie, Chella has escaped her captors and is in the forest somewhere. Jak ran off and is with her.

"The Korim hunters are on the trail of the people who did this to the Fellie; we should have a report from them soon.

"This man is Doo-ka, chieftain of the Fellie, he speaks for them." She turned to her companion. "Chieftain, this man is Micha of Nova. He's our chieftain; he speaks for the Novans."

The old Fellie leaned on his spear and looked Micha over, then smiled. "This young one is an able leader, Micha. She brings honor to your Clan. Deann has given us help and offered more should you give approval. What say you?"

"I'm proud of Deann; she's my daughter's chosen companion. Michella chose well. We'll honor her promise, Chieftain. First we have business to attend to, but then we'll return to help your folk rebuild and replant." Deann blushed shyly and beamed.

"Deann, your mission remains the same: Get Chella back. Take your people and get it done. We'll take care of the rest."

"I'll take the young Novans and one Korim hunter. I'll leave everybody else here to help the Fellie. Here comes Alise now. They must have found the scumbags." She turned and called out. "Alise, over here. Did you find them?"

"We did, Captain Deann. They're not so far away. There is another ship blocking the entrance to a cave. They're gathered there waiting for better light to attack."

"How many are there, Alise?" asked Micha.

"As many as forty, Chieftain Micha, but they're in a bad place to defend. High ridges run on both sides and would be hard to climb. There is no way out for them. I can take you there now."

"I need you with me, Alise," said Deann. "Doo-ka, can one of your folk lead the Novans?"

"I'm not as infirm as I look, child," chuckled the old fellow. "In my younger days I fought beside and against the Korim in the long wars. I know this place you speak of. I'll lead the Novans to their quarry. Go find your mate, Deann." She nodded and leaped away, shouting for her crew to gather.

They swiftly gathered by the long hut. "Barah, Tarah, Ellie, Nellie, Pally and Alise with me. Owen, take your rifle and go with Micha. He may need an extra sniper. Allore, stay here and care for these people."

"Forget that, Dee. I'm coming with you, Chella may need a healer too. Besides, we're a team."

"Agreed. Nellie, can you get us a direction?"

"I can't pinpoint her, Deann, but I can get a general direction."

"Do it. You and Alise take point. Lore, grab your kit and some spare clothes for Chella. Everybody carry weapons and extra supplies."

"Hawk, stay here with your family. We've got this." He nodded his thanks and went back inside to his companion's bed where the child waited silently. The child would not speak again in his lifetime.

A tall, well-muscled, Fellie carrying a long spear approached. "Deann, I am Ru-tar, son of Doo-ka. I know these forests well. I would like to accompany you."

"Thanks, Ru-tar; I appreciate the help. Are we ready folks? Nellie, lead on."

Nellie had already chosen her direction and headed towards a well-worn path into the forest. The sun was high in the sky when they found Michella and Jip by a small stream. Michella was in the water scrubbing herself vigorously.

"Chella," shouted Deann and Allore as they all rushed to her. She didn't respond; she just kept scrubbing at herself. Deann jumped in the water and took Michella in in her arms. "Stop now, Chella. You're making yourself bleed. Stop now, my lover. We're here. We've got you."

"I can't get myself clean, Deann," sobbed Michella, as she collapsed in Deann's arms. "The things they did to me, I can't wash them away. I can't get myself clean..."

"Yes, you did, Sweet Woman, yes you did," soothed Deann. "You washed it all away. Come on now. Let's get you out of the water and warm you up. We've brought you food and clothes. Lore will check you over. Come on, my love."

Deann continued to sooth Michella as she helped her out of the water. Allore took over then, drying her off and checking for injuries. She put healing balms on all of Michella's cuts, bruises, and the burns on her breasts. Slowly, under all the loving care, she began to allow herself to relax. She began to weep great heaving sobs that shook her entire body. Deann held her while she released the emotion of the past number of days.

As Michella lay in Deann's arms, recovering, Palentine reported in to Micha. "Pally to Uncle Micha."

"Micha here."

"We've got Chella back. She's pretty shook up, but Allore says she'll be fine."

"Understood. Thanks Pally. Micha out."

As soon as Michella's emotions settled down, Allore gave her something to drink. It tasted vile, but she drank it, complaining the whole time. She was coming back to herself. Once she got dressed, she wanted weapons. The rage was returning, but she had a grip on it now. "Lore, that medicine tasted like skeeter; got any more?"

"You need food now, Chella," grinned Allore. "Here, eat this."

"Does it taste bad?"

"Worse than the medicine," giggled Allore.

Michella shook her head and smiled. "I love all you guys, you know that. Thanks for coming to get me."

"I'd tear the galaxy apart to get you back, Chella," said Deann, as she hugged her, "we all would. Do you want to go back to the ship now and rest?"

"No, I have two more people to kill first," said Michella, as she rose to her feet, the rage rising within her again. "Three people took me, one's dead. I have two more to go and then I'll rest."

"Understood. Ru-tah, do you know the place where they're holed up?"

"I do, Captain Deann. It's not far from here."

"Take us there," said Michella as she took the comms unit from Deann's shoulder pocket. "Michella to Micha."

"Chella, are you all right?"

"I will be. It was two men and that woman Ayra who took me."

"Ayra? Kella's sister?"

"Yes. She tortured me, Poppa. I want her alive until I get there."

"Understood. I'll do my best."

"We'll be right there. Michella out."

———⬥———

BIX FOUND JIN'S BODY and screamed a protest. His best friend lay on the ground, his belly ripped open and his skull caved in. he was holding the body and crying when Ayra arrived. "Skeet," she muttered, as she whipped out her blaster. "I guess our little bird wasn't sleepy."

"I'll rip her heart out with my bare hands," declared Bix, as he rose to his feet and gently lay his jacket over his dead friend.

"Shoot her from a distance, Bix. She's a witch spawn. You can't handle one of them without weapons; they're way too strong. She took his boots so she must have run."

"We trapped the entrance, remember," said Bix. "She knew that. She's got to be in here with us somewhere. Get some search lights from the ship."

"What are you going to do?"

"Say goodbye to the only friend I ever had," Bix replied sadly.

"All right, but make it fast and keep an eye out, she took his weapons too."

Ayra returned to the ship for lights as Bix said a farewell to Jin, then turned his weapon up to full and fired. The body was pulverized instantly. He then piled stones over it and laid his depleted weapon on top. "So long, Jin. I'll see you the next time around."

"Ready?" asked Ayra, as she passed him a light.

"Ready," he replied, switching on the light and pulling out another weapon.

They searched the entire cavern in vain. "She must have been watching when we set the traps. She's gone out through," sighed Bix.

"Now we're completely and thoroughly screwed. Those are Tekka's men out there. Looks like we'll be joining old Jin sooner than later."

"We're still breathing," growled Ayra. "I'm not giving up yet. Get your sorry buttocks into that ship."

They raced inside and fired the engines. A hail of weapons fire struck the hull, but it had little effect as the ship began to rise. Cursing and threatening, the men charged, but the ship rose into the sky. As they turned to run back to their own ships they ran right into Nova Clan with predictable results.

Old Doo-ka's long spear pierced one man then the battle was on. Micha and his crew of mercenaries made short work of the city bred criminals. Several retreated into the cavern for shelter, but Keira launched several rockets in and the cavern collapsed. There were no survivors.

———◦———

"WHAT THE NINE HELLS is that?" asked Deann as they neared Micha and crew. She heard the sound of engines firing up.

"Ship rising," said Allore, as she pointed to the sky and the escaping ship.

"Ayra," snarled Michella.

Deann grabbed her comms. "Deann to Warbird."

"Warbird here, Rathbone commanding."

"Poppa Rath, they're taking off. Get the bird in the air. Run them down and cripple their ship, but don't destroy it unless you have to. Chella wants them alive."

"Understood. Warbird out."

In surprisingly short time the Warbird was in the air. She ran down the enemy just before they entered the anomaly. A volley from the big ship's forward guns destroyed their engines and the escaping ship hung helpless in space. Two fighters dropped out of the Warbird.

"Attention unknown ship, this is the Warbird, Rathbone of Urn commanding. All personnel suit up and eject into space; we'll pick you up." There was no response. "As you wish. I'll give you three minutes to change your mind then I'll destroy your ship." A minute later two suited figures left the ship and leaped into space. They were gathered up by the fighter ships and brought back to the Warbird.

"Prisoners aboard, Captain."

"Strip them of weapons and put them in the brig," replied Old Rath. "Gunner, blow up that ship." With a wide grin of delight, Bim hit the red switch. Two missiles struck the enemy's fuel tanks and the ship exploded. "Good shooting, Gunner, now go back to pilot and take us back to base.

"Warbird to Micha."

"Micha here."

"An Imperial fighter just slipped past me. You've got incoming."

"Understood Warbird. Ignore that fighter, stick to your mission."

"Understood. Warbird out." Bim was still grinning as he landed the Warbird on the same spot she left a few hours ago. There was an Imperial fighter standing close by.

———⊙———

"LOOKS LIKE THE EMPEROR finally got here," said Micha. "Is everybody ready?"

"We're ready. Are you sure about this Micha?" asked Lessa.

"I am, Lessa. It's me he wants and this has to end. I promised Brenna we'd try Chella's idea first. Personally, I'd prefer to have the Warbird just shoot him down, but what can you do?

"Micha to incoming Imperial fighter ship. It's about time you got here, Emperor. Are you ready for a re-match?"

"What do you propose, Hound?"

"There's an open field near where our ships are landed. I'll wait for you there. Let's get this done."

"You take me for a fool, do you? Why would I just land in the middle of your trap?"

"No trap, Emperor, just you and me one on one. The others won't interfere."

"Call my daughter and granddaughters there, Hound. I want them to see what happens to those who betray me. Frankly, I don't care if your people get involved or not, the results will be the same."

"I'll be waiting. Micha out."

"Sire, is this wise?" asked Lizera.

"Don't fret, Lizera. "I've had several modifications made to this body since my last encounter with the Witch's Hound. I'm now completely indestructible. Once I finish with him I'm going to crush that witch. Her tricks won't help her this time.

"After that, I'm going to take great pleasure in killing Rathbone slowly. You and the gunners just keep an eye on the rest. Shoot any who look like they might want to get involved before I'm ready for them."

"As you command, Sire," she replied softly, but her face told him she thought he was being foolish. He snorted in disgust and turned back to the screen.

Passing the Test

Micha stood alone in the open field, waiting as the Imperial fighter settled to the ground. Lessa was busy giving orders that he couldn't hear. Rathbone slipped back away and disappeared into the Ravage. "Lady, the boss gave his word on this," said Zartah. "He won't like it."

"I gave no such word, Zartah," she replied tightly. "I've augmented the ammunition of Rathbone's weapon. Should Micha fail, I'll step in. Should I fail, Rathbone will finish Loran once and for all. This man's madness ends here one way or the other. Don't interfere."

"I wouldn't dream of it, Lady," he sighed. "Gorda and I also have a back-up plan for this one. We all agree Loran has to be stopped."

"So, Hound," called Loran, as he descended from the ship, Lizera and the two gunners close behind him, "are you ready to die?"

"I killed you last time," said Micha, as he began to move to his left slowly, warily.

"I recovered," replied Loran, as he sent a bolt of energy from the palm of his hand.

The dirt where Micha had stood exploded and sizzled, but he'd leaped aside and rolled easily back to his feet. A few more blasts dodged and he was much closer to Loran, yet he hadn't fired a shot. "There's something I'm wondering about," said Micha, as he dodged another energy blast.

"Oh, what might that be?" asked Loran, as he chuckled and sent another blast at Micha. He wasn't trying all that hard to hit him; he was enjoying the game and completely confident in his ability to succeed.

"A short while back we interrogated one of your spies," said Micha, as he warily moved right. "She had a chip in her head. Lessa destroyed it, but it grew back."

"So?"

"Well, you used to have a chip in your head, but I'm pretty sure you've had it removed by now."

"Indeed I have, Hound. What's your point?"

"Well, I was wondering if yours might have grown back too," said Micha, as he whipped up his hand and pointed the remote device at Loran. Loran screamed a protest and tried to react, but he was too slow. He froze in mid action and didn't move again. Micha walked up and taped the emperor's forehead with his knuckles. "Yep, I guess it did."

He turned to Lizera and the gunners. "You folks have a bit of a problem now. Drop your weapons and we'll talk about that." Their weapons hit the ground. "Good. We'll just leave the emperor here while we go over there for a chat in the shade."

He led them to a shady spot, and they meekly followed. "Hello, Lizera," grinned Hawk. "Fancy meeting you here."

"Hawk, so this is what you look like," she sighed in reply. "Looks like you win again."

"It's better to be lucky than good," he replied. "Micha, this woman is the emperor's chief of intelligence."

"You should have advised him to stay in the empire," said Micha.

"I did," she replied. "Are you going to kill us?"

"Only if I have to. I'd far rather not have to do that. The problem is, I want to keep this place a complete secret, so I can't have you running around with that knowledge."

"Then you have no other option," she replied.

"Actually, I do," grinned Micha. "There's an anomaly about three weeks from here. Go through it and you're in another galaxy with no way back. We're shipping the emperor through that anomaly. I can send you with him. I have no idea what you'll face there, but you'll be alive with a fighting chance. It's that or the firing squad, take your pick."

"I'll go through with him," declared one gunner. "A slim chance is better than none." Lizera and the other soldier agreed.

"All right then," said Micha. "We have a plan. Rath, put these folks in the brig and stow the emperor in the launch bay somewhere."

"Gotcha, Boss," grinned Rathbone. "Come on, Jorge. We'll lock up these fine folks, then we'll fetch the robot."

"Didn't we just do that a while ago?" grinned Jorge.

"That was twenty years ago," chuckled Rathbone.

"Well, I sure hope he doesn't come back in another twenty years," sighed Jorge, a huge grin on his face. "He's one heavy bugger and in another twenty years, I'll be getting too old for all that lifting." The others were still laughing as they led the prisoners away.

That was when the Warbird returned with her prisoners. Old Rath brought them out of the ship at gunpoint. Everyone stood as they were brought forward.

"All right, people," said Micha as he faced them. "You two are the last of Michella's kidnappers. You'll face her justice. They're all yours, Chella."

"Now wait just a minute," began Ayra, "think about this Micha. Kella's not going to like this and you need her..."

"No, I don't," replied Micha. "What I need is for my people to be safe. I need the rest of the humans in this galaxy to understand what it means to attack Nova Clan. We're a small clan. We can't afford to play games. Chella, step up. What do you want to do with them?"

"Give Bix a weapon and tell him to step out. If he kills me he goes free."

"I'm not playing that fool game, girl. Just kill me and have done like you did with Jin."

Michella moved with the speed of a striking cobra. Her blow spun him around and her arms encircled his neck. A quick twist and she let his dead body fall to the ground. "I am Michella of Nova," she snarled, as she kicked the body aside, "and I will never submit to the slave collar.

"Now for you," she said, advancing on Ayra. The woman tried to break and run but Krak'sul caught her and threw her to the ground at Michella's feet.

"Have the courage to die with honor," he growled.

Ayra scrambled to her feet and lashed out, a knife in her hand. Michella easily avoided the blow. She grabbed the woman's wrist and snapped it. Ayra screamed and dropped the knife. "Please don't kill me," she begged, as she backed away from Michella.

"No? Perhaps not," said Chella. "I've thought of something better to do with you. Throw her in your brig with the others, Poppa. We'll send her out with the emperor and his people."

"Consider it done," said Micha as he nodded and Ayra was led away. "I think we're done with business here, people. It's time to help the Fellie rebuild their homes and farms."

Five days of hard labor later, the Novan farmers were all satisfied that they'd done what they could to set things right. The Fellie marvelled at the speed of the repairs and the farming skills of the Novans. When the day came to leave, Micha and Edie called Michella aside.

"Chella, are you going to be all right?" asked Edie.

"I will in time, Mamma. I still have nightmares, but Deann is so sweet to me. Nellie's working with me to get my head straight."

"Chella, you've got to get a hold on it," sighed Micha, as he hugged his daughter tightly. "You're the captain and your people look up to you. You need to be strong for them."

"I know, Poppa, I know. I'm good. Besides, I've got a great crew and Deann to help me out. We'll be just fine."

"All right, Chella. We're going to send the emperor on his long journey then I want a few words with Kella. After that we'll do a quick Gap run, and then meet you back here in about eight weeks."

"Thanks, Poppa. See you both in eight weeks."

As Michella headed for the Warbird she saw Hawk saying goodbye to his companion and child. She saw the sadness in their eyes and the last of her rage melted away. She realized love was stronger than hate. It was love that turned Deann into a warrior captain. It was love that made her crew risk everything to get her back. Michella realized then how much she had come to love these people, all of them, not just the enhanced she had grown up with.

With that thought in mind she approached Hawk and his family, smiling. "Hawk, we'll be coming back here in about eight weeks. You can bring your family with you if you'd like. We won't be making any stops."

They were all looking at her with surprise and delight as she entered the ship. "Make up your mind, we're leaving," she laughed, as she stepped out of sight.

Michella stepped onto the bridge to find Deann in the captain's chair. She was issuing orders and people were swift and efficient as they instantly obeyed. She knew her decision was the right one. Suddenly Deann noticed her and stood up. "Sit down, Captain Deann."

Puzzled, Deann approached her. "What's on your mind, my love?"

"This is your ship now, Deann; this is your crew. I'll be quite happy being your number two."

"You'll always be my number one, silly Chella," smiled Deann. "Now stop all this foolishness and take the chair."

"Dee..."

"Take the chair, Chella. I'm on guns. You know how I love to play with weapons. Chella, you're our captain. We're your crew. I can handle an emergency, but I'm too single minded to be a good captain. Now get in that chair and let's go play in the Gap."

The bridge crew all cheered as she took the chair, blushing. "Tarah, take us up and head for Arcalian space."

"Arcalian space, aye," grinned Tarah, as he eased the big ship into the air. Behind her she overheard Old Rath talking to Deann and smiled. How she loved that girl.

"Congratulations, Deann," Old Rath said, as the ship rose from the ground, "you passed the test. What did you learn?"

"Now you say I passed the test? Wait, I get it. The test wasn't could I seize power and lead people, it was could I step aside afterwards, right?"

"Right as rain," he grinned. "Power is just another weapon in your belt, Deann. It is easy enough to use, but hard to put down."

"It wasn't that hard, Poppa Rath. I can deal with anything in an emergency, but Chella is the smart one. She's the right one to lead us overall. She's the one to lead us into the future."

Old Rath patted her shoulder fondly. "Take the forward guns," he grinned and stepped past her to be at Michella's side. "Where are we bound, Captain? What's our mission?"

"I want to hunt up Zemma for a chat."

Two weeks later they found Zemma and her new ship. She was attacking five ships at once and winning. Michella grinned as she called for comms. "Attention all ships, this is the Warbird, Nova Clan. Cease fighting at once. This is Nova territory. We'll adjudicate the dispute."

"Whoa, Warbird," came Zemma's voice. "Thank the gods you're here; I was just passing by and was attacked by these pirates."

"Lies," came another voice. "This is a Guild convoy. With permission, I can come aboard the Warbird and show you Kella's personal seal."

"Frankly, I have no love for the Guild," said Michella. "I don't give a rat's hairy backside whose seal you carry, and I don't trust Kella anymore. Here's what will happen now. You'll hand over as much of your cargo to Zemma as her ship can hold. Do this and you can go your own way. Refuse and you'll face two ships instead of one."

"You can't mean this," sputtered the man.

"I surely do. Decide."

There was a moment's silence. "You give me your word there'll be no killing?"

"I do. Zemma, you hear that?"

"I have no problems here at all, Warbird. As long as they do as you ordered, there'll be no killing."

"There you go, Mister Guild. Start handing over your cargo."

"Micha will hear of this..."

"I'll tell Poppa myself," purred Chella. "Zemma."

"Here."

"From now until further notice, any ship in this area of the Gap is fair game unless they are Nova Clan. The Guild no longer has my protection. I have no idea what Poppa will do, so..."

"Understood. What's this going to cost me?"

"I don't want ships coming in here, Zemma, and I can't be everywhere at once. Also, I may need a favor one day. Play fair with me and I have no problem with how you make a living."

"I'll play fair, girl. I owe you one."

"So Nova Clan has turned pirate," came another voice.

"No," replied Michella, "Nova Clan claims this territory. This is my route and I make the rules. My rules are simple. Only Nova Clan comes in or goes out. From now on, everybody else dies. Spread the word. Michella out."

Bim switched off the comms. Michella sighed and relaxed into her chair. "Okay folks, I was making that up as I went along, but here's the reasoning. By shutting off this path through the Gap, the Fellie world is kept safe, and Nova Clan has a sanctuary to go to.

"Deann, keep your guns warmed up just in case. There're six ships out there. The first one to flinch gets blown to Andromeda."

"Aye, aye, Captain Chella," smiled Deann.

It took a while, but Zemma eventually had as much of the cargo as she could carry and she saluted the Warbird then moved off. The Guild ships headed out in a different direction. Once they were alone, Michella gave the order to head back into the Gap.

<hr>

AS THE RAVAGE AND SHIELD neared the anomaly a ship suddenly approached. It dropped a small speeder which came right at them. "Incoming speeder, Boss," said Jorge. "It's Kella."

"Bring her aboard," said Micha, as he rose from his chair, "send her to the meeting room."

"Aye boss," grinned Jorge. "Attention speeder, this is the Ravage. The boss will be in the kitchen waiting for you."

"Understood," came the reply.

Micha was enjoying a mug of his favorite bitter drink as Kella entered. Most of the old crew were there as well. "Micha, I'm glad I caught you. We've got problems."

"More than you know, Kella," he replied. "Grab a mug and sit down."

She filled a mug then joined them at the table. "Forgive me, Old Friend," she sighed, "but I sense hostility here. Micha, there are things happening and we need to share information."

"You first."

"All right. First, I've discovered another rebel faction in my organization. My sister is leading it. I don't know what the hells is going on in her head, but I promise I'll shut it down. You should know it's being backed by criminals and, rumor has it, even the emperor.

"Second, I just got word that Michella has joined forces with Zemma and they've taken down one of my convoys. What she doesn't know is, that wasn't really one of mine, it was something Ayra cooked up and forged my seal to. What concerns me is that she's joined the pirates and has attacked a Guild convoy.

"Micha, I need these routes through the Gap. You need my connections. It looks like our families have gone crazy. What do we do here?"

"My turn, Kella. I have no idea what Chella is up to, but we'll finish our little errand here then go find out. I do have a hunch, though. I'm betting she wants to hurt you and the Guild."

"Why? What did I ever do to her?"

"Nothing, but Ayra did. Ayra hooked up with two cutthroats and they took her prisoner. I think they were trying to sell her to the emperor. Ayra tortured her, the men raped her, but she got loose. She killed the two men and I have Ayra here in my brig, along with the emperor and a few of his folk. We're shoving them through the anomaly at Passage One to be rid of them forever.

"Ayra's here?"

"Chella didn't kill her, Kella, but I know she wanted to."

"Oh gods, Micha. I swear I didn't know anything about any of this. If I'd known I'd have put a stop to it myself."

"That's true, Micha," Ena said softly.

"I know, Ena," sighed Micha. "I trust Kella, but I made a bad mistake trusting Ayra. Do you want to see her, Kella? We're about to load them onto their fighter ship soon."

"Yes, I would, Micha," replied Kella, a hard edge in her voice.

Ayra sat on the bunk, staring at her boots. She didn't even look up when Kella spoke.

"Why, Ayra? Why did you turn on me, your own sister?"

"Why? You have to ask me that? You who were always Papa's pet while I did all the hard stuff to make you richer? It was me who built the Guild. It was me who found the third passage through the Gap. It was me Thronk truly loved, and you killed him. Tell me, spoiled baby, why wouldn't I take your toys away?"

"Ayra, are you truly that bitter about Papa making me the head of the Guild?"

"I'm the oldest, Kella. I'm the one who took all the chances. I should have been head of the Guild. You're damned right I'm bitter."

"Why did you torture Michella?"

"Because she's just another spoiled brat like you, that's why. The whole time I was prodding her bare ass with the slave brander, I was pretending it was you." She looked up with a snarl on her face. "I'd kill you if I had the chance."

"That's a chance you'll never get," sighed Kella, as her shoulders slumped. She turned and walked away without another word.

Lizera sighed as she was taken into a small room and deposited in a chair. Lady Arlessa sat facing her. "So, it's my turn to be interrogated, is it? There's no need for torture, I'll talk. You're shipping us out to another galaxy; no information about this one has relevance anymore. What do you want to know?"

"You appear to be an intelligent woman, Lizera," smiled Lessa. "That's why I have a gift for you."

"A gift?"

"Yes, a gift and some information you may find useful on the other side."

LORAN SUDDENLY SAT up, swiftly taking in his surroundings then leaping to his feet. Through the view screen of the fighter ship he could see dozens of strangely designed ships floating awkwardly in space. "Where are we? What happened?"

"Sadly," said Lizera, "you faced the Hound and lost again. They've sent us through an anomaly into another galaxy. Apparently, there's no way back, at least not from this point."

"Yes, he had that damned controller. The chip must have grown back."

"So it seems," she said drily. "However, I did manage to acquire it before they shipped us out." She tossed it to him.

"Well, at least that's something," he snarled, as he first inspected it to be sure it was the right one, then crushed it in his hand. Both gunners swallowed hard at the power in that hand. "What do we do now, Mistress?"

"Now, I need you to find a way for us to survive here. First we see to our survival, and then we turn our attention to other matters."

The two gunners' and Ayra's mouths fell open at that and they stared at the emperor. Could they all have been so blind? It was the woman who was in control.

"Yes, Mistress," replied Loran, "it shall be as you command. I'll begin by exploring some of these ships nearby."

The end, or is it?

About the Author:

Prudence MacLeod is a spiritual seeker, dog trainer, Reiki Master, interior designer, and personal trainer who has turned her hand to writing. She is an avid chess player and has recently become addicted to World of Warcraft.

In her own words, "I have roamed far and wide for over seventy years in this realm, and I have seen much; some I wish I had not, and a great deal that I would love to see again. Some days I feel like Bilbo Baggins, for I have been there and come back again. No, I haven't written a book about my wanderings, but much that I have experienced, observed, learned, surmised, or imagined, is woven into the tales I have written. I do hope you enjoy them."

AND NOW FOR A PEEK at the final tale in the Nova Series:

Red Nova

by

Prudence MacLeod

The days of fracture and bitter loss were destined. It began with the creation of the Gap. The two most powerful witches in history defeated the armada of the Iron Emperor, but in so doing they created a region of space that did not always conform to accepted standards of behavior. To protect his people, Micha led the Novans into the Gap and claimed it for their territory.

During those early days, Micha's daughter was taken, made slave, tortured and raped. Her bonded companion, Deann, took command of her lover's ship and retrieved her, and for a while all was well ... and then the great ship appeared.

The Great Ship

M ichella struggled to sit up on the bed. She found the captain's cabin a bit small these days and quietly wished she'd stayed on Vakay until after the baby was born. No, dammit, he would be a nomad, best he be born aboard a ship. Her ship. "Help me up."

"Sure," replied Deann, offering her hands for Michella to grasp. She pulled the pregnant woman to her feet easily.

Michella stepped closer and pulled her lover to her. "Dee, please tell me what's eating at you. I hate this distance that's come between us. Please talk to me."

"It's nothing," replied Deann, as she turned and started to step away.

Michella held her fast. "That's skeet and you know it. Now enough of this. It's been going on for months. Tell me what's wrong."

"Fine, I will." Deann had spun back to go nose to nose with Michella, fire in her eyes. She placed a hand on Chella's swollen belly. "That's what's wrong. We once agreed we would each bear a child of our combined DNA just like Lady Arlessa and Brenna. You were taken, went through hell, were raped, and impregnated. I went through hell to get you back. Now you insist on bearing that thing inside you, knowing what its father was, what he did to you. I don't understand, Chella. I just don't understand."

Michella didn't respond to Deann's anger. "My love, I'm so sorry you've been hurt by this. I wish you had told me sooner. Dee, I love you to distraction, you know that. I want to bear your children, not just one, but several. This one, however, is an innocent. Yes, his father was a right evil bastard and I killed him for what he did to me, but this child isn't him. Dee, that whole experience was evil, all of it, and it haunts me still.

"This child will be born with the Novan marks. He'll be raised Novan; he'll be Novan. He's not his father. Dee, this is the only bright spot in that whole experience. A baby is a beautiful thing, you've said so yourself many times. I want to bear the child so something beautiful will come out of what I went through. That's why."

Deann's anger and hurt melted away. "Chella, I'm sorry. I wish you had told me sooner. Maybe you're right about this, a child is a blessing. No matter what else his father was, he was a smart man."

"I wish I'd known how much this was hurting you, Dee. I honestly had no idea. You know I'm still a bit messed up by it and I get a bit lost at times ..."

She got no further. The klaxon blared then Old Rath's voice barked over the ship wide. "Battle stations. Battle stations. Captain to the bridge. Repeat, captain to the bridge."

Deann tried to help Michella, but Chella pushed her ahead. "Go, go, I'll get there as soon as I can. Go!"

Deann sprinted away, leaving the door open behind her. She came pounding onto the bridge and threw herself into the captain's chair. "Report!"

"We've sighted a ship, Captain," replied Old Rath. He was grinning at his protege. "Damn thing is half the size of a planet."

"Hail it."

"Trying," said young Bim. "No response. Captain, there's some sort of energy field around that thing. I'm not sure if our hails are getting through."

"Sensors?"

"Nothing, Captain," replied a woman's voice. "It's not moving. It's just sitting there like a dead duck."

Michella stopped at the door of the bridge and watched, a smile of delight on her face. Deann would play second fiddle but give her an emergency and she took over like she was born to it. How Michella loved that girl. "Hey there."

Deann hopped out of the chair. "We've got an intruder, Chella. We think it's derelict, but not sure yet. No response to our hails and it's not moving."

"Huh. You deal with it, sweetie. I'm not feeling so good. I'm going to wander off to the infirmary and see 'Lore. She must have something vile tasting that will fix me up."

"Need a hand?"

"No, I'm good. You deal with the intruder, and I'll go visit my sister." She turned and waddled away.

Deann turned to Old Rathbone. "What just happened?"

"You just got promoted, Captain Deann."

"Great." Deann sighed then resumed the chair. "Okay, people. We've got a quiet intruder. It's big enough to be a moon and it's blocking the way. Opinions? Options?"

"Personally, I'd like to take a look at her up close," grinned Hawk. "First man?"

"I agree with Hawk, but I wouldn't send him over."

"Hey now," said Hawk, as he rose from his seat at the weapons station. "Care to explain that?"

"I'm first man," grinned the old fellow. "I don't have to explain a damn thing to you. Captain Deann, shall I explain my reasoning?"

"Please do," grinned Deann.

"Hawk's the best gunner we've got. If that thing suddenly comes to life ..."

"Yeah," grumbled Hawk, "that plus I can contact the king and get an Arcalian Fleet here two weeks faster than anybody else."

"That had crossed my mind," said Rathbone.

"Okay, so we're agreed somebody has to take a look at that thing, yes?" asked Deann. They nodded their agreement. "All right then, I'll go."

"The captain belongs on the bridge," said Old Rath.

"I'm expendable," replied Deann. "The true captain is in the infirmary, still very much alive. I'll go. Comms, ship wide."

"Comms, aye. Ship wide ready, Captain." Bim was grinning. He loved being on the bridge and being a part of the crew. Deann returned his smile.

"Attention, all hands. We've encountered what appears to be a derelict ship. It's the size of a moon. I'm going over for a look. Pally, Barah, Alise, and Nellie, you're with me. Pally, prep our best fighter and make sure she's loaded for war."

Old Rath gave Deann a questioning look. She relented. "Chella is here, so I'm expendable. That ship is an unknown, so I want an engineer and a witch with me. Barah is our best pilot, I might need his skills to get out."

"And Alise?"

"If I'm trapped over there and there's anything alive on it, a hunter would be handy, don't you think?"

"I do think. Not taking a healer?"

"I'm the healer. I've spent a lot of time in the infirmary helping Alore. I can't take her with me, Chella needs her now, but I can manage if I have to."

The old man nodded his agreement. "You chose well. Do you want a warrior?"

"No, you're first man, you have to stay here too. I won't take any chances, Poppa Rath, I promise."

Deann left the bridge and headed for the fighter bay. She stopped off at the infirmary to let Michella know what was up, then continued on her way. That was the last time Michella would ever see the Deann she knew. The woman who would return to her a few weeks later would be very different; older, wiser, and a lot more savage.

The crew was waiting for her when she reached the bay. She climbed aboard the fighter and Barah took her out. Deann could see that Pally, like his father, had stocked the small ship with as many supplies and spare parts as she could carry. "Approaching derelict ship," said Barah, as they drew nearer to the monster that hung in space. "Repeat, approaching derelict ship. Warbird, acknowledge." There was nothing but static.

"The energy field around her must be interfering with the comms," mused Deann. "Is it affecting us?"

"No, we seem to be fine, Captain," replied Alise.

"Damn thing is just too blasted big," muttered Deann as she gazed out the view port. "Any sign of a docking port?"

"None so far," replied Barah. "There's some arrays up ahead, might be something there."

"Take a closer look. We still okay, Alise?"

"All good, Captain Deann."

Suddenly the small fighter powered down and lurched sideways. "Skeet," swore Barah, as he tried to regain power. The small fighter was pulled inexorably to the huge ship. A port opened and they were pulled inside. As soon as the port closed behind them their power came back up. "Dammit, we're trapped inside."

"Easy now," said Deann. "It must have been an automatic docking system. Once it had us safely inside it released us. Probably was used for bringing supplies aboard. I don't see a launch bay or anything else handy. Before we go exploring, nose her up to that port again and see if it will let us out." It didn't.

Barah started cursing again, but Nellie laid a gentle hand on his shoulder. He settled down immediately. "Well then, it looks like exploring is our only option unless you want to try shooting our way out."

"No, somehow I don't think that would work. I'd like to conserve our weapons for now. Let's go exploring. Alise, anything interesting on sensors?"

"We seem to be oriented along the long axis of the ship, Captain. "I'm picking up a lot of damage, some rubble, plenty of plant life and some animal life. For a second I though I had a human life sign, but I can't be sure."

"Hmm, Nellie, you get anything?"

The small witch closed her eyes and let her awareness reach out. A few minutes later she opened her eyes. "There's lots of animal life, some alien that I don't understand. It's not Korim nor Fellie, and there's a number of humans. They aren't near, but they're on this ship."

"Okay, so let's go see if we can find the humans. They should have lots of information about this monster that can help us. Alise, keep an eye out for another port to the outside, too. We might get lucky." They didn't.

They flew deeper into the massive ship. "I wonder what's keeping the lights on?" mused Pally.

"I was wondering that myself," said Deann. "Sensors say anything good about air in the place?"

"There's an atmosphere and it's breathable," replied Nellie.

"You sure about that?"

"Dee, there are humans in here running around without atmo suits. We can breathe the air."

"Good to know. Thanks Nellie."

"Stop," said Alise. Barah stopped and hovered the ship high in the air.

"Talk to me, Alise."

"Captain, there's an open space ahead where we could land. There's a forest close by with many animals. There are plenty of human life signs, ten close by and sixty or more farther away. There are five ships about the size of the Warbird with the humans. Also, there are about thirty alien life signs closing on the ten humans. The humans are watching us. They're unaware of the aliens approaching."

"Nellie, hail them."

"Comms are down, Captain."

"Skeet. Barah, drop us down by our cousins. We'll have to do this the hard way."

Don't miss out!

Visit the website below and you can sign up to receive emails whenever Prudence MacLeod publishes a new book. There's no charge and no obligation.

https://books2read.com/r/B-A-ZKBBB-EDURC

BOOKS 2 READ

Connecting independent readers to independent writers.

Also by Prudence MacLeod

Telling a story is like knitting a sweater. Start with a ball of possibilities, pull out one small thread and begin. With luck and patience you will create something quite wonderful.

About the Author

On a far off windswept island Jennifer Crandall sits with her dogs and cats creating fantastic stories for all to enjoy. She publishes as JL Crandall, Prudence MacLeod, and Jenni Leigh.

Read more at https://www.prudencemacleod.com/.